People & Trees

A Trilogy

Akram Aylisli

Translated by Katherine E. Young

Plamen
Press
Where Words Ignite

Washington, DC

Plamen Press

9039 Sligo Creek Pkwy, suite 1114, Silver Spring, Maryland 20901

http://plamenpress.org

Translation copyright © 2024 by Katherine E. Young
Adamlar və ağaclar ©1969 Akram Aylisli, and heirs
People and Trees©1969 Akram Aylisli, and heirs

Published by Plamen Press, 2024

Printed in the United States of America

10 9 8 7 6 5 4 3 2 1

Publisher's cataloging-in-publication data

Names: Aylisli, Akram, author. Young, Katherine E., translator.
Title: People and Trees / Akram Alylisli;
Description: Silver Spring, Md: Plamen Press, 2023
LCCN: 2024946758

Identifiers: ISBN 978-1-951508-41-8 (paperback)
ISBN 978-1-951508-43-2 (pdf) | ISBN 978-1-951508-44-9 (epub)
ISBN:978-1-951508-42-5 (hardback)

Edited by Rachel Miranda

Cover design copyright: © 2024 by Walter Carlton
Translator's photo copyright © Samantha H. Collins

This is a marvelous read. The world evoked by Akram Aylisli in his trilogy, *Tales of Aunt Medina, The Tale of the Pomegranate Tree*, and the titular *People and Trees* (with the brief not-quite epilogue, *The Tale of the Silver Tweezers*) may seem strange to western readers, but soon enough grows familiar. And familiarity breeds not contempt but wonder: how does he manage to do this? How has he managed to make the villages of Azerbaijan so compelling a home that we shudder to leave? And the list of characters evoked by our youthful narrator, Sadyk, son of Nadjaf—from Aunt Medina to Mukush, from Aunt Nabat to Avez and Merdzhan, from Yakub and Yusuf to Uncle Nazar—seems cut from stone and hollowed out of wood; they are elemental and of near-mythic stature. It's the high task of fiction to make a dark world visible and make, of that darkness, bright light. Aylisli (brilliantly translated here by Katherine E. Young) is a master for us all.

—Nicholas Delbanco, author of *Why Writing Matters*
and *Still Life at Eighty: A Memoir*

In *People and Trees*, Akram Aylisli writes with a lyrical prose that affirms there are "mountains as light as down," even as he tells stories of destitution, disappointment, and abuse. His book combines local history with a fairytale's universality, the real with the imaginary, the human with the natural. Katherine E. Young's translation does wonderful justice to this vision.

—Peter Orte, ADA University, Baku, Azerbaijan

This triptych is beautifully and specifically placed in the immersive landscape of village life in Azerbaijan amid the roiling forces of the 1940s; it captures a childhood that is grim yet magical, an ethereal fairy tale that will resonate with modern readers. One can feel the love and attention that went into this translation.

—Leslie Pietrzyk, author of *Pears on a Willow Tree*

Akram Aylisli's *People and Trees*, translated by Katherine E. Young, for the first time brings to English readers the compelling story of young Sadyk, who observes and narrates his life in the mountains of Azerbaijan. One of Azerbaijan's most noted writers, Aylisli here tells the story of life in early Soviet Azerbaijan in three novellas and a short epilogue. Beginning with the departure of many of the men to fight in World War II, the story focuses on the lives of the women left behind, who must raise the children and seek emotional and physical comfort as best they can. Through his lyrical prose and close attention to detail, Aylisli draws the reader into the physical setting of the looming mountains and into the interior and emotional landscape of the community.

—Joanne Leedom-Ackerman, author of *Burning Distance* and *The Far Side of the Desert*

Akram Aylisli's poetic writing combines the mysterious (the life of trees) and the familiar. *People and Trees* is a story about village women—the "aunts" and "grandmothers" who play a formidable role in holding together an otherwise male-dominated society during and after the Second World War. As I read *People and Trees*, I recalled faces from my visits with rural Azerbaijanis displaced during the Karabakh conflict in the 1990s. The relationships among the people in Aylisli's fictional village also remind me of my own "aunts" and "uncles" as I grew up in midwestern Illinois in the late 1940s and 1950s. I enjoyed reading *People and Trees* for its dreamlike imagery of a long-forgotten time and place—mysterious Azerbaijan and familiar America. You don't have to know Azerbaijan to appreciate Aylisli's skillful, poetic use of words; he reminds us just how small a planet Earth is in terms of our collective human experience.

—Richard Kauzlarich, U.S. Ambassador to Azerbaijan, 1994–1997

The multiple themes of *People and Trees*—the story of young Sadyk, his family, and their village neighbors; Azerbaijani culture straddling World War II, impacted by both war and the Soviet system; the war's losses and the changes they wrought—are carefully interwoven into an artfully crafted story. This is an important trilogy of novellas that needs to be read and studied in light of current world events. The translation, the trilogy's first into English, provides an accessible text that opens the story in such a strong, knowable way; its quiet power enters our imaginations and holds us throughout.

—William Miller, the Alan Cheuse International Writers Center

In simple but powerful prose, Akram Aylisli has conjured a village in full, a world so visceral and immediate you can taste the dried mulberries, feel the heat of the samovar, and hear the guns of war, never far away. You can also sense the unspoken tensions among villagers, the duplicity of local politicians and, most of all, the abiding bond between aunt and nephew that infuses every page of this tender and endearing coming-of-age novel, fluently rendered in Katherine E. Young's excellent translation.

—Eric Weiner, author of *Ben & Me*

Akram Aylisli's *People and Trees* offers a poignant exploration of the complex relationship between people, place, and memory in Soviet Azerbaijan. What stands out to me as a folklorist is Aylisli's masterful use of landscape and communal memory as narrative devices. Aylisli weaves folklore-like elements into the lives of his characters, reflecting the timeless struggle between tradition and modernity. His portrayal of village life is layered with symbolic references to nature that serve as metaphors for resilience, cultural heritage, and the passage of time. This trilogy not only preserves the oral traditions of Azerbaijan but also questions the intersection of political history and collective identity, making it a significant contribution to both literature and the study of folklore.

—Debra Lattanzi Shutika, author of *Beyond the Borderlands: Migration* and *Belonging in the United States and Mexico*

With striking detail and clarity, Akram Aylisi gives us a vivid account of a people grappling with change. *People and Trees* is told through the eyes of a child, a sometimes-unreliable narrator: interesting and tactile characters jump off the page, but we can only know them as well as the boy understands them. The subtle power of this story lies in the fact that Sadyk is a mirror for his society, navigating issues that range from gender relations to the loss of traditional ways of knowing to the ever-present tension between war and peace. Who will this boy—this society—become?

—Itoro Bassey, author of *Faith*

Contents

Translator's Note

People and Trees, Akram Aylisli's first trilogy of novellas, appeared in its original language, Azerbaijani (Azeri), in 1970. It was published in Russian in 1971 in a print run of 100,000 copies. The novellas quickly appeared in other languages of the former Soviet Union and Eastern Europe either singly or as a trilogy. An Azeri-language film version of the middle novella, *The Tale of the Pomegranate Tree*, debuted in 1984; Akram Aylisli shares screenwriting credit for the film. *People and Trees* has been republished many times over the years in various languages; this is its first publication in English. It joins a later trio of Aylisli's novellas, *Farewell, Aylis* (Academic Studies Press, 2018), and a stand-alone edition of the novella *Stone Dreams* (Academic Studies Press, 2022).

The Azeri-language literary tradition, with its strong roots in Persian and Turkish culture, dates back many centuries; in the last two hundred years, it has also come under the influence of Russian and Soviet culture. While Akram Aylisli writes in Azeri, his literary career, beginning with his years studying at Moscow's famed Gorky Literary Institute, is closely tied to Soviet and Russian literary culture centered in Moscow and Leningrad/St. Petersburg. The colonial language of Russian has served Aylisli well, not just during the Soviet period but also after Azerbaijani independence. In 2012, when Aylisli's novella *Stone Dreams* could not be published in its original language in Azerbaijan because of the work's political and religious themes, a Russian literary magazine published the entire novella in Russian. The international uproar over that publication resulted in death threats, threats of bodily injury (including a bounty offered to anyone who would cut off Aylisli's ear), and the burning of Aylisli's books throughout Azerbaijan. The harassment of Aylisli by Azerbaijani authorities, including trumped-up legal charges first assessed in 2016, continues to this day.

Aylisli himself translated *Stone Dreams* and other late works into Russian; the earlier *People and Trees*, on the other hand, was translated into Russian by Tamara Kalyakina, whose skill in translating Aylisli has often praised. My English translation comes via the Russian. Accordingly, names, toponyms, and culturally specific words in this work originally written in Azeri—a Turkic rather than Slavic language—have unavoidably passed through the linguistic and cultural filter of Soviet-era Russian. As I am not a scholar of Azeri, I generally hewed closely to the Russian-language versions of these items, sometimes adjusting those versions when words such as iwan had already made their way into English. The Russian language itself plays a role in these novellas; Aylisli often uses the interplay between the local Azeri spoken by his characters and the Russian spoken (not necessarily correctly) by teachers, Party officials, and other authority figures to comic effect.

I have profited immensely from the support and advice of numerous organizations and individuals in translating this book. Without the financial support of London's Pushkin House, which awarded me a 2022 translation residency, and the Granum Foundation, where I won a 2022 translation grant, this book would not exist. The indefatigable Thomas de Waal consistently championed this translation, prodding gently when prodding was most needed. My translator colleagues Lisa Hayden, Olga Bukhina, and Shelley Fairweather-Vega have been extraordinarily generous with their time and suggestions for some of the trickier passages. Charles H. Varner, Jr., provided invaluable insight into traditional agricultural and animal husbandry practices. Peter Orte kindly suggested several changes based on his knowledge of the Caucasus region and of Azeri. My colleague Liza Prudovskaya read every word of the manuscript and saved me from numerous pitfalls; any remaining errors, of course, are my own. I am also indebted to Olga Zilberbourg for her fond reminiscences of reading this book during her youth and her innocent question about when I planned to translate it...

As of this writing, Akram Aylisli, who is 86 years old, continues to live under de facto house arrest in Baku, a victim of one of the most repressive governments on the planet. It has been one of the highest honors of my life to translate the work of this consummate artist and man of conviction. Readers who value creativity, free expression, empathy, compassion, and human dignity are encouraged to learn more about Aylisli's case, which has been championed by international human rights organizations such as PEN International and Human Rights Watch, and to speak out on behalf of Akram Aylisli and others who are persecuted for no other reason than expressing what their consciences will not allow them to repress.

Katherine E. Young
September 2024

People & Trees:

A Trilogy

Tales of Aunt Medina

For my Mother, Leya Ali-kyzy

Part One

1

My mother died the day I was born, and for the first two months, Aunt Medina had to carry me from house to house where there were nursing children. During winter evenings my aunt loved to talk about that time; listening to her in the warm darkness of the room, I saw clearly how she walked along, slipping and stumbling on the icy path that stretched beside the irrigation canal toward the spring. If Aunt Medina took me out in the yard before bedtime, I tried not to look at the mountain towering above our path—it seemed to me that the stars were whispering about something with its peak, as if they were plotting evil. I heard the whispers of the stars later, too, in a dream: Aunt Medina was carrying me to the mother of Selim, Azer, or Fikret, the same ones with whom I played pebble jacks during the day, and above us the stars were whispering to one another. I also dreamed that I was suckling from the clouds and from fat, gray cows that looked like heavy clouds.

Spearmint curled along the path, blackberries ripened in dark clusters, and later, when fall set in, the walnut trees lining the irrigation canal covered it with their yellow leaves. Perhaps Aunt Medina had carried me here all of one time, but for some reason, of all the roads along which she wore herself out to get milk for me, I fixed on this one in particular: now and then it seemed to me that the traces of her feet were sometimes still visible on the narrow path.

Aunt Medina really loved talking about my early childhood, and on long winter evenings when everything else had already been talked over, she invariably started a story about me: how I grew up gloomy and unsmiling, how I got the measles, or how I climbed the tall apple tree and fell out of it without a scratch. One time I overturned the cradle, another I was almost scalded to death when I knocked over a boiling kettle. It was a good thing the physician's assistant lived close by—my aunt scooped me into her arms and lugged me to him. The physician's assistant has been dead a long time, but to this day, even without knowing what he looked like, I can't forget him—that's how often I heard that story.

Aunt Medina was even happier to recount how, as a foolish little fellow of two or three, I kissed the neighbor's little girl Khalida, who for some reason had been brought into our yard by her mother. When my aunt recalled that event, she looked satisfied, proud; her eyes shone happily. A similar expression flitted across my father's face when I said "naughty words" to Khalida. I remember that myself; at that point I was already five years old.

It was very hot: Khalida and I sat on a thick branch of the walnut tree, hidden by its dense leaves. I don't know what suddenly came into my head, but I seized the little girl by the hand and announced to her that she was my wife. Khalida began to sniffle, crawled down from the branch, and returned to her mother in a flood of tears. Aunt Sona didn't hold back for long; she swiftly appeared and immediately attacked my father. "He's starting early!" she shouted. "No bigger than a midget— and already talking about a wife!" For some reason I remember only those words, although Aunt Sona scolded for a long time and shouted many other words.

Naturally, my father didn't respond in kind—he wouldn't argue with a woman. He put on an angry face and scolded me sternly, although he could see that I didn't understand a single thing. However, as soon as Aunt Sona left, his face became completely different: I guessed that he wasn't angry. On the contrary, he was proud of me and had scolded me that way in front of her as a caution. I remember his eyes then very well, the kind of weather there was that day, the color of the leaves on the walnut tree. The only thing I can't remember is how I came up with the idea—I was really little, still running around without pantaloons. I got pantaloons only later, not long before my grandmother's death.

That day my grandmother led me in from the street, stood me up on the seki—the large, flat stone lying near the irrigation trough—washed my feet thoroughly, and dressed me in something that looked like pantaloons. That something had been sewn from a woman's coarse calico pantaloons, sewn, moreover, with a lot of extra room—I would have fit into either one of the legs. The pantaloons had a beautiful, colored drawstring running through them that my grandmother had pulled out of an old khurdzhin bag.

It was hard for me to tell how I looked in my new clothes, but there was a fly in front with buttons, just like on real trousers, and that was enough to instill confidence in me. Furthermore, my grandmother unquestionably liked the way I looked; quite satisfied, she smoothed and straightened me for a long time and turned me around to look at from all angles. Finally, she rolled up the pantaloons to the knee, tightened the drawstring, and ordered me to hold onto both ends of the string when I needed to take off the pantaloons.

Utterly happy, I dashed out into the street, my hand on the buttons. But my joy was short-lived. My bare-bottomed buddies, clustering around me on all sides, caught on in an instant and turned me into a laughingstock. Neither the fly nor the buttons fooled them. With a howl, I bolted back home, whipped off the "women's pants," and flung them at my grandmother. The next morning, running out into the street in my shirt like always, I felt my own nakedness for the first time in my life, was ashamed, and turned back. My grandmother tried once more to tie me into the hateful pantaloons, but I was adamant. For a long time after that she pestered me with those pantaloons. Even when she was seriously ill, she didn't leave me in peace; having barely opened her eyes, she'd start to moan, demanding that I put them on. It turned out that my grandmother was tormented more by my stubbornness than by her illness.

One day my father woke me at dawn and, taking me firmly by the hands, set me on the bed.

"Go release the mill water," he said sternly. And he added in a loud voice, as if to immediately drive away my sleep, "Your grandmother has died!"

I went to the mill, climbed down in the deep basin, and released the water. When I returned, the yard was already full of women. They washed my dead grandmother, placing her on that same stone where not long before she'd tried my new pantaloons on me.

I rejoiced that my grandmother was gone and that there was no one left to accost me with those accursed pantaloons. Then again, I didn't know that now I'd have to spend whole days by myself.

That summer my father was selling muskmelons from the collective farm at the bazaar. Aunt Medina went to work in the fields, disappearing until it got dark. Leaving at dawn for the district center, my father would close the gate with the upper latch, which I couldn't reach, and I remained locked in for the whole day. I had cheese and bread and as much water as I wanted gurgling along the irrigation trough all day.

Luckily for me, our house stood in the upper part of the village, and all the other homes, beginning with the two stuck onto the foot of the mountain opposite us, were spread out before my eyes. The road to the district center twisted along the slopes in the distance beyond the roofs of the houses.

I was entrusted with protecting the yard from "mischief makers," but I paid much more attention to the birds. Hundreds of jackdaws nested in the leaves of the hundred-year-old walnut tree, and I watched for hours as they clambered out of their nests, flew after prey, and returned to their hatchlings. Sometimes I chose a bee for myself, one of the hundreds of absolutely identical bees, and kept my eyes trained on its singular flight.

If I began contemplating the trees, then I instantly remembered my grandmother. As soon as I glanced at the apple tree from which I'd once fallen without even a scratch, then and there I heard my grandmother's irritated voice: "Eat like a normal person! Bite and toss, bite and toss—who eats apples that way?" For some reason the willow tree leaning over the irrigation trough didn't inspire my grandmother with confidence: she thought a willow had no place in a yard. On the other hand, she loved the pear tree that sprawled by the gate; she called it "the imam tree" and reckoned that a person who ate its fruit would find healing. The mulberry tree that towered up behind the house also enjoyed my grandmother's good opinion. "It's a gift from God," she'd say, "that can feed us in difficult times." She spoke disapprovingly of the apricot tree that grew on the mountain among the zerish bushes with their small, sour berries: "What a waste! Just upsets the stomach!" She never said anything about the walnuts, but those mighty trees, rising in a wall along the path below, also reminded me of my grandmother; that was the place where she disappeared with the pitcher to wash herself.

I sat for whole days in the yard. I sat there and knew that not far off in the neighboring yards there were ponds with clear, blue water and naked kids lolling around them on the yellow ground. How I longed to be with them! To chase along the stony village street, clamber among the rocks, thieve from partridge nests! Besides, now I had pantaloons. Real pantaloons made from thick, dark material that Aunt Medina had bought in the village co-op. And although these pantaloons didn't have a fly or buttons, there was absolutely no doubt that they were pantaloons made for boys.

From our yard it was possible to go through to two neighboring ones: to Aunt Sona and Grandmother Shaiste. Aunt Sona's wicket gate was always locked—ever since the time they'd broken the leg of our tailless hen, my father hadn't allowed anyone from their family to come into our yard. The hen had accidentally wandered beyond the fence looking for food, and they broke her leg with a stone. Our other neighbor, Grandmother Shaiste, could come through our yard at any time, and as she was very old, each time she appeared in the yard I hoped she'd forget about the wicket gate. However, that never happened; the gate was always closed.

All summer I sat locked in, dreaming of just one thing—to find myself on the street among the boys. And then it happened. For some reason Aunt Medina came home in the middle of the day and, opening the gate, set me free. I raced out into the street, started running—and suddenly stopped. There was nowhere I wanted to run: the street no longer attracted me. As if there were no more blue ponds, or hot, yellow earth, or birds' nests in the rocks behind tall gates.

I can never walk calmly past a store where they sell birds. Not because catching birds or even shutting them in a cage seems such a crime to me. It's just that, having seen a bird shut in a cage, I can't escape the feeling that it's no longer a bird, it doesn't fly—even if they let it go, it will have lost its taste for flying forever.

Being locked in became much easier. I spent whole days without moving, observing the bees or watching the crows. Sometimes I'd simply drift off, sitting there. The sun would slowly begin to sink, I'd follow it, trying not to miss the moment when it hid behind the mountain. The sun set, and the hundreds of jackdaws that had dozed all day in the thick leaves of the walnut tree took off with a clamor into the sky. It was very interesting to look at them—the jackdaws alone would have been enough to keep me from being bored. But I could also climb the mulberry tree and wait until the drummer, Imamali, and his three sons appeared on the sandy road that wound around the mountain in a bright belt. They'd stand in a row near Grandmother Shaiste's house, turn to face the village, and Imamali would start beating the drum. His oldest son, Alish, played the zurna, and Velish and Malik joined in on pipes. Imamali was a remarkable drummer: he thumped the wooden sticks on the drum with such force that the mighty, rumbling boom spread through the whole village.

A little later the herd slowly began to descend. The cows moved sedately, unhurriedly, as if listening to the wail of the zurna. Then the herd entered the village, a few minutes passed, and our Lyska was already mooing at the gate, waiting for my father.

My father returned home when it got dark. Even without seeing him, I knew he was drawing near—his heavy boots thumped dully along the stony road. Every day he brought me a present—a small, striped muskmelon. Those muskmelons could have come from a matched set all the same size and color.

While my father made a fire in the hearth, heated water, and brewed tea, I amused myself by rolling my melon around the grass. Then we spread out the palas carpet and sat down to supper.

Later, just before bedtime, Aunt Medina arrived. Silently milking the cow, silently boiling the milk, silently preparing qatiq—she was always silent in front of my father. Placing the small, smoking lamp on the seki in front of the irrigation trough, Aunt Medina would start on the dishes... My father smoked, propping his elbow on a pillow, and I tried not to look at his big, black boots standing near the palas—for some reason I was a bit frightened of them.

Finishing her work, my aunt left, holding the lamp in front of her; the flame fluttered for a long time in the darkness like a light, orange handkerchief. I nestled into my father's warm side and drifted off listening to his loud snoring.

* * *

One night my father returned from the district center earlier than usual: the sun still hadn't set, the jackdaws hadn't yet taken off into the sky, the herd hadn't yet returned from the pasture.

He spread out the palas, threw the pillow on it, jerked off his boots and put them in their regular place, and smoked, propping his elbow on the pillow. Then he called me to him, pressed my head to his chest, stroked it, and smoothed the hair behind my ear.

The jackdaws rose into the air—my father was silent. Music thundered on the slope, and my father was silent. Lyska arrived and stood mooing in front of the locked gates, and my father didn't budge from his place. Then he suddenly got up, went up to the gates, opened them, but didn't let the cow into the yard: on the contrary, he led her off somewhere.

A little later my father returned, but he didn't bring Lyska with him: our Lyska, red, with the big white spot on her head. Tonight she wasn't in the cowshed, breathing loudly and endlessly chewing her cud.

My father poured water into the tea kettle and put it on the fire. He went into the house, collected the palas carpets spread on the brick floors, took the two pile carpets down from the walls, put all of them in large sacks, and tied them tightly with rope. He dragged bags of flour from the pantry, put them in the hallway, and covered the openings of the beehives with fresh manure. Then he went up to the lemon tree, glanced at me—I understood immediately that something quite out of the ordinary was about to happen—and cut the single fruit off it.

My father had brought the shoot of the lemon tree from somewhere far away and planted it in a bucket. Each year the young tree flowered, and there were many blooms on it, but each fall only one lemon ripened. My father guarded that small, greenish lemon like the apple of his eye: it hung among the glossy, dark leaves until the tree

7

bloomed again, and my father showed it to everyone who came to our house. Getting ready for work, my father always fussed around the young tree, and Aunt Medina and I were strictly ordered to stay away from it. Now the young fruit wasn't any bigger than a walnut, but the lemon was yellow in my father's hand; it seemed as if he'd stolen it. My father brewed tea, took the knife from his pocket, cut the lemon into two unequal parts, and laid the bigger part in my glass.

He took a sip from his glass of tea and glanced at my surprised face. For a moment it even seemed to me that he was just about to smile, but I couldn't bring myself to ask what all of this meant.

My aunt arrived. She was also surprised to see that we were drinking tea with lemon, but she didn't ask anything either. She poured the qatiq she'd prepared the previous evening into a bowl. Then she climbed up onto the iwan, the long terrace along the front of the house, and put water on to heat. Picking up the oil lamp, she went toward the cowshed to do the milking.

"Medina!" my father yelled to her. I flinched at that unexpectedly loud shout. "Don't go. I sold the cow. I'm leaving tomorrow."

Aunt Medina's shadow shivered on the grapevine and froze. Then my aunt ran down the stairs and came toward us. She always walked slowly, with the sluggish, lingering step of a person who has lost something she very much needs and long ago gave up hope of finding—now she was approaching quickly, at full speed. She stopped short, as if she'd run into a wall, and sat down. I'd never seen Aunt Medina sit down, and here she was sitting, arms folded across her chest, her eyes fixed on the piece of lemon floating in my father's glass.

"I packed up some things. Mukush can come get them in the morning."

My aunt nodded.

They were silent.

"Beshir will pay you three hundred rubles for the cow."

My aunt looked silently at my father.

They were silent.

"Thank God, Sadyk isn't nursing. He'll grow somehow..."

My aunt hugged me and pressed me to her chest.

They were silent.

"You won't have to feed him for free. I'm leaving four sacks of wheat for the little fellow."

My aunt cast a reproachful glance at my father.

They fell silent.

Then my father spoke, and my aunt listened. And the night listened to what he said, and the trees listened, silently bowing their heads. And when my father fell silent, the stars started whispering with the mountaintops, and today there was something especially ominous in their whispering.

"Tomorrow I'll speak with Mukush," began my father after a long pause. "I'll say what I must. I stand guilty before you, Medina: I've driven you into this wretched hole. If I don't come back, forgive me, for the love of God!"

My father hung his head. And it suddenly struck me that they looked very much like one another, my father and his sister. Aunt Medina began to cry. My father turned away and coughed a few times.

My aunt lifted her eyes to him as if she wanted to say something, dropped her eyes, lifted them again, and again lowered them.

I'd always thought that Aunt Medina didn't talk with my father out of timidity, but when we went up to my aunt the next morning, it occurred to me that it simply wasn't necessary for them to converse—they understood one another without words. Otherwise, why would my aunt have brought the tea quickly to a boil—she didn't actually know that we hadn't eaten breakfast. Spreading out the tablecloth, she first set out a bowl of qatiq—before breakfast, my father always drank qatiq. Then four plates appeared on the tablecloth, four spoons, and four glasses; my little cup also stood there.

My aunt tidied up the plates. I sat on the palas and looked at my father. I couldn't hear what he and Mukush were talking about; they stood under the mulberry tree on the opposite side of the yard, hidden by its heavy leaves. My father's boots were the only things I could see; they restlessly trampled the yellow ground, as if they were two big, black hens. My father was in a towering rage. When our unfortunate crested hen, flapping her wings and hopping for dear life on her broken leg, had flown over the fence and darted for the henhouse, I'd understood from those boots then, too, that my father was livid—never before had his boots thundered like that on the brick floor. That time the boots had stomped twice along the thicket of Russian olives that separated our yard from the neighbor's. Then my father turned around, stood in front of the willow, leaned back against it, threw his cigarette butt to the ground, and stamped it out furiously for a long time with his boots.

From where I was now, on the roof of the cowshed attached to the house, I could see the irrigation canal with its silver ribbon extending along the slope toward our house. I knew that Grandfather Aslan was sitting right now on the knoll at the very end of the irrigation canal. He'd sit there every Wednesday. Grandfather Aslan had a marvelous garden, and on Wednesdays, according to the schedule that had existed in our village since time immemorial, he received his allotment of water; he always sat at the lower end of the irrigation canal and kept an eye on the water. An underground channel extended from the irrigation canal at that spot, and it was constructed in such a way that if water flowed into it, it wouldn't flow along the irrigation canal until a deep basin near the dam had filled up. The boys knew this; as soon as Grandfather Aslan left his post, they'd immediately remove the old jacket the old man used to plug the pipe leading to the underground channel and flee.

Not wanting to hang back, I'd also pulled the plug from the pipe a time or two, but when the water rushed down, foaming and chattering, I grew unbearably sorry for Grandfather Aslan, and the consciousness of my own daring no longer gave me any pleasure.

Now Grandfather Aslan will get up and walk along the irrigation canal with the grub hoe on his shoulder. He'll chase the little girls away—how much water they're taking, the thieves! He'll shout at the women also trying to siphon some off—when else would they wash themselves, he'll say, if not on his day? He'll walk from house to house and knock at the gate with the hoe, threatening the boys who pulled his plug from the pipe. Then Grandfather Aslan will get tired, sit down on someone's doorstep, and leaning back against the wall, tell stories about how he worked in the oil fields, how he established Soviet power in Baku, and how he, Aslan, was summoned by Lenin himself. The older kids, those already going to school, will anger the old man with their skepticism about his story. Someone will be found to dispute his claims, to argue that Lenin had never even been to Baku; the old man will stand his ground, get angry. The dispute will escalate to a quarrel, Grandfather Aslan will wave his grub hoe at the kids and leave. Then he'll sit on the knoll again, again he'll knock on doors with his hoe, and again he'll tell stories about how he worked in Baku and met Lenin himself... In the meantime the paths will be watered, and the women, having washed themselves, will go out into the street to pass the time, pink and satisfied. And all of that will come to an end only in the evening, when Grandfather Imamali's drum begins to thunder on the slope of the mountain. And in a week a new Wednesday will arrive, and it will all start up again.

For some reason that morning I felt especially, unbearably sorry for Grandfather Aslan. And for the herd boy, Safar, who'd just driven the herd onto the slope of the mountain and was walking by himself, whistling and kicking at stones along the way. And for Mukush's old boots standing under the tree so dirty, covered in clay. And for Aunt Medina. And for myself. A man appeared on the road: he was walking to the district center, driving a donkey. I even felt sorry for him.

My father and Mukush returned to the roof. Both were sullen, angry. My father looked Aunt Medina in the face, and once again it seemed to me that they understood one another without words. Then my father hoisted the sack of things he'd brought out from the house, perceived that the sack had become heavier, and again looked at my aunt, as if saying goodbye to her with a glance. After that, he didn't look at anyone. He lifted me in his arms, carried me down the stairs, put me down on the ground, kissed me, and left.

I went back to the roof. The strip of sunlight rising along the mountain in the distance slowly began to spread along the slope. Then the sun thrust its head out from behind the other mountain opposite. My father's silhouette appeared on the road—my father came around the bend where the man with the donkey had just been. Then the herd appeared on the slope, and I started looking for Lyska.

Mukush dragged various things out of our house right up until the noon meal. He loaded them onto a donkey and dragged them on his humped back, covered in sweat. I ran with him, step for step—I liked running back and forth through the village.

2

The house where I now lived had been built at the opposite end of the village, also right by a mountain.

That round, grayish mountain was not nearly as high as ours, and when I'd looked at it earlier from the roof of my father's house, the mountain reminded me of a giant sheep bending its head to peacefully nibble grass. Up close, the mountain looked completely different. It wasn't round and smooth in the least: giant, multicolored boulders, crevices, the bare wreckage of cliffs—it wasn't easy to climb at all. Of course, I scrambled up, but I was absolutely certain that the climb wasn't accessible to others, and that the villages, forests, and cliffs along the other side of the mountain that I saw from there were my own discovery, that no one except me suspected their existence. I sat on the heights of the "sheep mountain," looked at the village roofs turning yellow in the distance, at the kids running around the twisty paths, at the men with white turbans on their heads—they were winnowing grain on the threshing floor—and was amazed that these people were just like our people, our villagers, and that they lived so similarly.

Mukush had a big garden, but it didn't give me any pleasure to walk around it. Mukush had devised a way to siphon off a great deal of water, and he showed such zeal in watering the earth that it was always wet around the trees; that was probably why the damp smell of rot always hung over the garden.

Above the house, at a little distance from it, grew two old, half-dead mulberry trees. A little further beyond them, thick vines of cucumbers turned yellow. Not far from the cucumbers, Mukush tethered his black donkey under a walnut tree, and the donkey spent the whole day grazing on the thick grass, shifting from foot to foot and lazily waving his tail. Whenever Mukush returned home from anywhere, the donkey, hearing his master from afar, turned his muzzle in that direction, opened his jaws wide, and wrinkling up his face like a person who's about to sneeze, started to bawl. He bawled until Mukush appeared at the gates.

Every morning before the sun came out, Mukush untied the long-eared fellow and set off with him into the mountains. After an hour or two he drove the donkey home, laden from head to tail with brushwood. There was already nowhere to put the brush: Mukush had heaped up whole mountains of dry branches behind the house and in front of the cowshed. My aunt was angry that it was impossible to get near the cowshed, but Mukush continued hauling brush and piling it up, hauling and piling it up, and soon he'd filled the entire yard with brushwood.

Having dumped yet another load of brushwood behind the house, Mukush would sit down in front of the pile of old shoes and proceed to work at cobbling. Finishing his repairs, he'd take his shovel and sickle, sit on the donkey, and tapping the donkey's stomach with legs so long they almost reached the ground, set off for work at the collective farm. He returned at lunchtime, carrying a large load of grass on the donkey. There was always a sack of fruit stashed away in the grass, and although what he stole from the collective farm orchard couldn't really be called fruit—it was completely unripe— he diligently dried his spoils. Mukush put the hard, woody green apples and pears and tough medlars not yet juicy with sap in straw to ripen; he dried apricots on the roof. The greater part of all these goods went bad, not having been able to ripen; the rest vanished only later, after ripening. Fruit was strewn all over the yard, mixed with the brushwood that Mukush continued to haul from the mountains every morning.

Each evening the zurna sang from the slope of the mountain, and the drum rumbled happily; each evening the jackdaws took off into the heavens; each evening we seated ourselves on the palas spread out on the roof of the cowshed and silently set about dinner.

Then my aunt and I went into the lean-to. My aunt spread out the bedding, blew out the lamp, lay down, and pressed me firmly to her. Usually she lay awake for a long time. I didn't always fall asleep immediately either; we lay, nestling close to one another, and were silent.

13

At the back of the yard, behind the withered mulberries, the flame of a cigarette gleamed in the dark like a wolf's eye. That was Mukush, smoking. Each evening he seated himself between two big rocks. The pebbles and sand around this spot were stained with filth, and such a foul smell emanated from there that Aunt Medina never went any further in that direction than the withered mulberries. Later I found out that Mukush fertilized the earth under the cucumbers each spring with soil taken from this spot, which was why there were so many yellow leaves and so many cucumbers on the vines.

Aunt Medina never ate the cucumbers from our kitchen garden, and each evening, having seen Mukush in his customary place, I also promised myself not to touch those nasty cucumbers. But when daylight arrived, I'd forget about my resolution—the neighboring kids begged Mukush for a cucumber from morning till night, and I also began to want one. At noon Aunt Nabat would arrive in her dark dress burned by countless cigarettes, panting from the heat, and seat herself in the shade. If Mukush happened to give her some overripe, yellow cucumber, she'd take it, not noticing the grower's frowning face, and eat it with the utmost pleasure... When the heat of the day lessened, Mukush would pick two buckets of cucumbers and carry them to the square to sell. Some evenings he didn't manage to sell his wares and brought back full buckets. However, Mukush never allowed us to give those cucumbers to anyone: he fed them to the donkey. The donkey didn't much care for cucumbers, and they lay in a heap in front of him for several days, yellow and swollen. Then they began to rot, and they lay around the yard for a long time like the brushwood and the stolen green pears.

Having sat the requisite amount of time between the rocks, Mukush invariably came toward us, and my aunt would press me tightly to her. Mukush cautiously cracked open the door, looked in, and left, violently slamming the door. This sequence was repeated every day. Each evening my aunt spread out his bedding in the big room, and each evening he always came to us. I saw that Mukush wanted to sleep here, with us, but at first I didn't understand why he wanted to do that.

Once Mukush looked in at us, as usual, and seeing that I wasn't asleep, angrily slammed the door. However, he soon returned, having already changed into a long, white shirt that went down to his knees. I raised myself a little, looking at him in surprise. Mukush pretended not to see my glance, turned his back, went up to Aunt Medina, and pulled the cover off her. I was frightened and screwed my eyes shut... Then he left. The next day when Mukush took off his dirt-stained shirt, I saw bluish bite marks on his shoulders.

For several days in a row Mukush came into our room before going to bed and pretended that he thought I was asleep. While waiting for his inevitable appearance, I watched the flame of his smoldering cigarette, and it seemed to me that it wasn't a cigarette, but Mukush's eye, red from anger, glowing in the dark. From there, he looked at me with burning hatred—because I was responsible for his not being able to sleep with Aunt Medina. Now I knew why Mukush never talked to me, wouldn't take me with him into the orchard, had never once set me on the donkey. It's true that I tried several times to climb onto the donkey when Mukush wasn't there, but the long-eared fellow kicked so devilishly that I had no doubt: on leaving the house, Mukush had very firmly ordered him not to let me get near.

3

At the end of the summer Mukush went into the district center three days in a row. He left home at dawn, returning only after dark. The first day he took a full cargo of fruit—dried from what he'd stolen—to the bazaar on the heavily loaded donkey. The next day he led a young ox to market, the one he was supposed to hand over to the collective farm. The final day Mukush hauled two cockerels to the bazaar, tying them together by the feet. Coming back from the bazaar, Mukush didn't say a word to anyone, morning or evening, and Aunt Medina just looked gloomily after him and muttered something under her breath.

My aunt and Mukush were almost always at loggerheads, and I grew accustomed to the idea that that's just the way things were. And that, in general, being husband and wife was as bad as things could get: it was for precisely this reason that everyone had scolded me when I'd said to Khalida that she was my wife.

Each evening Aunt Medina and I set out for our old house at the opposite end of the village. As soon as she unlocked the gate of my father's house, she was immediately transformed: her face brightened, her eyes became happy, her voice grew resonant, and she'd start to sing. Absently humming a little song, she'd water the lemon tree, lift the stones that had fallen from the wall and try to fix them in place, sweep and water the yard, and light the lamp, without fail—people should know we were here, that the house wasn't abandoned: we shouldn't let our enemies rejoice. Sometimes, coming up to the house, we'd find Lyska at the gates. Several months had passed since my father sold her, but the cow still couldn't forget her old home or her old masters, and she mooed for hours by the locked gates, falling silent only when we approached. My aunt stroked her udder gently, smoothed her head, and I, clasping her neck, kissed her slippery nose and her big, sad eyes. Then we went into the yard, locked the gates behind us, and the cow still stood and mooed until Beshir's boy came and drove her away.

I was very sad to hear how Lyska mooed at the gates, but as soon as I found myself in my father's yard, I'd start to scamper about and get up to mischief, like a puppy released from its chain. I chased after butterflies, flung stones at the crows, climbed the walnut tree in which I'd once said "naughty words" to Khalida, and stuffed my shirt full of walnuts. I nibbled them in raptures the whole way back, scattering green shells around me.

And once more in the evenings the jackdaws took off with a clamor into the sky, and again the drum thundered on the mountain to the wailing of the zurna, and the herd returned to the village. And in her dark dress burned by countless cigarettes, Aunt Nabat climbed onto her roof and from there talked things over loudly with Aunt Medina, also standing on the roof. Meanwhile, Aunt Nabat's son, the teahouse worker Yakub—a handsome young man—sat at the top of the mulberry tree, munching berries and softly singing a song. The song was always exactly the same:

> Come out, come out, my love,
> Gazelle, don't torment me,
> Your brows are black as arrows,
> My wounded heart now bleeds...

Mukush, who'd gone to the mosque all summer with full baskets of cucumbers, stopped trading them. He collected the beans that grew where the sun was hottest in the yard and piled them in the hallway. He dug up the potatoes, pulled out the onions, tore the yellow cucumber vines out by the roots; mixed with the brushwood, they cluttered up the yard even more. He dragged in two good-looking lambs from somewhere and let them graze in the yard.

Every day I shinnied up a tree, tore off leaves, and then rejoiced, looking at the lambs who'd eaten my treat with gusto. But I just couldn't forget our Lyska. I kept an eye out for her when the cows walked past us on the way to pasture and when they returned to the village. Scrambling up the mountain, I looked for a long time at the other villages and at the road winding around the slope of the mountain: my father had always returned along that road, bringing me a striped muskmelon... One evening Teacher Sariya arrived: she visited all the yards with her blue notebook. Carefully covering her enormous, round stomach with a white handkerchief, the teacher talked with my aunt, went up to the apple tree growing right in front of the cowshed, plucked several unripe apples, and ate them, puckering up her mouth; she said that this year Sadyk was enrolled in school and made a big, red dot with a red pencil in her blue notebook.

4

When I remember my first day of school, the thing that immediately bubbles to the surface of my mind is the giant schoolyard: burning-hot earth strewn with nutshells and quince cores. To this day my bare feet retain the dry heat of that sun-scorched earth.

The next thing that comes to mind is the teacher, Ali-muallim. Ali -muallim walked into the classroom holding a long ferule and the class register in his hands. He said, "Good morning!" loudly to us, opened his register, called the roll, and taking the ferule in hand, got up from his seat.

"Hands on your desks!" he commanded loudly.

We followed his command, and Ali —small, dark, and very strict— walked along the rows attentively examining our hands. The teacher was not pleased with our hands. He walked between the rows, shook his head with displeasure, and smacking his ferule on the desks, sternly spoke distressing, even terrifying words. Teacher Ali announced, for example, that as we were in school now, we were forbidden to stain our fingers by removing the shells from nuts. We were to wipe our noses with handkerchiefs, cut our nails, launder our shirts, and carefully comb our hair. And we were not to walk around barefoot—we were in school now. And we were forbidden to play knucklebones—we were in school now. Teacher Ali walked between the desks and listed what we should and shouldn't do, and I listened and thought that to be in school was probably no more enjoyable than being husband and wife.

During the first break I went out into the yard, slipped through the kids enthusiastically munching quinces, and looking fearfully around, stole through the gate. The little kids congregated there, the ones still too young to attend school. I pushed through them and broke into a run. By the river I stopped and caught my breath. Then I looked at the small river, at the gray building at the foot of the mountain that resembled the grazing sheep, and immediately my nose picked up the smell of rot, the stink of befouled stones. I turned around, and just as quickly as I'd raced there, I ran back to school.

At the last break Teacher Sariya came into the classroom. She held her dark-blue notebook and the red pencil in her hands. Covering her belly with the white scarf, she walked among the desks, looking affectionately at the kids. She patted the head of one with a very clean, white hand, smiled at another, asked a third about his mother, and then sat on the chair that Ali-muallim had relinquished to her and started to write the names of those whose fathers were at the front in her blue notebook. Over the next few days, all of those whose names had been written down were called to the teachers' office, and they handed us a shiny new pair of galoshes.

Real fall weather set in. The trees were stripped bare. Now Mukush loaded not brushwood but dried leaves on the donkey—he raked them in the collective farm orchards.

I also rode to the orchard with Mukush. For some reason he began taking me with him, even sat me on the donkey, and if a quince turned up among the fallen leaves, he gave it to me. Mukush was somehow different; recently I'd even begun to like him more, but my trips with Mukush were not to Aunt Medina's liking.

At first Mukush took me to the orchards only so that I could look after the lambs, but later he got hold of a small sack from among some old junk and began collecting leaves on my account; at night I walked proudly among the kids, happily dragging a sackful of rustling leaves.

It was too bad that my aunt was angry with Mukush—I liked riding with him to the orchards so much! There were a lot of orchards, and there was such thick grass there, and reservoir ponds in which you could skip stones, and whole mountains of dried leaves! And every living creature: hedgehogs, rabbits, field mice. You might even see a fox in the orchard!

And I could run wherever I wanted there, especially because I didn't have to worry about burrs while wearing my galoshes: I could run across sharp stones, climb the cliffs. Lying down to sleep at night, I stood the galoshes close by, right next to the palas, as my father had once done: I so badly wanted my beautiful, shiny galoshes to look as much as possible like his boots.

Mukush and I would return after dark. First Mukush emptied the sacks of apricot leaves into the storage shed, then took the saddlebag stuffed with walnut leaves that were suitable only for fuel and, shaking out the leaves, removed firewood from underneath them. I drove the lambs into the cowshed; we sat on its roof and settled down to dinner.

And then the zurna wailed anew over the mountain; the jackdaws again took off into the evening sky; Aunt Nabat, standing on the roof in her wide, dark dress, exchanged shouts with Aunt Medina; and Yakub, climbing into the mulberry tree, slowly drew out his song... Then, suddenly, everything changed—they began to call meetings in the club every two or three days. A new, unexpected source of entertainment appeared for me.

We all three went to the club: Mukush, my aunt, and I. Usually Mukush went a little earlier: either he needed to speak with some people on the square, or else he was on the watch near the teahouse for buyers to whom he could sell eggs, cucumbers, or something else. All the same, when we entered the club Mukush was already sitting in his place: he always sat in the first rows with the men. My aunt sat a little distance away, where the women always sat, and I elbowed my way toward the boys: they stood in the corner near the broken benches. Facing the crowd, five people sat behind a long table covered in red fabric. In the middle was Uncle Murtuz, chairman of the collective farm. The chairman was quite short, noticeably shorter than those who sat beside him, but he seemed—I don't know, maybe it was only to me—the biggest and tallest. On the table in front of the chairman lay an enormous pair of field binoculars: Uncle Murtuz never parted with those binoculars. It was said that the chairman saw everything through his binoculars, including those who loafed around during working hours and those who stole what belonged to the collective farm. Up until that fall I hadn't for a second doubted the reliability of those observations; however, my faith in the power of the chairman's binoculars had recently begun to waver because if everything everyone said about the binoculars was true, then Uncle Murtuz would surely have seen Mukush stealing fruit in the orchard and carrying it away covered in armloads of grass or dried leaves.

Two people sat on either side of the chairman—three men and a woman, Aunt Zokhra. Aunt Zokhra sat unmoving, her eyes fixed on the poster with the slogan "Death to the German Invaders!"

Next to Zokhra is the director of the school, Nuftaly-muallim. He's wearing a yellow striped shirt and a tie fastened with a wide knot around his long neck. The chairman of the village council, Uncle Abutalib, is also here, naturally, behind the red table of the presidium. The only remarkable thing about him is his cap with its long visor and the big red ears that bend down under its weight. On the other hand, Imamali, the father of Alish, Velish, and Malik, immediately attracts attention. First of all because the collective farm watchman is generally a notable person— he's a musician, after all—but the main thing is that he's a person of extraordinary neatness, even a bit of a dandy. Even if large patches show on the sleeves of his neatly laundered silk jacket, his papakha is completely new. He twirls his moustache all the time, although it curls in different directions even without that. And Imamali's face is fresh, just shaved, his bearing so proud and his general appearance such that you can't even imagine him smiling.

The meetings were organized mainly for the reading of newspapers, but before the beginning of each reading, Uncle Murtuz invariably spoke about collective farm business. The chairman of the village council never spoke at the meetings, never gave a speech: he just nodded his head, the movement of his long visor expressing full agreement with what Uncle Murtuz said. After the chairman of the collective farm spoke, the floor was given to the director of the school, who read the newspapers. The school director read loudly, crisply pronouncing numbers and the names of cities; the phrases "German fascists," "killed and wounded," and "women and girls raped" occurred more often than others, and they remain fixed in my memory. When the school director said the word "killed," I always remembered my grandmother's funeral and, above all, the old women washing her body. On hearing the word "wounded," I immediately pictured our tailless hen: frantically beating her wings, she flew across the fence and, falling on her broken leg, hobbled into the henhouse...

After the reading of the newspaper, the floor was given to Imamali. He drew himself up to the fullness of his tremendous height and began his speech, thrusting out his chest as he did when he beat the drum. He spoke loudly, impressively, trying to use the bigger words from the newspaper.

"Comrades," said Imamali, smoothing his moustache with his hand, "the invaders came onto our land to enslave us! To destroy our homes, to dishonor our wives and daughters—that's what they want! It hasn't turned out that way! The plans of the German fascists have failed shamefully! Why, my dear fellow countrymen? Why, I ask you? Because first, they ran into the wrong people! We aren't some kind of lowlife scum—we're Soviet power! Because second, we're seventy-two free nations joined together! We have 'internationalicity'!"

"Third, fourth, fifth..."

Imamali usually listed no fewer than ten points, bending back a finger with each one. Then he put a hand over the eye with the patch and said:

"Comrades, I lost this eye fighting for Soviet power. But I'd also give my other eye for that, without a second thought! I'd give everything: home, belongings, sons, I'd give life itself for Soviet power, for our Motherland! And here's the word of a Communist: while I live, I won't leave these mountains. I'll beat my drum to the bitter end! Azerbaijanis have never been cowards! Let those who slander be silent! Our nation was and remains first among others! And this is how I'll conclude, comrades: may the worldwide Azerbaijani nation live forever on this earth!"

At this point Uncle Murtuz would stand up and extend his hand to the speaker. "Thank you, Imamali!" he said with feeling. The chairman of the village council nodded his visor in agreement. "Thank you, Imamali," came shouts from here and there in the hall. "God grant you good health!" Everyone liked Imamali's speech very much; the director of the school alone experienced some uneasiness listening to him, but he couldn't bring himself to correct the old man.

Then the questions began. The school director answered these questions, which were asked by particular people—always the same people. Suddenly, Mukush stood up.

"You read there," he said in an undertone, not looking at the school director, "that Odessa has fallen. How far is it from there to Moscow?"

Aunt Medina lowered her head. The school director looked at the ceiling, as if the number of kilometers from Moscow to Odessa were written there—he always looked at the ceiling before answering a question—and turned his gaze to Mukush. But Uncle Murtuz didn't let the school director answer.

"I'd be quiet!" he said loudly, glaring at Mukush. "You don't give a damn about Soviet power! Miserable excuse for a human being!"

A silence fell; I suddenly felt sorry for Mukush. And I wasn't the only one. Even Uncle Abutalib, contrary to habit, looked at Uncle Murtuz and reproachfully shook his visor. But that made no impression on the chairman.

"How many times have I told you?" he continued loudly. "Tie up that donkey! And you? Yesterday I saw that mule idling about in the collective farm mulberry grove again."

"My donkey didn't leave the yard yesterday," Mukush answered softly, not lifting his eyes.

Uncle Murtuz started to shout at Mukush; moreover, now the chairman of the village council was nodding his visor in agreement. Mukush was quiet. It was absolutely true that the donkey hadn't left the yard yesterday. Mukush had spent the whole day laying in fuel; he'd chopped down the old mulberry tree, sawed it up, and dragged armful after armful to the cellar, covered in sweat.

* * *

When Mukush felt at ease, he'd walk around the yard, thrusting his hands in his pockets and whispering something to himself under his breath.

"He's come to life!" Aunt Medina said scornfully on those occasions, looking askance at Mukush.

I felt that a very deep meaning was concealed in that phrase, saw it in my aunt's eyes, and I grew uneasy, although I didn't understand what was wrong.

That evening after the meeting, Mukush was in just such a mood. He paced around the yard, muttered something under his breath, as if he were memorizing poetry, and my aunt followed him with a hostile glare.

It was getting dark. Mukush's cigarette glimmered behind the trees at the back of the yard; he walked around and around, and I watched him in surprise, not understanding why he was so satisfied today. The donkey, tied like always to the tree on the edge of the yard, also seemed puzzled. He looked attentively at Mukush, shifting impatiently from leg to leg.

Then Mukush climbed up to join us and briskly began to circle the roof. His enormous shadow moved along the wall of the house, gliding over the withered cucumber vines.

Mukush was in an excellent mood, and any time he rejoiced, my aunt didn't like it. Now, setting the dishes on the tablecloth, she suddenly dropped the cup from which Mukush loved to drink tea. The cup broke; it seemed to me that Aunt Medina had broken it on purpose. The most interesting thing was that Mukush didn't even acknowledge the broken cup and continued to pace around the roof as if nothing had happened.

"Well, what is it?" Aunt Medina could hold back no longer. "Spinning like a top again? You think that if Hitler takes Moscow, you'll get your land back? Keep dreaming! You won't get anything!"

"Get your land back..." I immediately remembered the collective farm orchard, planted on four sides with walnut trees, and Mukush stretching out freely on the grass. When we rode there to collect leaves, Mukush sauntered around the yellowing grass, muttering something to himself under his breath, or lay for hours on that grass, looking at the sky and smiling blissfully. In one of those moments, Mukush unexpectedly told me that the collective farm orchard was his land: earlier it had belonged to his grandfather.

When Aunt Medina suddenly yelled about the land, Mukush lost his head: his eyes flickered, he rushed toward my aunt and with trembling hands tried to shut her mouth. However, Mukush soon calmed down, and when he sat down to dinner a little later, he wore the same face he'd worn back there in the orchard when, looking dreamily at the sky, he'd told me that the land was his.

That night I dozed off quickly and didn't see Mukush open the door of our room. I was awakened by a sharp jolting as my aunt shook me by the shoulders with all her might. I didn't open my eyes in time to see Mukush in the room: I only saw thin, hairy legs and the hem of his long shirt bolting through the doorway.

5

The bright yellowness of fall gradually faded from the mountains. It grew cold, and my aunt no longer laid out the palas carpet on the roof of the cowshed in the evening. As had happened in previous years, snow at first whitened only the farthest mountain peak—but every night it crept closer and closer, and soon it turned up on the neighboring mountain, very near. Heavy, gray clouds appeared from somewhere; the jackdaws disappeared. And finally one night even our mountain turned white.

One frosty winter morning we saw Imamali's oldest son, Alish, off to the front. The farewell took place during the first break at school. Imamali stepped solemnly across the spacious schoolyard. Elbows wide apart, he beat the drum unwaveringly. Alish, a tall, skinny fellow, walked behind him holding the zurna. It was obvious that he had to force himself to play. Alish's mother scurried along beside him. Running from one side to the other, she was trying to look her son in the face.

Velish walked behind his brother, head bowed low, red with

embarrassment, but the youngest boy, Malik, a solid, stocky youngster, was almost skipping.

Women poured out of the houses; people crowded the roofs. The little kids ran after them loudly yelling, "Hurrah!"

Alish went off to war, but each evening the music boomed on the slope of the mountain as before. Then, closer to spring, Aunt Nabat called out to Aunt Medina from the roof and pointed to the musicians. Now only two figures loomed on the road—Velish had followed his older brother to the front.

And three days later Aunt Nabat came to visit. She sat on the edge of the palas carpet, tucking the hem of the long dress with its cigarette burns beneath her, closed her eyes, and began rocking slowly from side to side.

"I can't bear it!" she said finally. "I can't sit at home. It's empty without Yakub in the house. Empty..."

That winter many left for the front. Many empty places were left behind among the desks in the upper grades, at the club, on the square beneath the big plane tree. On the other hand, Mukush's low, wooden bed covered by the red mattress was occupied almost all the time—he rarely left the yard in winter.

I didn't like it when Mukush stayed home—when he was there, my aunt was sad and silent. She didn't want to pop corn, didn't cut flowers out of paper, didn't tell stories.

If Mukush hadn't sometimes gone away from home, I'd probably never have found out that Aunt Medina could read. Once he went to the mill for the whole day. My aunt immediately came to life, cheered up, and suddenly began to recite poems by heart, the exact poems found in my *Native Speech* textbook. Then she began to sing them. Aunt Medina sang each poem in a special way, and each tune produced its own special expression on her face.

It was only when I listened to Aunt Medina sing poetry that I understood that she'd been a very good student. And that her teachers had been much better than ours—they'd taught her not only to read but to sing. My aunt loved to read, and she read very well, better than Ali-muallim himself. We had no books other than my *Native Speech*, and although my aunt read it from cover to cover several times, she never looked at the crumpled, worn-out newspaper that Mukush brought from somewhere twice a week, even if he wasn't home. Mukush forced me to read the newspaper. He was interested most of all in the word "Moscow" and in everything that was written next to it; he ordered me to read those parts several times, and he had enough patience to listen to how I stumbled in putting together the syllables of unfamiliar words. I did well only with those words I'd heard often at the club. I imagined that I wasn't me but the director of the school, that dozens of people were listening to me; looking at the newspaper page, I pronounced "German fascists" and "killed and wounded" with dignity.

At night Mukush didn't approach my aunt, although now we all slept in one room, but from the bruises that never left her face it wasn't difficult to guess what happened during the daytime when I was at school. More than once I noticed how old Nabat sighed, looking at my aunt's bruises. "Poor Medina!" the old woman said sadly. "What they say is true: the bear gets the best fruit! And Yakub has been carrying a torch for you for so many years. He used to turn pale when he caught sight of you!"

The red spots under my aunt's eyes turned blue, black, and then yellow, but it was as if she didn't notice them. She cleaned the rooms, swept the yard, carried firewood from the basement, and did it all calmly, silently, with the most unflappable look. When Aunt Nabat came to visit, they sat in front of the stove, and Aunt Medina patched my pantaloons, listening to endless stories about the letters from the front that arrived in the village.

By the way, our neighbor wasn't the only one who knew the contents of these letters. As soon as the mail carrier brought someone a triangular-shaped letter from a soldier, the whole village immediately knew who the letter was from and what was in it. We kids talked exclusively about soldiers' letters. Mentally they were always with us, like the ink-stained calico bags with which we ran to school.

Alish, Imamali's oldest son, secured pride of place for the number of letters sent. What's more, his letters were further distinguished by their thoroughness: in each letter Alish inquired about the wellbeing of his countless relatives and sent them all his best wishes. Two letters arrived from Velish, and in each he asked for wool socks. Aunt Nabat received all of one note from her son and constantly carried it with her: in the letter Yakub sent his greetings to Mukush, my aunt, and even to me. A letter also arrived from my father, very short: "First of all," he wrote, "I send greetings to everyone; second of all, I inform you that I'm alive and well and that I hope you are the same. Medina, look after the house and Sadyk. Bring the lemon tree inside—it will freeze on the iwan—and don't water it with cold water. Tell Mukush not to forget about the bees. There was a bit of honey remaining in the bucket, he should blow it into both hives. Medina, Sakina's ring, bracelets, earrings, and similar things are tied up in the blue bundle. If things get tight, sell them: don't let the child go hungry. There's nowhere to write me yet, they're sending me to the front."

The letter had been directed to me: soldiers didn't address their letters to women. However, Uncle Hasan, Azer's father, always wrote to his wife—but he was never like other people. In one of his letters he even wrote to his wife about a book. He wrote: "Have Azer check Shevchenko's *Kateryna* out of the library and read it to you." From then on Azer was nicknamed "Shevchenko." Each one of the letters from the front was special, unique, and always in some way reminiscent of the person who'd written it. From the way that Alish wrote, you could guess the way he looked: a tall, slim figure; clear eyes; and shining hair combed high. My father's letter reminded me of his heavy, black boots, while the gentle, affectionate letters that Azer's father sent his wife were as out-of-the-ordinary and surprising as the snow-white shirt peeking out from under his black jacket.

One more letter arrived from my father during the winter. This time he didn't write about bees or the lemon tree. Just the obligatory greetings and a request—to send warm socks. He wrote in detail about the correct procedure for sending a package to the front though.

For several days my aunt visited the neighboring houses to beg for wool, holding the ends of the scarf in her teeth so that her bruises weren't visible. Then she carded the wool piece by piece, spun it, and over several nights knitted my father socks and mittens by the light of the kerosene lamp.

Aunt Medina bore her bruises all winter without moan or complaint—however, she carefully covered her face with a scarf when she left the yard. Now I understood why my aunt had gone around bundled up to her eyes the previous winter and all the winters I could remember. When spring had just begun and it was still very chilly, Aunt Medina had already lugged the palas carpet up to the roof—there, she felt safe.

6

In the spring Mukush did everything that was supposed to be done at that time of year: where digging was needed, he dug; where sowing was needed, he sowed. Then—I remember this scene well—he collected the night soil in a rusty bucket, mixed it with earth, and scattered it over the little irrigation canals freshly dug between the cucumber beds. He also fertilized the trees—he dragged a sack of grayish powder from somewhere or other, and at night, lamp in hand, he sprinkled this powder under the fruit trees, glancing around in fear.

I still remember Mukush lying there in the collective farm orchard, stretched out freely on the sunny green slope, looking dreamily at the sky.

And I remember that slope, an ordinary mountain slope—the stream below, the almond tree a little higher, and the magpie's nest in it. And the ramshackle old chala, a simple structure somewhat akin to a hut or a shed. Once people had slept in it, they'd put the samovar nearby, at noon they'd grilled kebabs. Mukush told me all this—here, on what he still considered "my grandfather's land," he was full of life, talkative, even affectionate. It was too bad that my aunt never saw him like this. And Mukush told the story so well that when we spread our coarse calico dastarkhan covered in innumerable patches on the grass, I didn't see onions and bread, but skewers of kebab. Even the scent of roasted meat felt entirely real.

That spring Mukush never set foot beyond the orchard: he planted many new seedlings and cleaned out all the irrigation canals.

One day Uncle Murtuz appeared in the orchard. As usual, Mukush was lying under a tree and looking at the sky. He hadn't expected the chairman at all.

"Well, Mukush?" the chairman called out to him. "You're making plans again?"

Mukush sat up quickly, tucking his legs beneath him. Uncle Murtuz sat down, too, next to him. He pulled a cigarette from his pocket and smoked, silently tapping his boot with a small branch.

"You've screwed up, Mukush," he finally said softly.

"How's that?" asked Mukush plaintively.

"You sold the young ox?"

"I sold it, there wasn't a crumb of bread in the house..."

"I see; that means you bought grain?"

"I did, Comrade Chairman: three sacks. We ate it."

"And the grain they distributed for days worked?"

"We polished that off, Comrade Chairman. Two small sacks were left. We'll get by somehow, God bless you! We'd be lost without you, Murtuz!"

"You're not the kind who gets lost," the chairman said in a low voice, looking narrowly at Mukush. "You're fat with the blood of someone else! So: you're saving up grain. Are you planning to feed Hitler? Well, then. Your father also fed bandits..."

Mukush didn't dare answer; he just shook his head mournfully. Uncle Murtuz stood up.

"I've looked into your doings, Mukush. You don't operate honestly. You sold that young ox and got a scrap of paper in return? You thought no one would notice? Some lousy paper for that beauty! Well, guess what? That paper will cost you dearly! And the ox didn't come cheap for me, either—you know?"

And Uncle Murtuz pointed to a powerful, full-grown ox pulling a plow up the mountain slope. Mukush opened his eyes wide in amazement—it was his ox, the very same one he'd dragged to the bazaar with a thick rope tied around his neck. The chairman didn't say anything else. He turned around and, lashing his boots lightly with the small branch, began to descend to the river; his binoculars bounced, hitting him in the chest. I thought that perhaps the power of the binoculars hadn't been make believe after all.

So long as the chairman and his binoculars were still visible on the mountain, Mukush was silent. Then his dry lips trembled, and his face twisted.

"Drop dead!" he whispered. "May you never see the light of heaven!" And he spit after the chairman.

At supper Mukush sat like a dead man; all night he coughed, smoked, tossed and turned, and endlessly repeated the same thing: "May you drop dead!"

The next morning Mukush didn't get up. He refused tea, didn't eat any breakfast, and lay on the bed all day, as if it were winter outside. Next to the bed, Mukush placed a jar—for spitting. He smoked and spat, spat and smoked.

Toward lunchtime the village council sent a woman to fetch Mukush. As soon as she opened the door, Mukush began to cough, and he coughed until she left without saying a word to him.

Later they sent for Mukush once more; this time, a man appeared. Mukush also coughed incessantly in front of him. No matter how hard the messenger tried, he wasn't able to get Mukush out of bed, and he left, muttering angrily under his breath. Mukush forbade us to remove the jar of spit.

When the lamps had already been lit in the evening, Uncle Murtuz arrived. Moreover, he didn't come alone: the chairman of the village council was with him. Before entering, Uncle Abutalib neatly removed his old, patched galoshes; Uncle Murtuz came into the house in his boots.

Mukush didn't get up to meet the visitors. Groaning, he just turned from his side onto his back and coughed. Ceaselessly moaning and coughing, Mukush motioned for his visitors to sit and pointed for me to bring the cushion. I brought the cushion and laid it on the trunk, but Uncle Murtuz tossed it back into its previous location. The visitors sat on the windowsill and, exchanging knowing glances, looked at Mukush. He sat up slightly, spat into the jar, and shouted, turning toward the door:

"Medina! Where are you? Take this jar, empty it!" And he sank back weakly on the pillow. "Well, what can you do? It's the fourth jar—the poor thing can't take them out fast enough!"

I wasn't surprised that Mukush was lying and calling for Aunt Medina, knowing that she'd gone to the spring, but I didn't understand why Uncle Abutalib glanced at the jar, covered his mouth with his hand, and made a sound as if he were choking. Tears came to his eyes.

Uncle Murtuz went up to the bed and pushed the jar under the bed with his foot. My aunt came into the room out of breath, alarmed. She said hello to them, threw a quick glance at Mukush, noted that the jar wasn't in its place, but didn't say anything. She left, taking the samovar.

"No need for tea, Medina!" Uncle Murtuz shouted after her. "We're leaving now!"

In confirmation of these words, the chairman of the village council shook his long visor and turned to Mukush.

"Aren't you ashamed?" he asked.

"What's there to be ashamed of, Comrade Executive Committee?" answered Mukush in a weak voice. "Illness comes from God."

"And how did this one appear? Just yesterday God somehow visited illness on you?"

Mukush had a coughing fit, twisting around in place, indicating with his whole being that he couldn't say a word. Then he looked at Uncle Murtuz and reckoned that it would be better to speak:

"I got sick, Abutalib, I swear by your children, I got sick. I can't take it... For ten days now I've hardly been able to drag my legs. I've got to work somehow... And my chest is about to explode!"

At these words, something in Mukush's chest began to wheeze terribly. Uncle Abutalib was silent. For a minute even I believed Mukush was ill, but it wasn't so easy to outwit Uncle Murtuz.

"It's all a lie, Abutalib." Uncle Murtuz looked at Mukush with hatred and began to fidget angrily on the windowsill. "Every one of his words is hooey! Everything he does is a fraud! He steals fruit from the orchard—and gets away with it! He got a fake document for the young ox—again, it blows over. You think you're going to put one over on us now? You got sick, you say? You're not too sick to drag a three-pood sack, but you're too sick to go to the front? He stole a sack of fertilizer from the stack at night!" Uncle Murtuz turned to Abutalib. "People saw."

"Is that so?" the chairman of the village council asked with infinite wonder, in Russian, and he began remonstrating with Mukush.

It's unclear how long that conversation might have continued, but Uncle Murtuz was evidently tired of it—he went up to Mukush, tore the blanket off him, and threw it aside.

The chairman of the village council grimaced with displeasure, and Uncle Murtuz probably regretted his action—Mukush lay naked on the bed, exactly as his mother had birthed him into the world. Although he wasn't embarrassed in the least. Pulling on the blanket, he sat up and, no longer coughing, calmly asked:

"And why are you sending me to be a soldier, Murtuz? It wouldn't hurt you to try soldiering yourself."

"Me?!" Uncle Murtuz lunged threateningly at Mukush. "I'm not just waiting around for Hitler here! Each year I give the state five tons of cocoons. A thousand kilos of wool! I hand over wagons of grain to the front! If need be, I'll go to the front! But I'll send you there first because without me, you diehard kulaks will eat the collective farm alive!"

"It's you who's eating it alive!"

Uncle Murtuz didn't answer, but his face darkened. Clasping his hands behind his back, he walked around the room, tore a petal from the rose growing in a pot, chewed it, and spat it right in Mukush's face.

"Enough! That's it! If you don't change your tune by tomorrow, I'll send the recruiting officer. We'll tie you to the donkey's tail and drag you to the recruitment office! Let's go, Abutalib, there's no point in talking to him!"

They went out onto the roof, shook their heads at the sight of my aunt bustling around the samovar, and slowly descended the stairs.

Mukush pulled his pantaloons and shirt from beneath the pillow, got dressed, and went up to the window.

"Would you believe it?" he muttered, looking after the men departing. "And my father fed that bastard with his own bread!"

To which of the visitors these words applied—Uncle Murtuz or the chairman of the village council—I never found out.

* * *

My aunt came in with the samovar in her hands and placed it by the window; Mukush was walking from corner to corner. My aunt brewed tea, poured it into the cups; light steam rose from the cups. My aunt adjusted the wick of the lamp, placed it near the samovar—the lamp crackled, the samovar bubbled, we were silent.

My aunt brought dinner, took the plates from the alcove.

"Well, now, be happy," said Mukush. "I'm leaving."

My aunt silently dished food onto the plates.

"Better to be killed by a bullet than to see your evil snout day and night!"

My aunt didn't answer.

"What is wrong with you?! When you arrived here, it was as if a black stone had fallen on me. You destroyed my life."

"You destroyed it yourself," my aunt flung at him.

Mukush cast a baleful glance at her, went up to the window.

"I'll burn everything down! Everything! I won't leave you a piece of straw!"

"Burn it down."

Aunt Medina pushed a plate toward me and commanded me to eat. I couldn't eat—something was caught in my throat.

It grew quiet again. The wick crackled in the lamp, and the samovar bubbled by the window.

Mukush walked around the room without stopping. Steam was no longer rising from the tea glasses.

"Either go away or sit down!" my aunt threw out angrily. "Let the child eat in peace!"

"In peace?!" Mukush flared up. "And me? I haven't been able to eat in peace for seven years! I haven't heard a reasonable word for seven years! And what is it that I'm guilty of, in your eyes?!"

His voice trembled; his eyes filled with tears. My aunt was silent. Mukush sat down on the bed and spoke quietly, holding back tears with difficulty:

"For seven years I've lived only for you! I drag kindling from the mountain—for you—so there's a way to bake bread. I steal firewood from the collective farm—for you! And fruit to sell and put away something for a rainy day—for you! I think only of you! And you? How have you repaid me for my good deeds? Have you even once glanced affectionately at me? You call yourself a wife! You're my mortal enemy, not my wife!"

"It's your own fault."

"My fault? And what have I done to you?"

My aunt lifted her eyes to him and suddenly plunked down the glasses: they clinked. The saltshaker tipped over; salt spilled onto the tablecloth.

"What have you done?! You don't know what you've done? I'll tell you what you've done! You knew that I didn't care for you! That it would have been better for me to drop dead than look at your nasty face! You knew! Why didn't you leave me alone?! Why did you give my brother presents, drag in firewood for him like the vilest donkey? When you brought the pregnant cow, what did I say to you? 'Take away your gifts, I don't want to see you!' How many times I spat in your ugly mug! Why didn't you go away? Why did you hang around the mosque waiting for me after school? You stood directly in my way, you son of a bitch! Took me out of school! Teacher Khashim hasn't said hello to me for seven years! It's your fault! You and my brother! I was driven into this filthy house with blows, may it fall into ruin! You ruined my life, you monsters! Nadzhaf sold me! Sold me!"

She wept, repeating my father's name in a rage.

Mukush got up from the bed white, his eyes red; he went up to my aunt and kicked her in the leg with all his might.

"Drop dead, you daughter of dogs!" he hissed through his teeth. "Just..."

His legs were shaking. He flung the vilest curses at my aunt, doubled over, and left, clutching his stomach. The steps creaked.

Silently my aunt put the beans from his plate back into the pot, pushed my plate toward me, and sighing, began to eat. I had to eat my dinner too. All night a pair of big, black boots hovered before my eyes: I could even hear how they squeaked when they were walked in. And it seemed to me that it wasn't my father himself, but his big, black boots that were to blame that my aunt and her husband were unhappy and that Teacher Khashim hadn't said hello to my Aunt Medina for seven years.

Mukush probably spent the night sitting in his usual spot behind the mulberry trees, smoking one cigarette after the other; I woke up very late and thus didn't see him come in. Nor did I see how he left. But when I went out into the yard in the morning and looked at the mountains lit up by the sun, it suddenly occurred to me that Mukush didn't want to go into the army not because he was afraid but because he simply couldn't bring himself to leave our village.

Light, white tents spread out at the foot of the mountain—the almond trees were blooming. Arrayed like a bride, the reddish clusters of cornelian cherry that peeped out from all the orchards had never, it seemed, looked so beautiful. *And that's really only the beginning of what will happen when the willows leaf out, when the jasmine blooms! It's just at the point of blossoming—another day or two and fragrant bushes will turn white in Grandfather Aslan's garden. He'll break off a whole armful for the May holidays and stand near the school handing out flowers to the kids, both those who believe in his acquaintance with Lenin and those who don't. Then he'll ask the boys not to maraud in his garden, not to break the branches, not to trample the grass. In their joy the kids will promise, and then they'll come and trample the grass and break the branches all the same... The almond trees, the cornelian cherries— that's not all! The slopes haven't yet turned multicolored from the tulips, flocks of young girls aren't yet darting about collecting spearmint. And when the cow parsnip ripens, imagine what will happen then! And the quail will begin to build their nests, and it might be possible to catch a young quail in the grass! And that isn't all: the greatest beauty still lies ahead.*

Drunk on the sunlight, on joy, I happily clambered up onto the tip-top of a high cliff and looked down on the road from there—Mukush wasn't there. Grandmother Shaiste's house was right by the road, and just there, opposite her house, was where our musicians had stood every evening. This spring they no longer went out to meet the herd. All winter Uncle Imamali had taught his younger son to play the zurna, but when spring arrived and they began to put the herd out to pasture, Malik left. The old man was able to go out with his son all of one time to meet the herd; music was no longer heard in the mountains, although back at the club Imamali had resolutely promised that the music wouldn't fall silent.

I searched for our garden in the green mass of gardens. Surrounded by the branches of zerish bushes, the apricot tree towered over everything, all in white. "What a waste! Just upsets the stomach!" Could my grandmother really have been talking about this tree?

I scampered from one mountain to another; looked at the unfamiliar villages, astonished that life in them looked so much like our life; shouted something to the kids of that place, and understanding that they couldn't hear me, chucked stones at the dogs whose barks barely reached me here.

When I climbed down, a little red dress flickered on Aunt Sona's iwan. I wanted to shout, "All the same, you'll be my wife, Khalida!" with all my might.

I was celebrating, and I didn't know why. *Maybe it's because Mukush has gone?* The thought made me uncomfortable. And what about Aunt Medina? Because she was also glad: she was sitting now by the samovar and rejoicing that Mukush was gone.

First of all my aunt removed Mukush's bedding from the wooden bed, pulled pieces of canvas from under the red mattress and threw them aside—and a whole world opened up before me, suddenly liberated from its secrecy. During the long winter nights lying beside my aunt on the flimsy, quilted mattress, I'd trembled in fear before this dark, gloomy bed. Mice cavorted in the corner, squeaking, and it had seemed to me that terrible monsters resembling the djinns and devils of Aunt Nabat's tales were rolling around under Mukush's bed. Granted, as soon as he moved a muscle every single one of the bed's boards began to creak, and the djinns immediately fell silent, but as soon as Mukush settled back down, everything started all over again. I fell asleep and saw djinns and devils in my dreams: they were horned, with long tails.

Now all of that stopped. The den of djinns turned out to be an old bed assembled from boards from under which Aunt Medina cleaned out a mountain of old shoes, a piece of leather gnawed by mice, and a whole bucket of inexplicable odds and ends.

Then my aunt picked up the lamp, and I followed her down into the cellar, paralyzed with fear. Here various iron objects had been dumped: plows, pitchforks, shovels, many broken pitchers, and a countless number of strange-looking things that Mukush had undoubtedly inherited from his grandfathers and great-grandfathers. But besides all this junk we found two pails of honey, sheep's cheese, several sacks of grain, walnuts, tobacco...

That day I went to school with my pockets stuffed full of walnuts and gave them to all my classmates. Aunt Medina immediately gave one drawstring bag of tobacco to our neighbor; I hadn't seen Aunt Nabat so happy in a long time. She didn't visit for an entire week, and then she came and took away the second bag. My aunt also gave honey to our neighbors; I was reminded of when my grandmother died because Aunt Medina didn't let me eat my fill then either. For a little while the neighbors came to visit us every day to borrow a bowl of grain or a handful of peas, but I don't remember anyone repaying those loans.

My aunt dragged more than a dozen buckets of earth to cover up the spot where Mukush used to sit for a long time before bed. She swept the befouled pebbles into a pile with the broom and tossed them into the privy. Then she also tossed out the broom... At night Aunt Medina and I sat on the roof by the samovar and drank tea. That night it somehow bubbled especially cozily...

Dinner was also unusually tasty—my aunt cooked a full pot, and we ate it all up. The clouds billowing along the horizon were red that evening, almost scarlet, like the coals under the saj on which my aunt baked lepyoshka.

After dinner Aunt Medina climbed first onto the stool and then onto the wide windowsill, and she began to sing the way visiting artists sang at the club:

Pairs of beautiful women walk beyond rose gardens,
Bouquets of roses in their hands, fragrant red roses,
Loudly, clearly, they sing, "My darling, my darling, my darling."
And their joyful voices tear new wounds in my breast.
Joyful wounds. I'm only unhappy in this light-filled world,
I must go, I cannot, cannot stay here with them…

Now they sing that song differently, to a different tune, but I remember it the way Aunt Medina sang it. I remember the garden from that song—the roses in it smelled exactly like those planted in front of our house—and the girls in white dresses (for some reason they're always in white!).

My aunt sang, and I looked past her into the darkness of the window opening and saw the trees, not those that Mukush grew in his yard, but ours, my grandmother's. And it seemed to me that you just needed to open the door and you wouldn't see the yard littered with brush, but white roses, whole bushes of white roses.

Listening to my aunt, I saw not just white roses but also my father's black boots, and Khalida in her little red dress, and my grandmother, and Teacher Khashim, the same one who hadn't said hello to Aunt Medina for seven years. Then I imagined the stage at the club and Azer's father standing beside it in a white shirt with a turndown collar. There was Mukush hiding in an alcove and Aunt Medina passing by, casting a glance of loathing at him. There was Mukush tying a cow with a white spot on her head to a post and Aunt Medina standing next to the cow and shouting at Mukush.

My aunt finished singing, jumped down from the stool, hugged me, and began to laugh—she was happy. That evening she started singing again. All told, it was a special evening, the beginning of many things and the end of many others.

Part Two

1

Three months or so after Mukush was conscripted into the army, giant black cauldrons were brought into the village loaded on donkeys. Running up from the spring in her dark dress with the cigarette burns, Aunt Nabat argued to my aunt for a long time that they were going to build a commune and that these large vessels would be used to boil food for the whole village. Things didn't end with the cauldrons: after a few days, ten oxen harnessed in teams dragged a long, thick pipe along the mountain road. Every day some kind of iron contraption was carried into the village by horse, donkey, or ox: wheels, gears, levers... It soon became known that, in fact, a factory for producing silk thread would be built in the village.

Rumor had it that our chairman had orchestrated this whole business of the factory—all kinds of ventures were ascribed to Uncle Murtuz at that time.

At the meeting about opening the factory, Uncle Murtuz, speaking at both the beginning and the end, said straight out that he'd decided to build the factory and explained why it needed to be built in our village. The chair of the village council ordinarily just nodded in support of the chairman's words; however, in closing the meeting he couldn't contain himself, and he said, "The construction of this factory is evidence of the Party's high trust in the workers of our village."

After a few days large red letters appeared above the massive gates of the mosque: "Silk Thread Factory." The walls composed of bricks

39

of different colors were painted with a long slogan: "Women! Don't forget that with every thread you wind, you save one of your sons or husbands fighting for our great Motherland!" For some reason it seemed to me that Uncle Abutalib had composed the slogan: only he could have thought up such words.

Thus it happened that a giant factory smokestack, taller than the tallest plane tree, rose in our village and began belching black smoke. On the square in front of the mosque, onto which the kids had previously poured many buckets of water each evening at Uncle Aslan's orders to ensure cleanliness, large, oily puddles appeared; sparrows with oil-stained wings gleamed in our clear village sky.

If I could paint, and if I were trying to render the water that drained from the factory yard through long, thin pipes into the river, I wouldn't be able to find the right kind of paint: that wasn't even water, but some kind of strange sludge composed of a multi-scented stink. The fresh, green weeds turned yellow and dried up from that sludge, maybe not even from the sludge itself but from the evil smell that it spread all around. The stink penetrated everything; it seemed that even the pearly pebbles at the bottom of the river stank like rotting fish.

In the courtyard of the mosque they cut down dozens of lush acacias, and soon afterwards a long, ugly building appeared in their place—a storage facility for cocoons. Pigeons no longer built their nests near the mosque—they couldn't breathe the smoky factory air. The dead silkworms, boiled out of their cocoons, were dumped close by, in a pit that had formed on the site of a demolished house. Hens gobbled up the worms; an unbearable rotting smell began to come from their eggs. It must be said straight out that the factory did not beautify our village, but on the other hand, flour and sugar were delivered to the shop; they built a bathhouse, paved the highway, even began talking about electricity.

Because the factory was housed in the building of the mosque, which was a sin, the majority of our village women refused to go to the factory. Nevertheless, women workers were found. Some were persuaded by Uncle Abutalib, others were forcibly brought to the workshop by Uncle Murtuz, and there were also some like Aunt Medina: she didn't have to be persuaded or forced—she went on her own.

By that time we had only enough flour left for two or three bakes; my aunt had given the peas to neighbors early on, and the sheep's cheese stored by Mukush had long ago been exhausted. I'd divided the walnuts with my classmates the moment we found them, and for that, by the way, I received the idiotic nickname of "Walnut."

It seemed to me that working in the factory was far harder than at the collective farm, but for some reason Aunt Medina went willingly to her new job. She returned home cheerful, and she sang all the time: by then we'd already brewed herbs instead of tea for a long time, but even that didn't trouble my aunt much. The joyful expression never left her face.

Then Aunt Medina was given an award for outstanding work: she received a green dress with a stripe sewn around the pockets, and she was very proud of this gift. Now she'd stand in front of the mirror for ten minutes at a time examining her new dress, and in the evening she'd glance in the dark windows, seeking her green reflection in them. And she sang all the time. I simply couldn't figure it out: did the factory itself have this effect on my aunt, or was it all about the green dress?

Sometimes, on the coldest days, my aunt took me with her to the workshop. I settled myself somewhere in a corner under a window and watched how the little kids whose mothers worked at the factory scampered around the square in front of the mosque. Then I got bored with that activity and began to follow the silver drums that whirled tirelessly, winding the silk thread. These drums stood in rows, and two women walked back and forth in front of each row. In the back, behind the drums, huge cauldrons had been installed, the same ones Aunt Nabat had once mistaken for vessels to prepare food. It was in these same cauldrons that the cocoons were boiled, looked after by people who here were called supervisors. Besides the women workers and the supervisors, there were also trainees. The trainees caught a thread from the cocoon and hung it on a special hook. With a quick movement the women winders took the thread from the hook and, using all ten fingers, attached the thread to the whirling drums; the thread wound around, was connected to the next thread, and soon the drums disappeared under a giant skein of raw yellow silk.

Of the higher ups, I only had occasion to see the senior supervisor, Mamed, at the factory. He was lanky, like a plane tree, and round-shouldered. Bending over just the tiniest bit, Uncle Mamed walked up and down along the whirling drums with his hands behind his back; he hurried the trainees along, pointed out breakages to the women workers, surveyed the drums. It was explained to me that Uncle Mamed was responsible for looking after the machinery and supervising the work, but it seemed to me that mostly what he did was amuse the women workers. Women roared with laughter at his jokes; moreover, I noticed that if Uncle Mamed took someone by the hand, showing her how to fasten thread, the woman liked that.

As far as Aunt Medina, she must have enjoyed the presence of this cheerful person—she laughed heartily at his jokes. And from the time she started working at the factory, her mood in general was excellent.

Even coming home tired from work, Aunt Medina absolutely glowed with happiness. And her step became somehow different: young, vigorous. Whether she was adding coal to the samovar or looking at herself in the mirror, her movements were light, deft, and in some ways resembled those she made at the factory while standing in front of the buzzing drums.

I observed that at the factory, people generally did everything quickly: they moved around quickly, manipulated their fingers quickly, spoke quickly. Aunt Merdzhan alone, it seemed, never hurried: she walked up and down along the drums at an easy pace, connecting the thread with leisurely but precise movements. Glancing at the distant mountains, she softly sang.

Aunt Merdzhan lived in the district center; each day she went home for the night, and she always saved a lollipop or gingerbread cookie for me. Spotting me in the workshop, she'd pull a sweet out of her pocket and toss it to me, never forgetting to tease me at the same time:

> Sadyk, be my honey
> And give me some money!

I caught the sticky candies on the fly and stuck them in my pocket—I ate Aunt Merdzhan's sweets only when I got out on the street. Aunt Fatma, one of those women whom Uncle Murtuz had forced to work at the factory, had come up to me one day after work: glancing from side to side, she told me I shouldn't eat anything that came from Aunt

Merdzhan's hands. When I recounted that conversation to Aunt Medina, however, she got angry and swore at Aunt Fatma, but I no longer dared to suck the lollipops in front of everyone.

In the fall they tore down some ruins in the factory yard, built a kindergarten, and enrolled the little kids whose mothers worked at the factory. By that time I was in the second grade, but they also permitted me to enroll. I came to the kindergarten directly from school and immediately ate up everything I'd been allotted for both breakfast and lunch. It wasn't half-bad! However, the superintendent's son, a puny, pugnacious little boy, took a strong dislike to me: the imp either poured dirt into my bowl or tore off my hat and threw it in the mud. Pure chance came to the rescue. Trying to shame the scamp, the cook, Grandmother Sariya, told him that I was the son of an asker—a soldier—and that it was forbidden to treat me badly. The little boy thought for a moment, then suddenly grabbed my clay-smeared hat and, solemnly plopping it on my head, squawked: "Asker's son! Asker's son!" Fortunately for me, Askerov was the family name of the factory director, and the little boy had decided that I was none other than the son of the director. If he'd understood that my father was a simple soldier, I wouldn't have gotten rid of him so easily.

I grew accustomed to the factory yard quite quickly, the high walls of the mosque stopped weighing me down, and I began to like playing with the little ones more and more. We spent whole days scampering among the sacks of cocoons that filled the long, dim shed built on the site of the felled acacias.

The kids at the kindergarten were mostly not from our village, but newcomers from other places: in their conversation and demeanor, these kids differed markedly from us. For example, Azhdar, who lived in the district center, talked only about the war, and more than once he brought the little ones to tears with his strange stories. Noisy, talkative Gyulsum, who came with her mother from a neighboring village, loved more than anything in the world to talk about devils and djinns. One of the little boys who lived in the district center taught us to play "husband and wife," and as this game demanded a large variety of objects, we spent hours digging through the garbage, collecting various pieces of iron and sticks. It was an interesting game—everything as it was in real life. "Husbands" collected firewood, "wives" took care of children, wrapping the oblong stones they used for dolls in rags and baking imaginary lepyoshka on imaginary skillets. The best "husband" turned out to be the boy who'd taught us the game. Sticking a straw cigarette in his mouth and thrusting his hands in his pockets, he sauntered around the "frying pan" over which Gyulsum was fussing with a proprietary look. He cursed his "wife" harshly, spat in her face, even kicked her leg; however, as far as I could tell, Gyulsum didn't consider this an insult, but rather seemed to like such treatment, although she cried a little for show. Unbuttoning her little dress, Gyulsum pressed the stone wrapped in rags to a small, pink nipple, and then "put the baby to bed" and proceeded to bake lepyoshka out of mud. She also behaved like a real woman and housewife.

Everything was fine until the caregiver, Aunt Azra, found Gyulsum and her "husband" in a dark corner on the sacks of cocoons. They were doing "bad things." A gigantic scandal broke out, and we were no longer allowed to play "husband and wife."

Many of the kids in the kindergarten had very strange names: Danube, Marx, Ophelia—I remember them to this day. And I'll also never forget the bluish, watery kasha that I had to force myself to eat despite my constant feeling of hunger. And the berry kissel of a poisonous-red color that I'd never tried before. And Aunt Merdzhan's voice. She'd lean out the window, break into song, and glance sometimes at us kids, sometimes at the far-off mountains wreathed in haze. Behind her the heavy drums whirled nonstop.

Merdzhan's songs were sad, and at first I thought she was sad about her husband, who was out there somewhere beyond the far-off mountains fighting the fascists; later they told me that Merdzhan was unmarried, that she'd never had a husband and never would because she was a "whore." I first heard this word from that same town boy who was doing "bad things" with Gyulsum; after that, our village women, the ones whom Uncle Murtuz had brought forcibly to the factory, said it more than once, said it in a whisper, looking nervously around. Maybe that's why to this day I get the feeling of something secret and sinister in the word "whore."

2

Winter arrived, and the women who had to walk a long way to the factory began to quit work one after another. Uncle Murtuz and the chairman of the village council went from house to house to find apartments for those who remained. The places of the departed women workers were taken by our local villagers, but the kindergarten had free spaces, and several schoolchildren whose mothers worked at the factory were able to enroll. That's when Azer, nicknamed "Shevchenko," appeared in the kindergarten. With his appearance, an entirely new life began for me, and even the flavorless kindergarten kasha became much more appealing.

That thin, nimble boy, well-read and mature beyond his years, was the pride of our school. In the second grade—Azer sat in front of me, one desk over—he read so well that the teachers of the upper grades, wanting to shame overgrown idlers, took Azer to their classes and made him read aloud. Going out onto the street with a package of newspapers, Grandfather Aslan looked first of all for Azer.

Azer's father had left many books that Azer brought to the kindergarten; settling ourselves in some secluded corner, we spent hours poring over them. Sometimes the cook, Grandmother Sariya, joined us. She was a dignified old woman who at one time had completed a pilgrimage to the sacred places, so devout that she never failed to kiss the thick walls of the mosque on her way to work; she insisted that the kids do so, as well. Grandmother Sariya could have listened to us read forever, and we immediately became her favorites; if the director wasn't nearby, the old woman led us to the kitchen. We'd settle ourselves by the giant, still-warm stove and, glancing at the curved, soot-blackened ceiling beams, stuff ourselves with burned kasha or potatoes baked in the hot ashes. Sometimes Grandmother Sariya gave us a lump of sugar hidden somewhere in her breast pocket or pulled a newspaper intended for rolling cigarettes from her pocket and tore two pieces from it. Wrapping the remains of tea shaken from empty packets in the pieces, she gave them to us with strict instructions to tread gently along the road, no jumping, and to give the tea to our mothers without fail. If Grandmother Sariya had absolutely nothing left to give us, she'd slip us a couple of onions or the neatly folded wrapper from a package of tea. Azer took only the silver wrappers and forcibly stuffed the tea, sugar, and onion into my pocket.

People at the kindergarten tried not to upset Azer—official notification of his father's death had just recently arrived. Even when Azer beat up the superintendent's son who had tried, as was his custom, to pick on the newcomer, no one said a word to him. He could run out into the yard at any time, go out into the street—he could get away with anything. Even Aunt Azra, the caregiver, a hot-tempered and domineering woman, didn't dare scold Azer. Only Grandmother Sariya and I knew that Azer wasn't troubled by the notification—he didn't believe that his father had died—but by the fact that his mother had a new husband: Azer hated that man passionately.

When the workday ended, the mothers appeared at the kindergarten. Aunt Bilgeis also came for Azer, but he wouldn't even look at her. If his mother tried to kiss Azer, he pulled away and stepped aside, scowling. Returning home along the slippery, iced-over road, mothers held their kids by the hand; Azer never once touched his mother's hand.

Each evening after school we went to the kindergarten. Grandmother Sariya brought us something to eat, not, moreover, in the small children's dishes, but in those from which the grownups ate. We'd gulp down dinner in an instant and, finding a distant refuge, settle down to read a book. Azer read, I listened. Sometimes I was suddenly plunged into reverie, and looking at my friend's lips moving, I didn't see him but Uncle Hasan in his white shirt and black tie. Or I caught myself, having long ago lost the thread, thinking not about the characters of the tale but about Aunt Merdzhan, about why no one liked her, and why everyone called her such a terrible word that you couldn't even say it loudly. Maybe it was because she was pretty? I looked at the slippery road covered in ice and imagined Merdzhan walking along it alone in the darkness. Why didn't she ever spend the night in the village? Maybe no one wanted to let her? That was probably the reason. But why shouldn't I accept something from her hands? Maybe she had sores on her hands? Safar had them all over his body; they wouldn't even let him in the kindergarten. I tried to remember what kind of hands Aunt Merdzhan had and, not recalling anything, started again to speculate about what a "whore" might be... And Azer read and read.

3

It was a gray, dank winter evening. The horn blew. Merdzhan said goodnight by the factory gates and headed on her way. Aunt Medina glanced at Merdzhan's small feet, at the two pairs of thick wool socks—one pair was worn over her ankle boots so that she wouldn't slip—threw a glance at the mountains, at the road dissolving in the fog, and softly called out to Merdzhan. Merdzhan turned around, looking at Aunt Medina with a smile.

"How will you get there in this weather?"

Merdzhan lowered her head and began to look at her colorful socks. Then she turned and went on her way. My aunt called out to her again:

"Merdzhan! Come stay with us!"

Merdzhan turned around and looked at my aunt as if she'd just now seen her. Then she suddenly smiled broadly and exclaimed:

"Let's go!"

We talked loudly the whole way home. My aunt immediately lit the lamp, kindled a fire in the stove: it grew warm and cheerful. That night we even had a real dinner—Aunt Medina located a bag of beans Mukush had saved for seed under an old saddle in the basement. Not just that—she scrounged up a handful of pumpkin seeds and a dish of corn from somewhere. They put the beans on to boil; Aunt Merdzhan set about roasting the pumpkin seeds and corn. She stood by the stove chatting about something with my aunt, sang, and from time to time lifted her dress a little to warm her chilled legs. Sitting off to the side, I examined her hands attentively: there were no sores. Merdzhan's hands were white and plump, with thin, beautiful fingers. The corn kernels burst, popping cheerfully. Aunt Merdzhan threw them to me and sang:

> Sadyk, be my honey:
> Make change for my money!

Then my aunt put on the samovar and brewed herbs. Chattering ceaselessly, we ate our fill of the delicious, salted beans and drank tea with dried mulberries.

My aunt laid out three mattresses next to each other on the palas carpet. I lay down next to the stove, drowsy from the heat, and tried to imagine Merdzhan walking alone among the mountains in the dark with hungry wolves howling all around.

Fighting sleep, I tried to make out what Merdzhan and Aunt Medina were whispering about. Merdzhan was talking about her life, apparently, but at the same time, her story very much resembled a fairy tale, probably because it had roses, many roses, and a young man—tall, dark-haired, and handsome in his white shirt (I was already big enough to wear a shirt!)—who brought Merdzhan flowers.

"How good it is to be married!" Merdzhan continued dreamily. I immediately thought of the dark-haired young man in the white shirt. "How lucky you are, Medina!"

"You have no idea what you're talking about!" answered my aunt. "Some luck that is!"

And forgetting that I might not be asleep, helter-skelter, hurrying, she suddenly began to talk about what she'd never said to anyone else: about Mukush's courtship, about her wedding night, about the first morning in her husband's home...

And then and there the meaning of the incomprehensible newspaper phrase "they rape women" came to me, although I had thought before that rape was only committed by the fascists they wrote about in the newspapers; I hadn't known that it was also done after a wedding feast where music thundered... And it turned out that my aunt had had a beloved, the director of the club, who later became Azer's father.

"Never mind, Medina! You're not an old woman, you'll find another!"

"Absolutely not! You can do that with a hat—take it off one person, stuff it onto another! But marriage? I'm fed up with marriage! Completely fed up! Thinking of it makes me shiver!"

Perhaps they stopped whispering, or perhaps I fell asleep at that point, but I don't remember anything more. Waking up, I immediately saw the cheerful eyes of Aunt Merdzhan. She was shaking me and singing:

> Sadyk, be my honey:
> Make change for my money!

We breakfasted on beans left over from the night before, drank tea with dried berries, and went out into the street. It was very cheerful: Merdzhan scampered about and slid on the icy path. Then we separated, each going their own way: Merdzhan to the factory, while my aunt accompanied me to school.

"Aunt," I asked as we neared the school, "what's a 'whore'?"

"That's a terrible word, my son, don't ever say it!"

"Is Merdzhan a whore?"

"What are you saying?!" My aunt looked at me in surprise. "Have you lost your mind?"

I fell silent.

By the school gates I stopped and pulled my aunt by the sleeve.

"Aunt, who is Merdzhan?"

"A person!" answered my aunt sensibly. "A very good person! Go on, go on, my son," she said, nudging me in the back. "And don't go running around the streets: go straight to kindergarten when school is done! And I don't want to hear that word ever again!"

Merdzhan started coming to us almost every day. I rejoiced when she came. And it was also wonderful for my aunt. The most intimate conversations began at night when we put out the lamp and lay down to sleep. I would go quiet, and the women, thinking I was asleep, started whispering. I strained my ears, afraid to miss even one word, and then, without even noticing, I stopped listening, lost myself in thought, and fell asleep.

4

With the coming of spring Grandfather Aslan began to go out in the street more and more often with a stack of newspapers; he'd collected them all winter. If Azer didn't turn out to be nearby, the old man would sit down near some house and pull a newspaper from the pack.

"Come on," he'd say, holding it out to a passing boy, "read it. Something's wrong with my eyes, they're weak." No one contradicted him, although the kids knew very well that the problem wasn't with his eyes; it was simply that Grandfather Aslan didn't know how to read. Perhaps at one time he'd understood the Arabic letters, but the new alphabet was, of course, beyond his power. The old man listened intently, insisted on the reading of everything that pertained to the war several times over, learned it almost by heart, and in the evening when the old men gathered by the mosque, he astounded them with his expert knowledge of military affairs and his firm conviction that the war would soon be over.

It must be said that many people began to talk about the nearness of the war's end that spring. I, too, wanted to believe in a quick victory, but something prevented me. Maybe it was the fact that for us, it seemed the war had just begun, and although almost no younger fellows remained in the village, the war had only recently made itself felt in earnest.

The women began to quarrel more often; they argued while separating boys locked together in combat, created an uproar in the shop when sugar was brought in, and fought over the irrigation water, battering one another until the blood flowed. The kids weren't outdone by the adults—the boys' battles grew more and more fierce. The strong clobbered the weak. Even the dogs became unprecedentedly savage— there was simply no way to get past them. There began to be rumors about theft—that was the first time I heard such conversations... Famine began. It began gradually, and I didn't immediately understand that it was famine. If someone died in the village, people rejoiced, hoping to eat at the funeral feast, but funeral feasts were held more and more rarely... Khalida died. Either from hunger or from some illness, she suddenly turned yellow, dried up, and looked so terrible that I was already ashamed of the words I'd spoken in the walnut tree. Khalida died on one of the warm spring nights; she was lowered into her grave, and that grave was very small.

The houses were sharply divided into two categories: those where they baked bread, and those where there was no bread. In the houses that had bread, people hid it, and there were those who hid the smoke, contriving to give off less of it. And yet not everyone changed: quite a few remained whose souls the war could not maim. The Old Bolshevik Grandfather Aslan remained exactly the same Grandfather Aslan; just as before, when they'd climbed into his garden for jasmine without fearing any punishment, now they went to him for a piece of bread. The old man walked around the village saying that the war would soon end, made peace between the kids fighting, and sometimes, gathering them on the street, brought them home to be fed. If he had absolutely nothing to feed the kids, the old man would start to tell them about the last war, about the famine years and, of course, about Lenin; moreover, it turned out that Lenin had gone hungry for his entire life.

The black ceiling covered in soot, the dark walls, the lamp with smoke-blackened glass: even the neatly made bed, it seemed, smelled of soot... Grandfather Aslan's tiny little house couldn't contain his loud guests; they took over the bed, and the host settled himself on the earthen floor.

"Here's what happened," he'd say, tucking his legs beneath him. "One day Lenin sends for me..."

At this point one of the kids always snickered openly, but Grandfather Aslan would coolly continue his story, just turning his back to the scoffer. Talking about Lenin, the old man most often looked at me and Azer, perhaps because we never laughed at him.

On one occasion, seeing the kids off, Grandfather Aslan beckoned to me and leaned toward my ear:

"Tell your aunt not to bring that woman home."

With that, our friendship ended. I didn't go to visit Grandfather Aslan anymore.

It must be said that Grandfather Aslan wasn't the only one with whom I had occasion to quarrel because of Merdzhan. No matter how many times I wept, insisting that Merdzhan was a good woman, that she wasn't a whore, no one wanted to believe me. The boys tormented me most of all. They threw stones at Merdzhan and, running up to her, shouted, "Whore! Whore!" right in her face. Merdzhan acted as though she didn't notice the shouts or the stones flying at her, but although she walked without looking around, without even turning her head, it was evident how much it cost her from the way her hands hung helplessly, from her quick, scurrying steps. If one of the men appeared and the kids fell silent, not daring to use foul language, Merdzhan immediately turned around and smiled timidly at the boys. It sometimes even seemed to me that she was deliberately trying to get close to the children to convince them that she was no whore and that there was no need to fling stones at her.

They hounded Merdzhan, composed obscene poems about her; later Aunt Medina also began to be mentioned in them. It was a good thing that Aunt Nabat often went to fetch water; in front of her, the boys were afraid to harass Merdzhan. The old woman didn't waste any time: she grabbed a bigger stone and chased the kids all the way to the river.

"Just you wait, you sons of bitches!" the old woman threatened. "When Yakub returns, God willing, he'll show you how to call an old woman a whore!"

At first I thought that Aunt Nabat really did take the obscenities the boys were shouting as if they were meant for her, but I soon became convinced that the old woman was pretending in order to deflect the insults, as if Merdzhan were a little girl who could be fooled.

I still didn't fully understand the meaning of the word "whore," but I knew for sure that if the word was bad, it bore no relation at all to Merdzhan. Aunt Nabat was evidently of the same opinion because she visited us most often on those evenings when Merdzhan stayed the night.

In the summer Aunt Merdzhan rarely spent the night, but at the beginning of every month she always brought us all the flour that was allotted her at the factory.

When Merdzhan wasn't there and we went to bed alone, my aunt told me tales to pass the evening. She made up some of them herself; I could easily pick them out because they were always about school, the teachers, my father, Mukush, gardens that resembled the garden plot next to our house, fragrant white roses, girls in white dresses, and Azer's father—happy, smiling, wearing a pressed white shirt.

That summer the women fought especially aggressively over the irrigation water; Aunt Medina alone never took her turn. She distributed the entire harvest of fruit and herbs in our garden to the neighbors in advance, so long as they agreed to water the trees. She didn't once water Mukush's yard, and in the area where it had formerly smelled of damp rot, everything dried up: the seedlings withered without even opening their buds, the herbs didn't flower, the clover rose only palm-high—Aunt Medina didn't even seem to notice. When the cellar caved in, my aunt dragged out the trusses and burned them in the stove as if they were ordinary firewood, and cheerful, satisfied, she went off to the factory.

5

No one received anything at the collective farm in payment for days worked—people swore at the bookkeeper, the storehouse keeper, the guard. Those who were more canny dragged stuff home from the collective farm day and night now that the all-seeing binoculars of Uncle Murtuz were no longer around. The chairman had long since departed for the front; not a single letter had come from him.

Soldiers' letters in general had become fewer and fewer, as if the famine also extended to them. Aunt Nabat didn't talk about anything else: she even saw letters from Yakub in her dreams. Imamali wasn't himself—his sons wrote nothing. The only one not worried about the lack of letters was Aunt Medina. And Merdzhan wasn't expecting anything from anyone; she lived calmly and without worry.

The evening that Azer first visited me at home, Merdzhan was spending the night. Azer liked her so much that the very next day he hit one of the boys—who, as usual, had decided to tease Merdzhan—in the head with a stone. Covered in blood, the fellow launched himself at Azer with a roar. Azer wasn't afraid: he didn't run away. He snatched up another, bigger stone and went toward his opponent. The boy retreated. Then Azer dropped the stone and disappeared. I found him in the orchard—he was crying uncontrollably, lying under a walnut tree.

"She's not a whore!" shouted Azer as I tried to raise him. "Merdzhan is a good person! My mother is the whore!"

And he came toward me with quite a fierce expression, as if he knew beforehand that I would contradict him. I was frightened and for some reason climbed up on a stump, then fell off. I knew Azer couldn't possibly dislike Merdzhan, but what did that have to do with his mother?

Azer probably felt sorry for me; he helped me get up and said guiltily:

"Well, what are you afraid of? Of course, she's a whore! Would a respectable woman have married someone like that?"

If only I'd known that hitting the head of one the boys would rid Merdzhan of her tormentors once and for all! I'd suffered so much from the consciousness of my own impotence! Every shout, every filthy word the boys thoughtlessly yelled after her turned my soul upside down: I wanted to throw myself at the scoundrels, tear them limb from limb. I dreamed frantically about a rifle—if only I had a rifle! And about growing bigger! About growing quicker, getting bigger and stronger, like my father! Every night I prayed to God to make me a grown-up quicker, leaving my peers children. But even in my dreams I couldn't vanquish them. I saw our street, the kids. They flung stones at Merdzhan, and Aunt Medina was silent, looking fearfully around. I dreamed that the boys hit my aunt in the head: she died, and Aunt Nabat washed her body in the yard. That dream tormented me so often that I began to mix up what was in the dream and what was real. I prayed to God to give me wings so that I could fly and throw stones at the boys. Sometimes I flew exactly like a bird, but even in dreams I didn't lose my awareness that it was all just a dream. And when I finally understood that God couldn't free me from the torment of diabolical impotence, Azer unexpectedly did it—more precisely, not Azer, but the stone with which he hit the boy's head. The kids not only stopped shouting obscenities at Merdzhan: they weren't brave enough to approach Azer, or me, either, especially after we found an iron bar in the factory yard that looked like a crowbar. That piece of iron completely made up for the rifle about which I'd dreamed so passionately. Although Azer was nicknamed "the Madman" thanks to the iron bar, on the bright side, Merdzhan became untouchable.

Shortly before the factory horn each evening, Azer and I took up a position in the very niche where Mukush had once laid in wait for Aunt Medina; we held the iron bar at the ready, like spies on the trail of a source. The women workers went out through the factory gates, and each went her own way. The kids gathered in a knot in front of the gates and stared at Merdzhan's slender figure, at her white legs peeping out from underneath her dress, and they were silent—no one dared swear at her. When the women moved away, we left our place of ambush; the boys turned away, feigning complete indifference to us and our iron bar. Then again, there were also those who, seeing the Madman, preferred to slip away.

Placing the bar on his shoulder, Azer marched past the hushed kids with a crisp, soldierly step. I paced solemnly behind him—it must be said that this was a very pleasant sensation. Yes, God turned out to be weak compared to Azer with his iron bar!

As we moved further away, Azer passed me the bar, and although my shoulder ached from the weight of the iron, I carried it with the utmost satisfaction. The pain was pleasant; it reminded me that I was strong, that I had a weapon, that I could protect the weak. Azer's iron bar sometimes comes to my aid in my dreams even now: it's indispensable in dark city parks, where I lower it over the heads of bandits; chastise scoundrels I don't know who are harassing unknown girls; punish scumbags attempting to cut in front of the line; and drive bribetakers, bureaucrats, and bootlickers out of institutions. Many years have passed since that time, but even now I feel the pleasant weight of the iron bar on my shoulder; maybe that's the reason the ultimate triumph of good over evil seems attainable to me. The feeling never leaves me that this iron bar exists somewhere: sooner or later I'll get my hands on it, and then things will turn sour for all the champions of injustice and untruth!

Having marched triumphantly through the village, we'd scale the mountain behind Mukush's house and, satisfied that we no longer had to play the hero, lie down on the warm stones. Until very late, when the windows were lit in the village, we confided the secrets of our hearts to one another.

"Let's run away from the village!" Azer would say wistfully.

"Where will we go?"

Azer nodded silently toward the mountains.

"There are wolves there!" I made this argument each time, not hiding from my friend that I was more afraid of wolves than anything in the world.

"What about this?" Azer lifted the iron bar meaningfully.

"We won't have anything to eat!"

"We'll hunt," Azer would answer, without any particular confidence. "We'll catch a gazelle."

"We will not catch a gazelle!"

"Well, then we'll go hungry. I can go a month without eating! Wanna bet?"

I'd express doubt and begin to make the case to my friend that you can't do anything without food. Azer argued without any particular conviction, and then he'd confess that he himself wasn't certain whether he could live without food.

"Then what should we do, Sadyk?" he'd ask sadly.

I was silent.

This conversation repeated itself every day, and every day we silently climbed down from the cliff and silently parted, heading for our homes. The next day everything repeated itself from the beginning: school, the ambush in the mosque's niche, long conversations on the cliff...

By this time Azer and I were no longer allowed in the kindergarten, but Grandmother Sariya continued to feed us on the sly. Hiding a dish of food under her large, dark scarf, the cook would lug it to a hut on the edge of the kindergarten area. We ate; Grandmother Sariya didn't take her sad eyes off of us, and each time we choked on the food we were stuffing into our mouths with our hands, she also swallowed, as if she wanted to help us. The bowl was soon empty, the old woman smiled cheerfully, and her eyes gleamed cannily.

"It's all right," she'd say, deeply satisfied, hiding the empty bowl under her scarf. "Maybe we'll get a little meat tomorrow."

But there was never any meat: not tomorrow, not the day after tomorrow, not on any other day.

In the fall they gave the women workers bread coupons, and every morning, with no little trouble at the shop door, we traded our coupons for bread. To tell the truth, we ate it all on the spot; not a crumb was left for lunch.

One evening my aunt brought home a man nicknamed "Bear" who—in a businesslike way, without any unnecessary talk—dismantled the shed in which the stolen pears once had ripened. Then the sons of the bread cutter, Khamza, arrived, laid the trusses and crossbeams on their shoulders, and whistling, carried them home. For this, Khamza sent us a loaf of bread for several days in a row. Then there was no bread again, and after a few days I saw Bear on the roof of the lean-to as I was coming home from school. Dust rose in a column; dry earth poured between the trusses into the big room where Mukush used to sleep. I felt uneasy, but my aunt looked as if this had absolutely nothing to do with her; humming a little song under her breath, she coolly set out the samovar.

The trusses collapsed, the beams flew off with a roar, one after another, and my aunt stood near the samovar coming to a boil and talked animatedly about something with Aunt Nabat, who was smoking on the roof of her own home.

By winter only one room of Mukush's large, carefully tended home survived, the room in which the stove stood; however, this didn't affect my aunt's mood at all. We sat in our one-room house, read the books left by Azer's father, or took turns telling stories. Again and again Aunt Medina talked about school—that was her favorite story—and listening to my aunt, I invariably remembered the song she'd sung upon sending Mukush off to the front and saw the girls in white dresses and the paths lined with roses along which Aunt Medina had run to school when she was a girl.

Then Aunt Bilgeis would come into our room full of light, warmth, and stories, and glancing timidly at Azer settled beside the lamp, she'd wait patiently while he got up. They left, and the stories, just recently fluttering like moths around a flame, flew out of the room. I looked after Aunt Bilgeis, thinking about how she was now walking with her son along the cold, slippery road, shielding the lamp from the wind with her hand, and I no longer saw beautiful girls in white clothing, but the kids in flimsy little coats and worn-out shoes—hungry, pinched with cold—who'd walk along that road tomorrow to school.

Part Three

1

Malik, Uncle Imamali's last son, was conscripted into the army either in spring or early fall, I don't remember exactly which one, but in any case it wasn't winter or summer because everything was green all around. And a few days later Uncle Imamali climbed the mountain alone and beat loudly on the drum—that morning he'd received his second notice of a son killed in battle. The old man raged around the slope, beating the drum and calling his dead sons:

"Alish! Velish! Alish! Velish!"

That was the day Uncle Imamali lost his mind; at least, that's what people said.

My aunt sold my father's beehives, then took the palas carpets somewhere. That was in either the spring or the fall. During the last year of the war, those two times of year got tangled up in my head. The last letter from my father also arrived either that spring or fall—I don't remember very well.

On the other hand, I can say with certainty that the soldiers stationed among us "to prevent unexpected surprises from the east," as the school director put it, appeared in the village in the fall, the last fall of the war. I remember that the grass on which they sprawled for hours, resting after drills, was yellow; and I also remember that the soldiers who'd taken up residence in our empty house didn't touch the pears of the "imam tree," although they were at the absolute peak of ripeness: I picked them myself and carried them to the station.

59

A large portion of the soldiers was settled in the club; accompanied by a policeman, Uncle Abutalib distributed the rest among the houses. This act didn't pass without controversy; a few people even went to complain at the district center, but the majority of my fellow villagers met the soldiers with open arms. Aunt Medina lightheartedly gave Uncle Abutalib the keys to the house without a second's hesitation. As for Aunt Nabat, she immediately spotted an Uzbek soldier—"Just like my Yakub!"—and almost dragged him into the yard by force, not taking her eyes off the cigarette smoking in his hand.

Aunt Nabat was happy to see the soldiers because they had an abundance of tobacco; Grandfather Aslan because he could now stroll up and down all day in front of the club carrying a bundle of Russian newspapers under his arm and talking with the soldiers and officers in Russian; and the kids because things had become more cheerful. With the coming of the soldiers, a little bazaar sprang up in the village on its own: under the large plane tree in front of the club, people now sold sunflower seeds, eggs, dried fruit... After school the kids stuffed their pockets full of walnuts and hotfooted it to the club, yelling in broken Russian: "Nuts, who want? Nuts, who want?"

In the schoolyard, on the street, in the orchards, scuffles broke out everywhere: we couldn't seem to peacefully share the soldiers among ourselves. The tall, ruddy officer with the most stars on his shoulder marks was taken by Azer; naturally, he could have his choice—he had the iron bar. It was precisely thanks to the power of that bar that another possessor of stars—a young, blue-eyed officer—was chosen for me by Azer, although there was admittedly some justice for this decision: my officer, like the one who "belonged" to Azer, resided in my father's house. I was soon dispossessed of my officer. Of course, I myself was mostly to blame for this, more precisely, not I but my shyness—I never even made the acquaintance of my officer, although to do so would only have required me to enter my own home and say hello. In the end I had to content myself with the Uzbek who'd taken up residence with Aunt Nabat.

Later, when they were departing, the soldiers left quite a few valuable items behind in the village: boots that were still in very good shape; warm footcloths; in one house, they even forgot a shoulder mark. After the soldiers left I acquired a saddle and a can of boot black. To tell the truth, I threw away the boot black as useless and immediately forgot about the saddle—and someone stole it. On the other hand, I'll probably never forget the large, black kettle set up on the exact spot where my father had once spread out the palas.

Azer took me there: after a few days he'd made such good friends with the tall, ruddy officer with the most stars on his shoulder marks that he visited him quite casually, as if it were his own home. Among us, Azer was reputed to be a master of Russian: he even tore the Russian-Azeri glossaries out of all the textbooks and constantly carried them around in his pockets. Marshalling all his learning, Azer somehow explained to the officer that the house in which he was now living belonged to me, that I was his host. Azer's officer didn't bother discussing anything with me, he asked just one question: "Is your father a soldier?" I bowed. The silent, angry soldier stirring something in the kettle with a shaved plank of wood turned and looked at me in such a way that I immediately understood—those weren't just words, there was something in them, there was a reason the little son of the superintendent had immediately stopped tormenting me that time... In an hour the soldier's kasha was ready: I sat on the stone where my grandmother had once dressed me in my first pair of pantaloons and held a full mess tin of kasha in front of me. "My father's a soldier"— those words became a kind of password. Dozens of kids from all over the village began to gather in our yard. They all said, "My father's a soldier" and begged for kasha. At first they weren't refused, but so many kids turned up that the officer ordered the gates to be closed, and no one, other than Azer and I, was allowed to enter. Then the boys began climbing the walnut tree whose mighty branches hung over the walls surrounding our yard. If they weren't given anything, the kids sat in the branches for hours like outlandish birds, and they shouted the same exact thing in their various voices: "My father's a soldier! My father's a soldier!" The most desperate crawled over the wall and went straight to the kettle. Valida, the little sister of the dead Khalida, made use of the gap that our tailless hen had once dug under the wall and on her crooked, rickety legs hobbled right up to the officer with the most stars. She wasn't even able to utter the customary words, she said just "My father..." and began to cry bitterly. The ruddy officer took Valida by the hand, patted her head, and quickly began to load bread, potatoes, sugar—as much as she could carry—into the skirt of her little red dress. Still crying, the little girl headed back for the gap made by the hen. Aunt Sona glanced over the wall; her face was happy.

I no longer went hungry. Because I was the proprietor of the house, its gates—and, consequently, access to the soldier's kettle—were always open to me. Not only that: Avez, the Uzbek soldier quartered with Aunt Nabat, quite often brought me something in his mess tin. To be honest, there were certain complications with this situation. As soon as I sat down on the hillock behind the house with the mess tin in my hands, Aunt Nabat's grandson Rakhib immediately appeared on the roof, his eyes following every spoonful of kasha. Recently he'd been glaring daggers at me, and once he took a large brick from the roof and flung it at me as I walked to school; if the brick had struck me in the head, the soldier wouldn't have brought me food in the mess tin. I knew very well that Rakhib was no hungrier than I was, that Avez tried to feed him first, that with the appearance of the soldier in his house the boy had put on weight, grown rosy, that his cheeks had filled out as before, but still, the kasha didn't go down easily.

Avez was a kind person, and almost every day he brought kasha, but at first I didn't like him—there wasn't a single star on his shoulder marks. His face was swarthy, not pink like Azer's officer, and he didn't speak Russian with me. As a matter of fact, Avez very quickly began to speak Azeri, but that didn't please me—like all the kids, I wanted to speak Russian.

Avez was a strong, broad-shouldered person. No matter how much I peered into his kind, open face, I couldn't figure out how old he was: I think this soldier must have been the same age as my father. I suppose he generally looked like my father: the same thick, wide eyebrows and prominent nose. It was hard for me to tell—after all, I'd never seen my father in uniform. Incidentally, Aunt Nabat also noticed the resemblance.

If it had only been up to me, of course, I'd have missed my chance with this soldier, too, but Avez took a decided interest in me. He visited almost every evening and sat with me until dark; once he asked me to take him to the collective farm orchard, and when a film was brought for the soldiers, he invited me to go—we became friends without even noticing it.

More often than not, Avez and I spent the evening on the mountain behind Mukush's house. Sprawled out on the grass, we contemplated the other, unknown villages or, turning sideways toward the setting sun, talked about everything in the whole world: the war, soldiers, German fascists... Sometimes we drifted off to sleep after these endless conversations, and my aunt, arriving home from work, would come to wake us up. Avez smiled at my aunt meekly and guiltily; she answered him with a light, barely perceptible smile, and that strange, glancing smile didn't leave her face until night fell. Once Avez brought a loaf of bread and asked me to give it to my aunt. Hopping and skipping, I rushed home. My aunt didn't take the bread, but for some reason went up to the mirror and began contemplating her green dress, and again that light, barely noticeable smile glanced across her face. A few days later I caught that smile on Aunt Medina's face again. She was standing near the fallen mulberry tree—Mukush had cut it down not long before his departure—and baking lepyoshka on the saj. Avez was right there, chopping a door into firewood. On the way to the factory in the morning, my aunt and I spotted Avez at the gate of the neighboring house. Aunt Medina and the soldier looked at one another, smiled, and the bright and somewhat embarrassed smile didn't leave my aunt's face all the way to the factory gates. Even in the evening after work a remnant of that smile flickered over her face.

2

One night my aunt came home from work very cheerful, it seemed to me even excessively cheerful—she laughed loudly, and seemingly without any particular reason. My aunt laughed all evening. She laughed standing in front of the window, she laughed looking at herself in the mirror; then the laugh changed into a loud roar that shook her whole body, and it seemed to me that Aunt Medina had lost her mind. She roared with laughter for a long time, then began to weep, and her weeping was just as terrible as her roaring laughter. My aunt didn't sleep the whole night, but the next morning she got up and began to get ready for the factory. I lifted my arms the way Aunt

Nabat did and whispered: "Glory to the Lord!" I thanked God that my aunt hadn't gone crazy.

Even before I hadn't really liked it when Avez, smiling, looked Aunt Medina in the face; when I saw how self-consciously and fondly they smiled at one another, I felt disturbed and uneasy. Now I began to detest that kind, broad-shouldered man; I didn't understand what was going on, but I had no doubt that Aunt Medina's laughter and her terrible weeping were in some way connected with Avez. I began to avoid Avez, didn't eat the things he brought me, and seeing him one day lying in the orchard, I resolved to kill him with Azer's iron bar.

My aunt also tried not to see our neighbor; if she met him during the daytime, she couldn't fall asleep that night. Sometimes she sat up in bed and stayed that way for hours, staring at a fixed point; sometimes she'd suddenly begin to roar with a terrible, soul-chilling laugh. She'd put on the samovar and forget to fill it with water, or light the lamp without having filled it with kerosene and be astonished that it wouldn't burn... Now I took care of the samovar and filled the lamp with kerosene. In the morning when my aunt left for the factory, as usual, I lifted my arms to the heavens each time and thanked God that nothing had happened during the night.

It was a dreary, cloudy winter day. My aunt came back from the factory with Merdzhan. "Thank God," I thought. "Finally I'm not going to be alone when Aunt Medina begins to laugh in the dark." But that night my aunt didn't laugh. She and Merdzhan sat up late on the palas talking softly about something, and I loafed about the house, now and then looking out the window. Everything was quiet, calm. My aunt didn't cry, didn't laugh, didn't sit staring at a fixed point. Then we went to bed, and for a long time we lay there silently.

"You know, Merdzhan," said my aunt thoughtfully, "much more of this and I'll probably go out of my mind..."

"Because you're a fool," Merdzhan said calmly. "If you'd just give it a little more thought, you wouldn't let your life be destroyed. You've finally found someone worth waiting for! The fellow loves you, he dotes on you. And how handsome he is—a feast for the eyes!"

My aunt didn't answer. Merdzhan also fell silent. Then she sighed deeply.

"You don't comprehend your own happiness, Medina!" Melancholy and envy were in Merdzhan's whisper. "If only someone would love me like that! Who cares if he's Uzbek, or Russian, or Armenian! I'd leave with him, go wherever the road takes us! I'd sit by the train window... There are so many interesting things in the world, and we sit here like mice in a corner, knowing nothing about anything!"

Merdzhan said this so confidently that it was as if she weren't imagining but actually seeing everything she was talking about. And for the first time I suspected that she'd conjured up the young man with the roses in exactly the same way.

Once again it grew quiet. And then Merdzhan whispered again:

"Look here, Medina, I'll go to Avez tomorrow. I'll lay it all out for him. I'll tell him that you're pining for him, but that you're afraid of your husband."

"Are you crazy?!" exclaimed my aunt and looked at me in fright. "Don't you dare even think about doing that! If you do, I'll never look you in the face again, not until my dying day! As a matter of fact, I'm not afraid of my husband. I..." My aunt fell silent.

Merdzhan didn't ask who she was afraid of, but my father's black boots loomed in front of me. I thought that Aunt Medina probably also saw those boots in the darkness. The women were silent for a moment.

"You're absolutely crazy!" sighed Merdzhan. "He'd be such a good husband!"

"I don't need any kind of husband! My time has passed, Merdzhan: look how many beauties have grown up... And I have a child to take care of: I'll live for Sadyk. But it's hard for me, Merdzhan! Oh, it's so hard! I've truly almost burned up with shame... Almost lost my mind!"

My aunt didn't lose her mind or burn up with shame, and no one ever found out. I didn't tell even Azer about those horrible nights. Perhaps only Aunt Nabat guessed why her neighbor had dried out and blackened so much over the course of a week. It was a good thing that Merdzhan was there: she brought meat, eggs, and cheese from somewhere and insisted that Aunt Medina eat. However, she rarely stayed the night, and that really upset me because Avez came to our gate every evening, and every evening Aunt Medina sent me to drive him away.

"Get away from here!" I shouted, going out onto the roof. Avez silently turned and left. I returned to the room.

"Must you bawl like a donkey?" my aunt said, grimacing painfully. "You really shouldn't shout like that at a stranger in a strange land..."

I began to speak in a softer voice, then I didn't have to say anything: seeing me on the roof, Avez left immediately, but just the same, when I returned to the room my aunt would say, grimacing as if she had a toothache:

"Can't you do it more quietly? You shouldn't yell at a person that way!"

She couldn't sleep; it seemed to her as if Avez were standing under the window. In the middle of the night she'd suddenly rouse me, and I, shivering from fear and cold, had to go out onto the roof. There was no one in the yard; there was only darkness all around. "Go away!" I'd say to the darkness. "Go away! Go away, please!" I'd quietly repeat to the dark silhouettes of the trees.

That evening, as always, Avez left our gates with nothing. My aunt seemed calmer than usual: she lay silently in bed and immediately grew quiet. Merdzhan soon fell asleep; I also lay without moving a muscle, pretending to sleep, although I never fell asleep before my aunt now. I kept thinking that if I fell asleep, she'd leave and never return. If Aunt Medina got up in the middle of the night, I'd freeze—now she was leaving! I wanted to shout, seize her by the hand, but fear choked me: I couldn't shout or move, only tremble with a faint shivering.

My aunt got up. She lit the lamp, stood it in the corner on the palas, then picked up my school bag, pulled a notebook out of it, tore out a page, laid some book on her knees, and began to write very, very fast.

In the morning she led me behind the house and, looking around to see if Merdzhan was coming, with trembling hands thrust a letter into my hands. First and foremost, she commanded me very strictly not to read the letter under any circumstances, not even to unfold it: to put it in my pocket and wait until the soldiers set out for drill. She explained in detail where these drills were held and under which tree I must wait for Avez, how I should go up to him and say hello: say hello first and foremost.

As soon as Merdzhan and Medina disappeared inside the factory gates, I headed for the road along which the soldiers passed every morning, looking warily around me. I hid myself in a deep hollow by the roadside and sat there for a few minutes, shaking as if I had a chill. Then I pulled the letter from my pocket and began to read it. It seemed I was in no condition to collect my wits, but—a remarkable thing— that letter with all its corrections, with its crossed-out and rewritten words, with its tear-stained blurs, is to this day visible before my eyes:

"Treasured friend of my soul! I send you thousands of passionate greetings nurtured in the secret compartments of my heart trembling with love... Avez! I can't stand it anymore! Save me! And forgive me for tormenting you so much! If only you knew! If only you knew! I'm not afraid anymore! Have pity on me, Avez! This evening I'll wait for you by the river. Come!"

This was followed by several of the quatrains that are obligatory in love letters.

Covering my face with my hands, I cried at the bottom of the ditch. My aunt had decided to abandon me: she'd become a whore. More than anything in the world I wanted to rip up the letter, tear it into a thousand pieces. Why I didn't do that, I don't know. I thrust the letter into my pocket, wiped my tears with my sleeve, and ran to catch up with the soldiers.

I wasn't able to catch the soldiers—coming to meet me, trailing her headscarf behind her, disheveled, out of breath, ran Aunt Medina. She was white, covered in sweat, and her eyes blazed rather strangely.

"Where's the letter?!"

I pulled the letter out of my pocket and held it out to Aunt Medina. She immediately turned pink again, took several deep breaths, and sank onto a stone. Then she tore the letter into tiny pieces, hugged me, and we both started to cry.

That night Avez didn't come to our gate. Perhaps Merdzhan had spoken with him, perhaps Aunt Nabat had gotten wind of something, but the important thing is that he didn't appear. Lying down to sleep, Aunt Medina hugged me and pressed me so tightly to her that it was as if we hadn't seen one another for a thousand years.

"You won't abandon me, Sadyk? You won't forget me? Even when you get big, when you get married? You won't abandon me? We'll live well. Your daughter will grow up, we'll marry her off—I'll dance at the wedding. You won't abandon me, Sadyk? You won't abandon me?"

She was crying and stifling me in her embrace, and I couldn't answer a single one of her questions. But she didn't need answers.

"I'll never abandon you, Aunt," I thought, falling asleep on her warm arm. "I'll never leave you alone. I'll go to Baku, finish my studies, and take you there, to my home. We'll go to the theater or the movies every day. I'll buy you dresses with flowers, the most beautiful ones you can get in stores! And I'll bring you candy every day. What joy that you didn't lose your mind and become a whore: the kids would have teased me without mercy!"

3

The soldiers left as unexpectedly as they'd arrived. It was a blinding, glittering winter day. The first lesson of the second school shift had started. Azer and I had written out the assignment from the textbook and were now twiddling our thumbs, not knowing what to do with ourselves. Our Russia-language teacher, "Pussycat" Akhad-muallim, was dozing near the stove, leaning on his elbow.

We heard a shriek from the yard. This came from the little kids, the ones who'd start school next year—they spent whole days hanging around the outdoor gymnastics area. Then we heard the sound of motors—vehicles were driving down the mountain. The lids of the desks rumbled. Akhad-muallim lifted his head, looking sleepily at us. "The soldiers are leaving," he said indifferently and again lowered his head onto his hand. But he wasn't able to doze any longer. Azer, who invariably spoke only Russian with Akhad-muallim, emphatically raised his hand:

"Teacher, please, I go?" he said and, without waiting for an answer, headed for the door.

The kids who were more daring whisked silently past the teacher, and the others followed them. In an instant, Akhad-muallim was left all alone.

With shouts of "Hurrah!" kids ran out of all the classrooms and raced off to meet the vehicles. I ran to the factory. The area in front of the mosque was full of people. The women workers abandoned their machines, crowded around the windows, and shouted something, looking after the soldiers marching in formation behind the armored vehicles. The senior foreman paced up and down in front of the stopped machinery and grumbled testily under his breath. Aunt Medina didn't go to the window; she stood in front of one of the drums, mutely hanging her head. Merdzhan, on the other hand, made more noise than anyone. She climbed the barred windows almost up to the ceiling, stuck her head between the bars, and looking at the soldiers, sang something loudly. Her voice was drowned in the general roar.

For a long time afterwards our school director rushed around the streets with a stick in his hand, driving the kids to school just like sheep... When I was walking home, Aunt Nabat called to me. The old woman sighed sadly, lamenting that she'd had to part with a good person, and handed me a parcel wrapped in an old jacket. It felt as though there might be something valuable in the bundle.

"There are some groceries," said Aunt Nabat to enlighten me, "wrapped in newspaper. Don't throw away the newspaper: give it back to me later."

I ran behind the house, and with the same panicked horror that had enveloped me a few days previously when I'd read my aunt's letter in the roadside ditch, I ripped open the thread that made up the knot. To unpack it here was dangerous: my aunt would soon come home from the factory. I scrambled up the mountain, climbed down the opposite side, and only then began to unpack the bundle. Wrapped together in the newspaper with a loaf of white bread, I found a letter folded into a triangle. Beside myself, I grabbed that little white triangle and began tearing it into tiny pieces. Calming down a bit, I tried to collect the teeny tiny bits of paper, but it was too late.

Besides the letter and the loaf of bread, I found three cans of food in the bundle. "Gobies in Tomato" was written on two of them and "Eggplant Caviar" on the third. I searched the pockets of the jacket and pulled a red thirty-ruble note out of one of them and two small, elegant boxes that looked like packages of cookies out of the other. A different hand had written "Merdzhan" on each of them in blue ink. That stumped me, and I decided to open one of the little boxes. In it weren't cookies, but long, white cigarettes—I'd never seen anything like them—and inside the lid, "Farewell, Merdzhan!" was written in the same blue ink and handwriting.

If only I could have been sure that Aunt Nabat wouldn't say anything about the bundle! I'd have flung all those treasures into the gorge without a moment's hesitation! Even the bread! I sat above the river in despair, holding the accursed gift in my hands and not knowing what I should do. I knew only one thing for sure—if Aunt Medina saw it, everything would start all over again!

I watched as she returned from work; then Merdzhan's voice could be heard in the yard. The herd entered the village. They drove in the sheep. And I kept sitting on the mountain and listening to the evening sounds, trying to pick out Aunt Nabat's voice among them. I couldn't hear her, and I made up my mind: one after another, I tossed the cans of food further into the gorge, weighed down the jacket with a large stone, having previously stuffed the little boxes of cigarettes into the pocket. Only the bread remained. It would have been simplest to now eat the whole loaf, but as a matter of fact, my aunt had never swallowed a crumb in secret from me. I looked at the golden loaf, but I didn't see bread: I saw her face, her sunken cheeks, the dark circles under her eyes... I wrapped the bread in the newspaper, thrust it under a stone, and went home. That same night Aunt Nabat, calling to Aunt Medina from the roof, asked for the newspaper in which the bread had been wrapped. My aunt already knew that Avez had left some kind of bundle, but she thought it had contained only bread and that I'd eaten the bread. She didn't ask any questions.

What a good thing that I didn't bring Avez's gift home!

Aunt Medina put on the samovar, wiping off the glass in the lamp, and for some reason went up to the window. She was singing softly the whole time, but her song resembled a moan, the way people moan when a tooth hurts unbearably: they walk back and forth around the room and pick ceaselessly at something, trying to distract themselves from the unbearable pain.

Night fell. My aunt stood by the window and looked at a spot on the wall a bit higher than Merdzhan's head. Merdzhan sat in the corner on the palas and also looked at a fixed point. They were both silent. It was the first time I'd ever seen Merdzhan that way. Without changing position she slipped her hand into her bosom and pulled out matches, a cigarette—exactly the kind that lay in the little boxes that looked like packs of cookies—and started to smoke. I glanced at Aunt Medina with astonishment, not understanding why this didn't interest her. But it seemed that my aunt didn't see either Merdzhan or the cigarette. Only when Merdzhan struck a match and lit a second one did my aunt lift her head.

"Oy! You smoke?"

"I smoke." Merdzhan took a drag with pleasure. "For a long time already: I just hid it from you... And now there's no point. Why should I smoke in the toilet? Anyway, we're going our separate ways."

"Why?" Aunt Medina looked at Merdzhan, perplexed. "Has something happened?"

"Nothing's happened. The factory's closing."

"Closing?! What do you mean?"

"It's very simple: there aren't any more cocoons. There are five sacks in the storeroom, and that's it. The director has been scouring the surrounding area for a whole month trying to get cocoons. Of course, you don't know anything about it: you've been dragging around like a shadow."

This meant there would be no more factory! How I loved to stand by the barred windows! If you looked out from the factory windows on the snowy heights, the snow seemed somehow especially white. Maybe because my aunt was always cheerful, smiling, at the factory, and there was something in common between her radiant smile and the blinding whiteness of the snow. Honestly, though, I couldn't exactly define what constituted the resemblance.

Merdzhan silently smoked several cigarettes one after another, then stood up and went up to my aunt.

71

"Stop it, Medina," she said with a sigh. "What's the point of looking at the road? Mine went too. My handsome one, my hero, my beloved abandoned me, left..."

Merdzhan's habit was to sing, but this time she fell silent, frowned, waved her hands.

"Did you see the Russian fellow who sometimes visited Avez? So tall, so fair! He was mine, that Russian!"

My aunt lifted troubled, bewildered eyes to her. Merdzhan grinned.

"What are you looking at? Of course, he's not Majnun, and I'm not Leyla, but I don't give a damn about beautiful names. It was good, and that's all! So good! We'd lie next to one another on the grass, he'd cover me with his overcoat... It's dark... The water's noisy... And the sky's overflowing with stars! They twinkle, they wink at us..."

If I hadn't seen the boxes of cigarettes with my own eyes, there's no way I'd have believed Merdzhan—she said it all too prettily! Exactly as she'd talked about the young man with the roses.

Merdzhan started to sing. Then she began to smoke again. My aunt was silent all the while.

That night we went to bed much later than usual.

"He promised to take me to Moscow!" Merdzhan announced dreamily, looking at the ceiling. "But he didn't even come to say goodbye! They're all the same: Russians, Armenians, Muslims..."

They closed the factory on the eve of Nowruz-Bayram. Aunt Merdzhan went back to her home in the district center and didn't visit us anymore.

Part Four

1

March arrived. When the long-awaited spring sun finally peeped out after a year away, I immediately noticed that it was somehow different this spring—as if it hadn't been reborn strong, filled with life-giving light, but remained last year's sun: tired out. It had been over there where the war was going on, and now it didn't have the strength to either warm or shine on people. If it had been possible not to appear, it wouldn't have come out from behind the mountains at all.

The sun gave off warmth at half strength, lazily spilling its light across the slopes. Sick, hungry old people, yawning every now and then from weakness, crawled out into the sun's heat, exposing their bony sides to its warm rays, but it seemed to me that the sun was having just as hard a time as those old people: its head hurt, and it didn't have the strength to give off heat. The white roses just beginning to bloom in our yard seemed weak and sickly to me, and the old pear tree that had dried out without water seemed to have died from lack of nourishment.

That spring the smell of milk followed me around. The young grass turning green beside the irrigation canal gave off the scent of fresh milk, and the weeds that my aunt pulled out of the strawberry field also smelled of milk; each evening my aunt packed the most delicious grass pulled from the rows of strawberries in a sack, and I carried that sack smelling of milk to Uncle Beshir in exchange for a half-liter jar of qatiq. Each evening Beshir's wife sternly ordered me not to lick the cream off the top so that Medina, God forbid, could accuse Goydzhek of palming off skimmed qatiq on her.

As soon as the school day ended, I went immediately to find grass, not even bothering with my schoolbag of books. We'd fill up a sack of grass for the cow and climb up the slope where the sunshine beat down so splendidly and delicious guzukulak grass grew. In the evening when I brought home the qatiq from Beshir's, my aunt boiled that slightly sour grass and topped it with qatiq. That was our dinner.

Merdzhan sent us bread with the mail carrier several times. I remember that. I also remember how Aunt Nabat sold her last carpet to the storehouse keeper at the beginning of spring and brought home about three kilos of wheat; then they gave out cheese in payment for days worked, and for several days we ate only cheese.

I finished the fourth grade. Fewer and fewer kids remained in school; they disappeared one after another, and there was no possibility of bringing them back to school. Azer still came to school, but he was always late—his stepfather forced him to tend the sheep.

They started sending the schoolchildren out to the fields in the morning. They began by taking the girls to weed, although many of them were younger than I was. In April they sent me into the melon field too. Now Aunt Medina and I walked to work together. I was completely happy because my aunt was cheerful, and when she was cheerful, it seemed to me that the sun shone brightly, at full strength, the way the spring sun ought to shine. My aunt smiled, and I walked beside her, hopping on one foot, and rejoiced that everything had turned out so well and that everything around us was new, green: the grass, the almond trees, Grandfather Abbas's melon field...

Grandfather Abbas was a husky, large-boned man in his sixties. His face was fresh, his cheeks ruddy, streaked with bluish veins, and he generally looked as if he'd never even heard of the war. He couldn't bear to talk about it, by the way; he preferred to wax poetic about his watermelons. Judging from his stories, the watermelons were nothing if not remarkable: they were sent to the Kremlin every fall. Once Kalinin, the Chairman of the Presidium of the Supreme Soviet himself, had tasted a watermelon from Abbas's melon field, and he liked the watermelon so much that Grandfather Abbas was immediately given a medal. Now the medal was at home in the trunk, but when the war ended, he'd pin it on without fail... Our aunts and mothers didn't exactly believe these stories, but because of his cheerful disposition, they forgave Abbas his harmless twaddle, as well as his salty jokes and constant flirting with the girls. As for us kids, we adored the cheerful old man: it was easy, quick, to work to his funny sayings, and we fulfilled the three-day quota in just one day. Joking nonstop, Grandfather Abbas sent us to the shop, to the spring to get grass for his donkey, and we raced one another to carry out his orders.

One day the old man bet us—also as a joke—that he could eat up all the bread we'd brought with us and drink all the tea brewed for the entire group. The proposition was met with enthusiasm. With jokes and funny sayings, Grandfather spread out the rag that served him as a tablecloth, and we put the bread on it. Old Abbas stuffed everything in, to the very last crumb, drinking an entire teapot of tea. The kids laughed and shouted, "Hurrah!" in unison, but it seemed to me that there wasn't anything funny about it: the old man had simply wanted very badly to eat—the two pieces of barley bread he had with him were nothing for his large, hungry body. He ate his fill, and all the rest of us remained hungry.

Going to the melon field in the mornings, I took a bag that I stuffed with cucumbers, green plums, and cherry plums, and along the road to school at noon, I freely gave out presents to the kids I met—I knew very well what it felt like to sit out on the street and peer at the hands of everyone returning from the orchards.

The path leading to the melon field lay between the orchards, and nowhere else, it seemed, was there such beauty: fresh grass, violets, mint... But that spring I noticed a different, astonishing beauty along the path—she was ten years old, and her name was Zarifa: each day we walked together from the melon field to school.

We were hurrying to school, and I, as always, was dragging the bag full of presents. And suddenly Zarifa froze in front of someone's wide open gate. "What roses!" she exclaimed in amazement. "I've never seen any like these!" I looked: they were just flowers. Our own white roses were shut in the yard, and no one could see them—she might have frozen that same way, in fact, in front of our gate! And her eyes would have been the same as they were now!

75

Zarifa was the most beautiful of our girls; I thought of nothing else the whole day. Catching sight of Aunt Medina, I ran to meet her and immediately bewildered her with an unexpected suggestion:

"Let's move back home! Why are we living in ruins?!"

And I began to argue excitedly that there was no point in remaining here at Mukush's, where things were so bad, so ugly.

At first Aunt Medina brightened up, but then her face darkened, drooped.

"It's impossible, Sadyk," she said, sighing. "Everyone is already judging us…"

My aunt became thoughtful, evidently not knowing how she could convince me, but there was no need for that—my father's large boots already loomed black in front of my eyes.

"It's impossible," said Aunt Medina firmly. "Your father's a very strict person. When he returns, both of us would be in trouble."

2

If it's possible to call any May day in the mountains where we live typical, ordinary, then I'd venture to say that the war ended on a typical May day. But the thing is, all the days in May are atypical, different, and they don't resemble one another: on one, all the jasmine blooms in a single night; on another, hundreds of cherry trees flower all at once; on yet another, all the roses suddenly open up their buds. You wake up in the morning and the slopes that just yesterday were bright green are now a colorful patchwork of tulips. Each day has its own color, its own aroma, and even the sun in May is different each day, not resembling yesterday's sun. No, we don't have ordinary days in May!

The war came to an end. The war—which took place somewhere off to the north in ruined cities and in deep, frozen trenches, poisoning every living thing around it—came to an end. It came to an end on a vibrant May noon in the melon field of the collective farm.

But until that moment the war was still going on, and we sprinkled earth on the seedlings from which muskmelons would later ripen. The war was still going on, and Grandfather Abbas pinched the girls as before and made our mothers laugh with his funny sayings.

The war was still going on when we spotted Azer at the far end of the melon field tearing toward us at top speed. He rushed right along the rows, his feet getting stuck in the vines, and shouted something, waving his hands.

Zarifa was the first to see him, and just as she'd done when she saw the roses blooming, she clapped her hands to her knees in delight.

"Oy! Just look at him fly!"

Azer ran up to us. He gasped, couldn't say a single word. But the war really hadn't ended yet, and of course, Grandfather Abbas immediately grabbed him by the ears and toppled him to the ground—the old man couldn't forgive that kind of treatment of muskmelons. Azer's ears instantly turned scarlet, but he didn't beg for mercy, just silently tried to tear himself away. When Grandfather Abbas at last released Azer, he jumped up—red, disheveled, sweaty—and solemnly announced:

"War over is!"

He said it in faulty Russian; only the schoolchildren understood. They understood and immediately cried in unison, like roosters at dawn: "Hur-rah! Hur-rah!"

The old man didn't understand anything. He even wanted to seize Azer afresh by the ears, but floundering a bit, I hurriedly managed to explain to him what was going on. Then Grandfather Abbas again grabbed hold of Azer and, knocking him over into the grass, began to roll, tickling and pinching. The old man laughed, rejoiced, and tears flowed from his eyes.

The kids dashed back to the village in a crowd. They ran all over the melon field, paying no attention to the melon vines or to Grandfather Abbas. However, the old man apparently didn't see any of this either.

I rushed ahead of everyone. Azer was left behind, and Zarifa too—I had other things to worry about. I cannoned into a branch, hurt myself; my head buzzed, but I didn't even rub the injured place. I reached the strawberry field where my aunt worked, glanced over the high wall—there was no one there. Women and kids crowded along the road—they were shouting something, waving their hands. I rushed home: the lock still hung on the door. Seeing it from the yard, I sprang into the street again, ran past Aunt Nabat. Windblown, hoisting her skirt in her hands, the old woman was running to Grandfather Aslan's house as if he'd promised to give her tobacco.

She shouted something after me; I didn't catch it.

I found Aunt Medina in the yard of my father's house. She was sitting quietly under the tree, arms folded across her chest. I'd never seen her that way. Everything immediately flew out of my head: Azer running along the melon field, Aunt Nabat, the happy crowd in the street, and that the war had come to an end.

I sank down next to her in the grass. My aunt hugged me, laid my head on her knees, and ran a hand through my hair. We were silent. The water murmured softly in the irrigation trough.

"You understand, Mukush is coming back..."

Mukush: the name echoed dully, far away, as if from the bottom of a well, and suddenly began to come closer, becoming ever more distinct, louder, silencing the songs and stories and the path among the flowers along which my aunt had run to school as a little girl. And I saw winter—cold, wordless, with a big bruise beneath its eye. And dark, impenetrable night—for some reason it had thin, hairy legs. The stinking pebbles behind the outhouse. The yellow leaves on the cucumber vines. The jar of phlegm. Could all that really be there, lurking off in the distance beyond my aunt's bright stories?

I wanted to soothe her, to say that Mukush wouldn't come back, couldn't come back, but I kept silent, feeling that I'd start to cry if I spoke a single word. I couldn't speak, couldn't look at my aunt. Even when Mukush had been present, I'd never seen her so unhappy.

Always, whether I was full or there was absolutely nothing to eat, as soon as I caught sight of my aunt's white scarf from afar, a wave of hope would seize my heart, and I knew everything would be all right. Even when I lost the bread coupons, my aunt only smiled and shook her head. And how many times I'd managed to lose the key, and we weren't able to get into the house! My aunt would walk the route I'd run during the day, and singing something under her breath, she'd start looking for the key. And would always find it... Why had she suddenly become so small? When we'd left for work that morning, she'd been tall, sturdy, and her green dress hadn't been old or ragged.

I stifled sobs, unable to lift my eyes. My aunt took my head in both hands and looked me in the face.

"But I'm not afraid!" she said. "I'm not afraid, and that's that. Right?"

She looked me straight in the eye.

"Right!" I said in amazement. "That's right, Aunt! You're not afraid of anyone!"

She became more animated, brightened up, got lightly to her feet.

"And I won't go back there!" My aunt pointed to the half-ruined house at the foot of the sheep mountain. "I won't go back to that house. I won't go back!" She repeated these words loudly several times, straightened up, sighed with relief, and I suddenly understood that I'd been mistaken—she wasn't small at all. On the contrary: she'd grown even taller.

The Tale of the Pomegranate Tree

1

The first summer after the war, on the very day they let us out of school for the holidays—I rushed home, hopping and skipping, rejoicing that I was now in the fifth grade with a free summer ahead—our neighbor Aunt Nabat stopped me at the gate. She said very sternly that I was a grown-up fellow now and that my time for running idly around the streets had come to an end.

Balancing the pitcher she used to carry water from the spring on her shoulder, Aunt Nabat leaned it against the wall and started talking about the spikelets of grain that remain in the fields after the harvest, about how much firewood goes to waste under walnut trees; then she nodded at the ant hill, from which an endless stream of life flowed toward our wall, and she told me what sounded like a tall tale: that there was a hole under the wall where the ants kept their stores, enough to last each ant ten winters. Aunt Nabat explained to me that if I were a smart fellow, I'd use the summer to gather grain and haul firewood, and if apricots or cherry plums fell into my hand, then it wouldn't be a bad idea to lay a handful or two on the roof to dry out—come winter, it would be nice to chew on some during class breaks at school. Aunt Nabat explained to me in great detail about where to collect grain spikelets and in which orchards the most firewood could be found; I stood and listened dutifully, although after four lessons and a long, long meeting about the summer holidays, I was just itching to climb up into the walnut tree.

But matters didn't end with that conversation. In the very hottest part of summer, when everything all around was burning and cracking from the heat, Aunt Nabat suddenly started to frighten me with winter. "Run around, run around!" she'd say, seeing me on the street. "But winter really isn't going to wait!" That whole summer Aunt Nabat didn't leave me in peace, and finally I really did start to be afraid, as if it weren't winter coming but something unknown, something dreadful. Each time Aunt Nabat threatened me with winter she turned her face toward the mountains, and it seemed to me that it was precisely there, over the far mountains, that something ominous and unknown was hiding, something that would suddenly come upon us—and so far, Aunt Nabat was the only person who was aware of it.

In the heat the coolest place to be is by the spring, and kids always gather there. That summer after the war, Aunt Nabat tried to prevent me from running to the spring. Every time I showed up there, having stuffed myself to bursting with the apricots I needed to swallow in order to collect more pits to play yamki with the kids, Aunt Nabat's chador would invariably appear at the end of the street. All in black, terrifying, she slowly approached us. Setting her bucket full of small pieces of brushwood down on the ground, the old woman would lay a small sack of spikelets on top of it, go up to the spring, and splash her face with water for a long, long time. Then she'd put her mouth to the trough, and you could see how the water spurted down her throat to her thin, wiry neck; water spilled from the corners of her mouth, running down her chin, and poured over her dress. Wiping off her face with the end of her scarf, Aunt Nabat would start scolding me. Sometimes I was able to slip away, and Aunt Nabat could only threaten my retreating back; sometimes, having drunk her fill, she'd silently lean her shoulder against a tree and, rolling a cigarette, stare fixedly at me. That was worse than any scolding.

I don't know why, but in the end Aunt Nabat left me in peace. Perhaps the old woman grew offended that I always ran away from her, maybe she happened to see how the watchman thrashed kids caught in the collective farm orchard, but most likely she simply threw up her hands—why else would she have stopped saying hello to me?

In the fall Aunt Nabat's son, Yakub, returned from the army. He came to visit us the very first night. He flung his feet in their heavy, black boots across the wall and immediately appeared in front of the iwan. All of this made it seem as if he hadn't come back from the war, but simply absented himself for a short while: as if he'd been away from home not for four years, but four days. Yakub briskly said hello to us and began pacing around the yard, observing our domestic affairs. Walnuts rustled in the pockets of his soldiers' pantaloons. "A grown fellow," said Yakub, meaning me. "And he didn't break off the dead branches in time. And he hasn't watered the yard: the apricot tree has dried out. And the grass has turned brown. Why didn't he cut it when he was supposed to? The mulberry stumps should have been uprooted, and seedlings should have been planted. And he should have dug a ditch across the yard—look how big he's grown!"

My aunt stood silently to the side; she really didn't like the way Yakub was sauntering around our yard with a proprietary look, not paying the slightest attention to her. Yakub went up to the house, yanked at a piece of peeling plaster, threw it on the ground, kicked the rickety stairs with his foot—the walnuts rumbled in his pocket. For some reason Yakub didn't pay any attention to the broken window, although not a single one of its six panes remained in the frame. Then Yakub left. To avoid stepping on the stairs, he began edging along the wall itself, touching it with his side; rolling around in the pocket of his pantaloons, the walnuts rustled. Going out onto the street, Yakub began to nibble them, and I listened to the crack of the walnut shells and, for some reason, remembered Aunt Nabat's words: "Poor Medina!" the old woman would say, looking at the bruises on my aunt's face. "To this day my Yakub carries a torch for you. He swoons when he sees you!"

Before two days had passed Yakub led in a nimble, black donkey from somewhere. Now it was out of the question to play with the kids in the street: Yakub was constantly bustling about the village with his black donkey. Now he was driving from the mill, now to the mill, now carrying hay to the collective farm storehouse, now bringing firewood to the schoolyard, and every time he saw me, he shouted that if he saw me loafing in the street one more time, he'd kill me.

I wasn't particularly afraid of Yakub, but all the same, I ran away when he started yelling like that. *First, Yakub is an adult, and grownups must be obeyed, and second, it pleases me just a little that he's shouting at me: shouting at someone means you're connected in ways a stranger wouldn't care about. Better to obey Yakub than have the kids think I've got no one.*

And in general I can, of course, dry sumac to eat with beans—just there the mountain is deep red with it—and break off the dead branches: just cut a stick of hazelnut and you can reach the deadwood from the ground. But seeing as no one wants to pay any attention to the thick, red A grades with which my teachers ornament my workbooks from year to year—because everyone thinks I'm a simple, good-for-nothing fellow, that I can't do anything and have no abilities, that I won't ever do anything—I don't. And that's that.

Coming home from school I'd throw down my bag, take out the barley lepyoshka that Aunt Medina had left for me, and slipping behind the neighbors' fences, I'd steal away toward the foot of the mountain. I'd climb the slope, lie down behind a broken-off fragment of the cliff so that I couldn't be seen, eat the lepyoshka, and loll around in the warm sand for hours, looking at our village.

From here, from the mountain, it was all in view, as if it lay in the palm of my hand: the earthen roofs; the little yards; the small gardens behind the houses; and further off, on the other side of the village, the orchards, farmland, and fields of the collective farm... *Laid out to dry, fruit turns yellow on the roofs. In the evening women will climb onto the roofs and collect it. At this hour trails of smoke, appetizing and not-so-appetizing, rise from all the yards: appetizing smoke from those yards where children are given stuffed eggplant and fried potatoes wrapped in wheat lavash to take with them to school, not-so-appetizing smoke from the other yards. The roofs, like the trails of smoke, I also divide into two kinds: the roofs of those who've returned from the war and the roofs of those who haven't returned. And when I start counting them up, I can't believe that the war has already ended, although I've read about it with my own eyes and seen many different photographs.*

It seems to me that the war is still going on, that it will end little by little: little by little, everyone will return home. My father will come first. Then, of course, Uncle Murtuz: how can the war end without

86

him? He often stood on this very cliff with his binoculars, looking at the village roofs. And when he climbed down, an unpleasant scene would inevitably take place near one of those houses. The thing is, our chairman Uncle Murtuz knew by heart how many fruit trees each person possessed, and if there was more fruit drying on a roof than there should be, it meant the fruit was stolen. Uncle Murtuz was very angry with those who stole fruit at the collective farm; he'd shout and make some notes in his red notebook. Having shouted to his heart's content, Uncle Murtuz went about other business, and we ran after him in a crowd, looking at the black binoculars. Uncle Murtuz didn't get angry at the kids because there were no "vestiges of capitalism" in us, and once we became members of the collective farm, we wouldn't steal fruit.

When the schoolkids marched in columns through the village streets on the first of May or the October holidays, Uncle Murtuz was always with them. He marched in front of the kids, and we little ones ran next to the column, bellowing loudly and happily. Uncle Murtuz shouted, "Hurrah!" and we shouted, "Hurrah!" In this manner we arrived at the administrative building of the collective farm. Uncle Murtuz would head for the statue of Lenin standing next to the building, unbutton his jacket, tuck one hand into his pocket, stretch out the other hand to us—exactly like Lenin—and loudly start to give a speech. Uncle Murtuz talked for a long time, and we'd clap until our palms began to burn and shout, "Hurrah!" until we were hoarse.

But even if my father and Uncle Murtuz return—that still won't be enough. For the war to truly end, Azer's father has to return. People have to gather on the club's iwan in the evening so that Azer's father can walk along that iwan, handsome, wearing his pressed white shirt, and show us how the strings of the tar should be played. And he has to walk along the street in the evening, catching small girls in his arms and tossing them in the air. Azer's father doesn't like playing with little boys: for example, he's never once set me on his shoulders. But all the same, until he returns, I won't believe the war is over.

From here, from the mountain, the large plane tree is easy to see. Earlier this was an extremely crowded place, and every evening Grandfather Aslan compelled the young fellows to haul water from the irrigation canal and, having thoroughly drenched the earth, carefully sweep beneath the plane tree. Now the old people still gather in the evenings; they sit, leaning against its gnarled trunk, dozing, yawning. Grandfather Aslan always sits in the exact same spot, and jabbing his cane into the ground, he twirls it wistfully—he, too, is still waiting for the end of the war. He's waiting until "our boys" return and there'll be someone to sweep under the plane tree; and when they sweep under the plane tree, he'll also make them sweep the street, the whole street, all the way to the school. But "our boys" still aren't returning, and there's no one to water the street, and after sitting under the plane tree, Grandfather Aslan leaves; next to the place where he was sitting, small, deep, round holes remain in the ground. Each time I walked past I looked at those holes the way people look at ancient writing. Grandfather Aslan's writing spoke of how the cursed war had turned everything to dust: even children had stopped listening to their elders. It was all hateful, he couldn't bear it, it was time to die, but death didn't come; if "our boys" had returned sooner, he'd have taken leave of this world in peace... In the morning they drove the herd through the village, and the cows trampled the marks where Grandfather Aslan had written about war and peace, but the next night would arrive, and Grandfather Aslan's writing would appear under the plane tree again.

Every time I look out from here, from the mountain onto the village, I'm reminded of how the crow who lives in the crown of our large walnut tree used to call out. The call of our crow was full of the blinding sun. The sun flooded the mountains, sweeping over the village with a wide stream of light, piercing the leaves with its rays and driving the crow out of her mind. Unable to hold back her delight, she'd exhaust herself in calling out; the branch shook beneath her, and the crow, shooting up, would fly directly at the electric line stretched near our house. My grandmother got angry at the crow—"The cursed thing's gone berserk, God forbid she brings the snow down on us!"—but I didn't hear anything in the crow's frenzied call besides frantic, irrepressible joy.

In winter the sun would disappear for weeks at a time, returning stealthily one night, and in the morning I'd be awakened by the joyous call of the crow—everything sparkling and shimmering all around. And although that kind of morning was a holiday for everyone—for the crow, for me, for my grandmother—my grandmother grumbled all the same: the crow was bringing on the snow, the damned sorceress.

My grandmother couldn't bear snow—she didn't own shoes. My grandmother had never had shoes; I always saw my father's giant boots on her dry, little legs. The rhythmic clomp-clomp of those boots constantly followed my grandmother, whether she was going down into the cellar for firewood, carrying the small bucket of milk, or returning from the henhouse with her skirt full of eggs.

When the sun grew warmer and the earth darkened in the yard, my grandmother plodded out there, dragging her boots: inhaling the damp, thawed air with pleasure, she'd look attentively at the sky, weighing up whether there were lots of clouds. If there was a fair number of clouds, then for some reason there was too little firewood in the cellar; but if clouds were few, then our firewood store immediately increased, and there was no need to conserve it. But whether there was a lot or a little, you still had to go down to get it, and my grandmother would drag her boots to the cellar—dinner had to be ready before my father arrived home. And while dinner cooked on the cast-iron stove, hissing slightly, my grandmother told me long, long, long tales. Most often she'd tell me about how she traveled to the tomb of the Prophet in Mecca, how they crossed the Araz River on rafts made from inflated skin bags, and what wonders there were in Mecca. The crescent moon there dressed in men's clothing, but the sun wore the clothes of a girl. And the sun's gold necklace wasn't visible to everyone, just those who truly revered Allah. Thanks to the Creator, my grandmother had been deemed worthy: she'd gazed on the gold necklace of the luminous one!

In wintertime my father always came home in a bad mood, and on hearing the rumble of the collective farm pails in which he hauled butter and farmer's cheese to be sold, my grandmother would instantly fall silent. My father came into the room and immediately started to find fault with us; he fumed that while he'd spent the whole day in the cold to earn a living, we'd been sitting in a warm room and eating the food he'd worked for. He peeled the wet socks off his feet, hurled them toward the stove, then grabbed the largest pillow from the divan, threw it down on the palas carpet, and propping his elbows on it, proceeded to drink tea. My grandmother retrieved the boots he'd kicked off by the front door and placed them closer to the fire. My father drank tea and, stretching his feet toward the stove, wriggled his numb toes: large, flat, they were scarlet now. And so long as the redness remained and

89

the perspiration couldn't form on his cold forehead, he stayed morose; he came to himself slowly, as slowly as the water steamed out of his woolen socks.

My grandmother thought this was normal—that all fathers were this way because it was difficult to earn a living. And that it was normal that she didn't have shoes, that she wasn't supposed to—she wasn't the one earning the money. All the same, my grandmother once did start a conversation about shoes. A mullah had appeared in the village, an actual mullah from the city, and my grandmother decided she had to visit the mosque just this once, although she'd be ashamed to stand before God. But when she started talking about shoes and God, my father flew into a fury and began denouncing Allah in such terms that my grandmother didn't know what to do with herself. My father yelled that Allah wasn't worth a damn, that he was the lowest son of a bitch there was, and that if he were a real God, there wouldn't be any collective farms or those cursed pails. Every time the conversation turned to God, my father for some reason started shouting about land, about cattle, and I was confused as to whether our land and cattle had been taken by the collective farm or by God himself. After the conversation about shoes, I had no doubt that my father would refuse to buy them for my grandmother, not because she didn't earn any money but because she loved God.

When I opened my eyes in the morning, my father's boots no longer stood next to the stove, and the pails that spent the night by the front door had also disappeared from the hallway—gone off to earn a living. But no matter how angry the evening had been, morning arrived all the same, and my grandmother was again dragging her boots to the cellar, the cowshed, the henhouse...

And my grandmother's marvelous tales, and the clomp-clomp of her boots, and the satisfied crackle of the cast-iron stove stuffed full of dry, resinous firewood—all of that echoed in the call of our crow.

And yet the crow's happy call first and foremost means summer. Evening in summer: women on the roofs all around. They've collected the fruit and are shouting something loudly to one another in their rich, ringing voices. The men are standing on their iwans, good naturedly shouting at their wives every so often and solemnly exchanging remarks. Everything is already ripe in the gardens, and they invite everyone who comes by to sample the fruit. Boys scamper about the streets with ecstatic shouts. And above all of this rises the incessant cawing of the crow.

Nowadays it's quiet in the village, and when the son of the melon grower climbs a tree full of unripe fruit across the river, where the melon fields begin, and shouts to chase away the birds, I take heart from his voice. The boy's shrill call reminds me a bit of those evening voices. I like it when the women shout out to one another, when they exchange remarks standing on the roofs. But that happens rarely these days; the women are mostly silent. As if they no longer have anything to chatter about; as if cats no longer kill chicks, dogs don't steal hides from the yard, and hens don't dash into henhouses that aren't their own.

Toward evening there are many women by the spring. And no matter how far away they are from me, I immediately recognize Yakub's wife, Sadaf: she's thinner than thin, and even the bones of her temple are visible. I always felt sorry for Sadaf, especially after Yakub returned and a huge bruise swelled up under her eye. The eye was painful, but Sadaf didn't hide the bruise, didn't cover her face with a scarf—she wanted to show everyone that she had a husband. These days it's rare for people to have husbands.

When the sun faded from the spring, the herd returned to the village. However, you couldn't really call it a herd, just ten to fifteen cows. The cows scattered around the village and stood mooing by those gates where there was always appetizing smoke. And when the sun faded from the mountains, Bald Safar would drive the lambs close by me; he shouted curses at them and continually talked about their mothers. Bald Safar was the youngest of the shepherd boys; we'd started school the same year. However, Safar completed just the first lesson. When the second lesson started, they kicked him out because he had scabs— his whole head was covered in sores. I really envied Safar, I'd always envied him, and now that he'd gotten himself a puppy, my envy was beyond all bearing. The puppy's ears had recently been cropped, and Safar boasted that he'd soon crop the puppy's tail. He spoke about this calmly, as if it were an everyday occurrence, but I thought about that tail day and night: wouldn't that be a pity, would it really be cut off?

Wagging his short tail, the puppy ran after Safar; they climbed down the mountain and disappeared, but they could still be heard for a long time as Safar walked around the village and shouted loudly at each gate, calling the owner. Then his voice would grow softer, and the lambs would fall silent. The slope on which I lay would turn from rose-pink to gray, and I'd climb down from the mountain and make my way home the back way, behind the houses. Hiding behind trees, I'd steal along the wall that separated our yard from the street, and only after jumping over it would I stand up to my full height. I'd try as hard as I could to bang the iron fastener on the gate—after all, no one besides Safar knew that I hid on the mountain, and my aunt didn't need to know that either: I let her think that I was in the street. If I came in from the street, no matter how late I turned up, my aunt wouldn't get angry. *She even says that I shouldn't listen to Yakub: some relative he is—a cousin by way of our wattle fence! But I listen to him anyway. Let him shout, it doesn't make a bit of difference to me—the upside is that those fortunate enough to bake lavash from wheat, those more fortunate than us, won't dare mess with my aunt. They're afraid to do that because Yakub is the strongest, toughest man in our village: he keeps everyone in fear. If Yakub hadn't yelled at me and called me to hold his donkey, the kids would still be creeping into our yard and breaking the glass with stones, just for the fun of it. No, even if Yakub isn't our relative, I'll listen to him anyway.*

Returning home from school one day, I spotted an enormous, black cloud far off beyond the mountains, and I understood immediately that this was the very thing with which Aunt Nabat had been threatening me. The cloud was indeed terrifying. For many days it moved slowly but inexorably toward the village, one night finally crushing the mountains beneath itself, filling the sky from edge to edge. For the first time in my life, the call of the crow that morning didn't give me joy: what if the crow really had brought on the snow?

A few days later my aunt brought home a handful of yellow paper sacks from work and used them to patch over the window. And going out into the street in the morning a few days after that, I saw that the trail of ants had disappeared—the ants had gone to start eating up their stores.

Winter had begun.

We removed the pillows, blankets, a piece of the old palas carpet, the cast-iron stove with the broken leg, and the kerosene lamp from the ruins of Mukush's house. We placed the stove in the center of the room, setting a brick in place of its broken leg. We put the blankets and pillows on top of the old trunk: to this day I remember the trunk in the corner of the room like I remember my own name. We covered part of the earthen floor with the palas, and every night Mukush's kerosene lamp burned on it.

After dinner I'd lay out my schoolbooks and notebooks by the lamp: my aunt sat a little way off with her back against the wall, patching up something from the rag bag. Sprawled on my stomach, I'd prepare my lessons. Sometimes my aunt would also open a book and prop it on her knees. We'd read quietly, and the lamp would quietly burn.

The neighbor women dropped in quite often—in wintertime it was pleasant to sit and chat after dinner in a warm room. As soon as guests appeared, I had to creep off to the side with my books. My aunt would put her book aside, but she didn't close it, simply set it face down, and the whole time the guests were sitting with us, my aunt's thoughts would remain there on the open page.

My aunt didn't enjoy chatting with the neighbors, didn't listen to what they said. And all the same, my aunt was delighted when they came. The thing was, that winter Yakub became a frequent visitor, and if my aunt and I were alone, he'd sit longer and talk more, and that was real torture for my aunt.

The women arrived chilled, ruddy with cold, and coming into the house, they'd immediately start to lavish praise on it: our house really was a good one, they'd say—a strong, old house—and heating the stove once a day was plenty.

Having complimented the house, the guests would gradually turn the conversation to other topics: whether sugar was better in loaf form or lumps, who had earned how much for fruit this year, and what could be brewed in place of tea. Aunt Khadidzha would remark that rose leaves were very good, especially if drunk with mulberries.

They also said that some kind of powder had appeared that looked like whitewash. The wife of Kadyr, who worked at the Zemotdel—the agricultural department—made milk out of that powder.

The women talked most of all about military pensions, and having begun this topic, they'd talk over the whole village, house by house. They knew for certain that more people on the upper street received a pension than on the lower street, that someone from the lower street had managed to obtain false documents; it was true that parents of educated sons received higher pensions than parents of those who were uneducated. Aunt Khadidzha got very upset when people spoke about large pensions—her son had been less than a year from finishing his studies when he went to war. But Aunt Ziver hadn't had anyone serve in the war, and when the conversation turned to pensions, her mood immediately soured.

The women tried not to talk about those who'd perished, not to recall their names, but this topic arose spontaneously all the time. As soon as the talk turned to those who hadn't returned, Aunt Khadidzha closed her eyes and began to rock slowly from side to side. Aunt Mesme sighed deeply, something wheezed in her chest, and she'd cough painfully for a long time. Aunt Ziver also made a sad face, although it didn't turn out very sad, not the way it had looked during the conversation about pensions.

I heard a great deal about my father every time the neighbor women came to visit. The women stoutly assured me that my father had been the bravest, strongest, and most worthy man in the village, although I'd never doubted that. Aunt Mesme never got tired of repeating what she'd seen with her own eyes: how my father, having come to blows with his fellow villagers over water, had beaten the whole gang black and blue all by himself. Another time he'd stolen six magnificent rams from the Karabakhers, herded them into the yard when the shepherds drove the flock near the house, and that had been that. Our street had smelled of shashlyk—roasted mutton kebabs—for an entire month. *When Aunt Mesme reminisces about shashlyk, I can see her mouth water, although if you believe what she says, she can't stand shashlyk, and if, God forbid, she eats a piece, she'll be sick for a week. Aunt Ziver, who happens to be a distant relative of ours, likes most of all to talk about how pious my father was—spotting her at the spring one evening, he'd seen from one* hundred paces off that she wasn't wearing stockings, and he immediately told her husband about it. That evening, as was right and proper, her husband had schooled her with a stick, and his stick was heavy. Aunt Ziver talks about this with pride and sadly shakes her head; now all the real men have gone, died out.

And what a good thing it would be if I were to take after my father! Easy to say, hard to do! The garden has to be the best in the whole village, I have to get to the shop before everyone else to buy sugar, and if the night is windy and the walnuts have blown down in the collective farm orchard, I have to be the first to get there. And it goes without saying that the yard needs to be weeded by hand so that the weeds don't take over. And it's come to this: I'm too lazy to gather the fruit that lies rotting under every tree! You might call it "free money"!

Aunt Mesme confidently foretold that I wouldn't turn out well at all: "You can tell from the egg how a chick will turn out." Ziver wouldn't agree with her, and as proof she offered a different proverb about chickens: "It's said: don't count them till the fall, when they're grown." However, in defending me Aunt Ziver looked with such aversion at the notebooks spread out on the palas carpet that I saw very clearly—she didn't believe what she was saying. *Well, what can you say to that? I don't resemble my father one bit, and I'm never going to!*

Of course, if my father had returned from the war, it wouldn't be so evident that I'm no good at anything—under the circumstances, perhaps even he wouldn't be able force his way through that scrum to the shop. And then they chatter on, they say I can't do anything, that I'm no good at anything, but do they consider my aunt? Will she let me steal walnuts or be squashed in the line for sugar? She can't bear these conversations. These neighbor women don't know how repugnant it is for her to listen to them. Neither by word nor gesture does Aunt Medina announce her displeasure, but I know what it takes for her to control herself: her lips turn pale, her pupils grow huge.

It was still worse when Yakub dropped in on us, and he showed up quite a lot. As soon as Yakub appeared in the doorway, my aunt would silently get up, grab the largest log from the pile he'd laid in in the fall—uprooting the sumac bushes in our yard—and shove it into the stove. It seemed that she wanted to burn all the firewood right that minute in front of Yakub so that he wouldn't show up at our house anymore.

When Yakub came into the yard, the wicket gate made of boards would rumble as if something heavy were striking it, and the iron fastener would hit the plate with a bang. And right then, almost simultaneously with that sound, the steps would start to creak. Yakub crossed the distance from the wicket gate to the house so quickly that I was absolutely amazed, but later I understood that he had very quick feet—that's how he'd come home alive from the war.

Yakub's pockets were always chock full of mulberries, Aunt Nabat's famous mulberries, which no one else was able to dry as successfully. Yakub came in and out freely, as if it were his own home; he'd saunter around casually near the window covered over with yellow paper, asking my aunt about this and that, rustling his hand in his pocket the whole time. If there were women sitting with us, his hand stayed that way, in his pocket; if no one else was around, Yakub took out a handful of mulberries and held it out to me and then put down another handful in front of Aunt Medina. Then he'd seat himself on the trunk, cross his legs, and begin to twirl the laces of his thick, woolen socks—he wore two pairs of them, one atop the other—around his finger. Yakub twirled the laces with his left hand and tossed mulberries into his mouth with his right; he chewed with pleasure, and he conversed with pleasure too.

My aunt sat by the wall, paying not the slightest attention to the mulberries in front of her and thinking about something else. No matter how loudly Yakub talked, I knew she wasn't hearing a single word. I was also bored listening to Yakub: he told us at least a hundred times about how he'd been a storehouse keeper in the army and how not just soldiers but even generals groveled at his feet because vodka is a god for Russians, and he'd held that god in his hands for three years and nine months. I was skeptical about the generals; however, I had no doubt whatsoever that while at the front, Yakub had sold all sorts of odds and ends under the table to his fellow countrymen. I believed Yakub when he said he'd looked for my father and Mukush at the front: he'd looked for them to peddle pilfered bread, boots, and sugar. But Yakub hadn't been able to realize his scheme, and every time he talked about it, something resembling sadness appeared on his wide, red face. Yakub would fall silent and turn pensive. And I grew pensive looking at him. I'd think about why he wore old socks on top of his nice, new ones. And about how many mulberries Aunt Nabat must have dried last summer, if Yakub was sick of them by now! Then I'd try to imagine the generals who "groveled" at Yakub's feet and marvel at the fact that storehouse keepers and storehouses apparently also existed during wars.

After all these stories with vodka and generals, Yakub invariably brought up my father. Moreover, when he brought up what a brave man the late Nadzhaf had been, he himself would become just as brave right before our eyes: his back straightened up, his fingers clenched themselves into fists, and his eyes began to sparkle. But then his glance would fall on me, and he'd silently hang his head. Yakub pitied me with all his heart and, unlike the women, disliked chattering about my uselessness. He'd simply bring his heavy fist down on the trunk and sigh sadly: "Ah! All fires end in ashes!" And I'd immediately imagine the ashes that fires leave behind: the cooled ashes filling the hearth, the pile of ashes just shaken out of the samovar, and the ashes flaking off the cast iron stove through little holes into the brazier.

Yakub talked for hours, and I didn't once observe that my aunt looked at him. However, Yakub never took his eyes off her. When the mulberries were finished and the stories were also coming to an end and it was time to leave, it was still more difficult for my aunt to endure his mute gaze. As before, she'd sit in her corner and just breathe very quickly, as if she were short of air: her ragged breathing was clearly audible in the quiet. Either Yakub didn't notice, or else he liked the fact that she was breathing like that. He'd stretch his neck, his thick, red lips would open slightly, quite comically; in those moments it seemed to me that Yakub was about to burst into song. He did indeed start to sing, but only after he was already out in the street, when the wicket gate had banged shut behind him. And until his loud, rollicking voice died out in the distance, my aunt sat without stirring. Then she got up quickly, seized the bedding from the trunk, and spread it on the palas, muttering angrily beneath her breath. She lashed out at the neighbors, railed against Yakub, soothed me: "They think they're so smart! They want me to send this boy to look after sheep. Just you wait! Not in a million years!"

Judging by the fury with which my aunt plumped up the pillows, it was evident that she very much wanted not just to give someone a piece of her mind but also to give that someone a good thrashing. Still grumbling, she'd bring the matches in from the hallway, shove them under her pillow, and lie down, putting out the lamp. In bed my aunt immediately quieted down—I had to get up early the next morning—but I knew she wasn't asleep, that she was lying there and arguing with the neighbor women, with Yakub, with Aunt Nabat...

Yakub's voice could be heard from the street, and that voice was hateful and loathsome to her, like the smell of the medicine the cleaning crew had poured onto the street when Leyla got sick with typhus and was taken to the hospital. My aunt tossed and turned, sighed, covered her head with the blanket, but like that stinking medicine, there was no way to rid herself of Yakub's hateful voice. All day, from morning to evening, from sunrise to sunset, that booming, imperious bass voice thundered over the village. In the evenings when the boys raised a ruckus by the spring, Yakub's joyous shouts and contented laughter could be heard a long way off—his son easily laid any opponent flat on his back. Not by the irrigation canal, not at the mill, not under the plane tree—nowhere, now, was there a voice louder than Yakub's; it penetrated even the closed windows in the school, and every time I heard it, I saw his well-fed, contented face, and over and over again, it came into my head that perhaps for Yakub, the war might truly be over.

Was it the beginning of spring or the end of winter? We hadn't yet packed away the stove, and the paper sacks that had once held sulfur were still stuck up over the window; in the dim light of the kerosene lamp, the damp, yellow paper resembled rawhide. The firewood laid in by Yakub was long gone; the mulberries Aunt Nabat had dried in such vast quantities last summer were also gone. The neighbor women no longer came to visit, and there was no talk of pensions, or sugar, or tea in our house. I lay on the palas, my notebooks placed in front of me. My aunt sat in her corner, leaning back against the wall. Yakub's large, strong legs, one crossed over the other, stuck out from the old trunk. On this night, contrary to his habit, Yakub was silent, and my aunt, who'd never said even two words to him, suddenly spoke first.

"Why did Sadaf leave you?"

"I'm the one who kicked her out!"

Yakub straightened up and looked proudly at my aunt. As if there were nothing more difficult than to drive skinny, little Sadaf out of her home, and he'd finally managed to do so. Despair flickered in my aunt's eyes. She fell silent. But she should have spoken, should have given voice to everything that seethed in her heart: "Don't you dare dishonor me," Aunt Medina should have said to Yakub, "don't you dare visit us again! You have no business in this house—and no matter what, I'll never marry you!"

Yakub left. My aunt looked guiltily at me: "Well, how can a person drive him away? After all, he's a man, not a dog!" And once more there was hope in her eyes: maybe he'd understand, maybe tomorrow he wouldn't come.

The very worst was the day when Yakub installed glass in our window. My aunt was at work, and I wasn't home either; when I arrived home, the glass had already been installed in the window frame, and the remnants of the yellow paper were lying on the floor.

My aunt returned from work in the evening. She walked in and froze, eyes riveted on the glass. Then she set the bucket she took to the field each day down on the floor and walked right back out the door. It got dark, lights were lit in the houses, and my aunt was still walking around the yard. That night she didn't put on the samovar, didn't light the lamp, as if the glass wouldn't be visible if we sat in the dark.

But the glass was visible, both that day and the following one. And there was yet another very bad day when Teacher Tovuz, the most senior of our teachers, took me aside during the break and, taking the cigarette out of her mouth, asked:

"Has Yakub taken your aunt as his wife?"

I didn't answer her, but all that day, right up until evening, I kept repeating the same thing in my mind: "No, Yakub didn't take her as his wife! No, Yakub didn't take her as his wife!" How could they not understand: if Mukush hadn't been able to force her to do so, would she really have slept with Yakub?

But they didn't understand. No one understood that. On the contrary, everyone was certain that my aunt and I just longed to sink our claws into Yakub. Sadaf, too, who'd shown off her bruises, and Aunt Nabat, who hadn't spoken to my aunt since the winter and didn't answer when I said hello to her. And she certainly wasn't angry because I hadn't collected the spikelets of grain or laid in firewood, she'd washed her hands of that long ago—how happily she'd kissed me when Yakub returned from the army!

Was it the end of spring or the beginning of summer? We'd already stored the stove in the cellar, and it lay there on its side because it had only two legs and couldn't stand up. The lamp glowed in its accustomed place, and as there was now glass in the windows and not paper that looked like rawhide, the shining moon could be seen. Moonlight spilled over the cherry tree; the ripe, red berries seemed white now. The light fell on my schoolbooks, which had been resting on the windowsill for a long time already. As usual, I was lying on my stomach in front of the lamp, although I didn't need to study my lessons. My aunt sat in the corner, leaning against the wall. Two large, strong legs in charyki—rustic shoes made of rawhide—stuck out from the trunk. Yakub was trying to persuade my aunt to allow me to go with him to the district center to sell those same cherries that now appeared white in the moonlight. And my aunt agreed. Surprising, but true: my aunt agreed with Yakub.

As soon as Yakub left, my aunt took my small notebook from the windowsill, tore a page out of it, added water strained from the samovar to the dried ink, picked up a fountain pen lying in one of the books, and having thought for a second, dipped the pen in the ink. And her face immediately changed. Lord, what other woman would rejoice so much to take pen in hand?! My aunt's face immediately became happy, and right before my eyes she turned into a little girl, a schoolgirl. I know that my aunt started school when Soviet power came to the village. At that time the teachers worked with the kids in the orchard under the trees. That wasn't for long, just at the beginning, but Aunt Medina always talked about her school in such a way that it was impossible to imagine her in an ordinary classroom behind a desk. Only in the orchard. And not in the ordinary collective farm orchard where we had botany lessons. This orchard was extraordinary: in it, everything was in bloom, and it smelled different from any other orchard. Here the teachers didn't write out math problems, didn't dictate grammar rules—they sang with the kids. And the lanes along which the children ran to school weren't the same as they are now. Or maybe they were the same lanes, but at that time they were drowning in roses, the very roses mentioned in my aunt's song. Azer's father had sometimes sung that song at the club too. And if it hadn't been for that song, and that school in the orchard, and Azer's father in the snow-white shirt, perhaps Aunt Medina wouldn't have hated Yakub. It even seemed to me that precisely because of that song, she couldn't do with Yakub what Mukush had unsuccessfully demanded of her.

And always, as soon as my aunt laid down the pen, the flowering orchard was lost, the lanes lined with roses turned into ordinary paths, and Mukush appeared in the niche in front of the mosque, lying in wait for my aunt. Then the heavy tramp of boots was heard. The tramp of black boots merged into the ululation of the black wedding zurna, and in the ink-black darkness, they led my aunt toward Mukush... Then I saw the old teacher Khashim on the road near the club, the same Khashim who wouldn't say hello to my aunt because she'd quit coming to school.

This time the joy didn't disappear from my aunt's face when she laid down the pen. My aunt placed the ink on the windowsill, folded the piece of paper into a triangle, gave it to me, and said I should carry it to Merdzhan. Merdzhan worked at the bread shop across from the market. My aunt described at great length how to find the shop, and then she said that the most important thing was not to show the letter to Yakub. And she ordered me very strictly not to lug the cherries myself, not on any account: let Yakub tie the bucket to the donkey's pack. If I got tired, he should put me on the donkey, too, but I'd need to hold on tight. When we went out on the steppe, it would be necessary to stop and eat without hurrying, and if I needed to relieve myself, there was nothing to be ashamed of—I'd sit down behind a stone, and that would be that. And for the first time in her life, my aunt said that Yakub was an ass and wouldn't understand any of this.

It was still dark when we left the village: the donkey in front, Yakub behind him, and then me. My pantaloons were immaculately clean and completely dry: just when had my aunt had time to dry them? My galoshes were also clean, shining; she'd washed them and lined the inside with newspaper so that the stones couldn't be as easily felt. But all the same, my feet hurt. Yakub wore his charyki—and the stones didn't seem to bother him, even though he was wearing only one pair of socks. It didn't hurt the donkey, either, to step on the stones—he picked up his hooves cheerfully, his new horseshoes gleaming.

I carried the bucket of cherries; Yakub didn't carry anything. I absolutely had to carry the bucket myself, of course, if I wanted to grow up to be like my father—at my age, he'd lugged sacks of grain along the mountain road.

It was a shame it hadn't occurred to me earlier—Yakub walked so fast, I shouldn't have filled the bucket to the brim. The donkey also walked easily; the two packs didn't weigh him down. He felt terrific and even swished his beautiful, black tail.

We walked along the steppe for a long time; it was gray, flat, endless. And all the time we were walking along that gray, flat plain, Yakub told me about my father. And for some reason it started to seem to me that my father's face had been gray and entirely flat, although I remembered very well—my father was hook-nosed, and his face was red, almost as red as Yakub's.

The sharp stones stabbed the soles of my feet unbearably. The stones were also gray, evil, and pitiless. Now the whole world was made up of these sharp, merciless stones, and the worst thing was that it was impossible to grind them down, smash them to bits, make them cry.

It was still a long time until sunrise: the sky hung heavy, low, gray. Up ahead loomed the mountain—huge, aloof. I had to carry the bucket to its very top. I very much wanted to break into sobs.

And not because my feet hurt unbearably and my back ached from the weight but because the whole world was made of gray, sharp, evil stones, and it was impossible to grind them down, smash them to bits, make them cry.

We walked from one telegraph pole to the next, and along the wires next to us stretched a low, pinched moan. From time to time Yakub lashed his military riding trousers with a switch in the spot where they puffed up like a ball; the donkey shuddered and lurched forward. The little, black donkey was not evil, not merciless, and he was afraid of Yakub's switch. He was a good donkey. I looked him in the eye more than once. There was sadness, pain, and melancholy in the big, brown eyes, but I never saw malice in them. If Yakub hadn't been there, I'd have tied the bucket to his back, naturally, but I'd also have brushed his withers, stroked him behind the ears, and driven the horseflies away from his stomach so that he wouldn't take offense.

Will you carry my pail, eh? It won't hurt, you've got a felt palan on your back! And my hands are falling off, and my back aches so much... Well, at least slow down!

Sometimes the young donkey would start to move his hoofs more slowly, but the switch cut the air with a whistle, and shuddering, the donkey again sprang forward. Yakub was preoccupied, he was in a hurry, he continually lashed the donkey—anyone with sense had to be at the bazaar before dawn: the early bird gets the worm.

Several times Yakub set about cheering me up: think, it's just a bucket of cherries! As boys, he and my father had hauled grain along this road—our village didn't have a mill then. Now, that was heavy! And no matter how many times they'd run into wolves here, it was nothing: they weren't afraid! My father was quite a fellow. And I should grow up to be just like him: fearless, strong, quick-witted.

Sometimes Yakub tilted his head back, looked at the sky, and began to sing, lashing himself lightly on the back to the rhythm of the song. Yakub sang because it was impossible for him not to sing: this summer he'd definitely become the storehouse keeper. He'd take me as his assistant, and then I'd eat my fill of cheese and almonds. We'd have enough of everything. We'd weigh out peas every week, and every week we'd have a pood: peas absorb moisture. Walnuts are a different matter, they have to be watered—they dry out. But here, of course, moderation would be necessary: the right amount of water for the walnuts, the right amount of sand for the grain—each has its own requirements. Yakub knew this with absolute certainty; his father had worked as the storehouse keeper for many years...

The big toe of my right foot grew completely numb—I couldn't feel it. My hands also felt like they were no longer attached to me. When we reached the base of the mountain, Yakub finally permitted me to put the bucket down and rest. But I didn't put the bucket down—I no longer felt any pain. I felt only one thing: I hated Yakub. I didn't know at the time that it was called hatred, but I didn't want to let it pass: the more I hated Yakub, the less I felt the pain—the top of the mountain already didn't seem quite so far to me.

On the mountain Yakub took the bucket from me—now the donkey would carry it. Yakub smiled and gently patted me on the head the way he patted his own son when the boy, tussling with one of the other boys near the spring, laid his opponent flat on his back. The bucket had been my opponent, and I'd conquered it. Then Yakub lifted my shirt and patted my shoulders, my shoulder blades. Tears choked me, but I didn't cry. I was happy, but I didn't want to rejoice—I was afraid to lose the thing that had given me strength, the thing called hatred. When we sat down to have a quick bite to eat and Yakub took out the fat, white chicken wrapped in a scarf, it grew harder not to unburden myself of that hatred because Yakub handed me more than half of the chicken; I managed to hold onto it, but only because the slope of the mountain was in shadow and the orchards couldn't be seen. When we walked among the orchards and the dewy leaves sparkled in the sun's rays, I couldn't help myself, and I let it go. And right up until the end of the road, up to the district center itself, the fear never left me that I'd also lost the letter, and I kept feeling about for it in my pocket.

I spotted the bread shop immediately, as soon as we sold the cherries and I was able to slip away from Yakub: it was right there, catty-corner to the bazaar. Finding it was no trouble at all. First, there was a sign right on the building that it was a bread shop. Second, everyone who walked out the door was carrying bread. And third, people were crowded around the shop, and my aunt had told me that the biggest crowd of people would be right smack in front of the bread shop. My aunt had also listed a heap of other signs, saying that finding the bread shop wouldn't be easy, and now that puzzled me. *Where, for example, are the cars my aunt talked about, the terrible cars rumbling along the street one after another? My aunt insisted that I wait for them all to pass, but there aren't any cars in sight. One comes past, but you can cross over and come back ten times before another one shows up... Maybe this isn't the right street? No, of course not, there's only one such street here: long, covered with asphalt. The others are like those we have in the village: narrow, made of stones. And the houses on them are the same country houses as ours.*

My aunt had said that an irrigation canal flowed along the street and that I'd have to walk up a bit to cross over—there was a little bridge there. *But what kind of irrigation canal is this? It's easy to jump over!*

People strolled along the street in front of the bazaar, trading in fresh herbs and cigarettes; the cars that so rarely drove by honked their horns deafeningly, as if the drivers took special pleasure in this. The shoeshine man, having set up his bench by the irrigation canal, was continually banging his brushes against it; evidently, he also took pleasure in this. Sometimes he'd even start shouting. The boys swarming all over the mulberry trees also shouted all the time; there were so many of them that it seemed that the tree might just break and all of them fall into the irrigation canal.

A few fellows were idling along the irrigation canal. Two of them had taken off their shoes and were sitting, dangling their feet in the murky, brownish water. When girls walked by, the whole group turned their heads, as if on command; if the girl wasn't wearing stockings, the fellows fixed their eyes on her legs, and the girl walked very straight and stared at a single spot. *Exactly like our girls from the upper grades at school when they perform at a party in the club!* It had always seemed to me that the girls were afraid they'd forget the words if they took their eyes off the poster hanging at the back of the auditorium. Here, as if in unison, all the girls kept their eyes fixed on the star attached to the little tower of a white, three-story building; from afar, the star very much resembled one of the stars on the Kremlin. *The star, the tower, and also, perhaps, the radio shouting something to the whole square—this is what people call a town.* And the clock: there was a clock on the tower beneath the star, also very much like the Kremlin clock.

I crossed the street, stood by the irrigation canal. It would have been a cinch to jump over it, but I'd promised my aunt not to jump it, so I headed for the bridge. At last I found myself in front of the bread shop. I hadn't been mistaken: it was the right bread shop. You could hear Merdzhan's voice from outside. Four dogs kept watch on the door; they ran after everyone who had bread in their hands. I started waiting. When all the bread was sold, Merdzhan shooed everyone out of the shop, swept the crumbs from the counter, threw them to the dogs, and locked the door with three large padlocks. Then she turned around and saw me.

I don't remember what she said, whether she asked about anything or not. I only remember that half a loaf of bread fell out from under her headscarf and that the dogs who immediately surrounded us didn't dare snatch it. Merdzhan picked up the bread, kissed it, and hid it again under her headscarf. And I also remember that the dogs ran after us for a long time, all the way to the big apricot tree with peeling bark. Here Merdzhan yelled at them, and the dogs immediately backed off. There were four dogs. Three were ordinary, homeless curs: skinny, ugly, dirty. The fourth was completely different—strapping, with a big head and strong chest, the kind shepherds have.

Under the apricot tree I stopped and pulled out the letter. Merdzhan took it, tucked it in her bosom, and we walked further along the irrigation canal. Merdzhan walked quickly. She didn't say anything, just looked affectionately at me. Everyone we met said hello to Merdzhan first. She answered their greetings, turned back, and looked at me with a smile: "Well, how do you like that, young Sadyk?" Merdzhan was wearing an elegant, yellow dress and high-heeled shoes, and the keys of the three locks clinked on the iron ring through which she'd put her finger. I liked the way they clinked.

I looked at Merdzhan's expensive shoes and remembered how she'd walked along the mountain road in winter: one sock inside, the other on top of her ankle boots. And how Azer and I had gotten hold of the iron bar so that we could clobber anyone who called Merdzhan a whore. And really, if these keys had been clinking on her finger then, if she'd been wearing this beautiful dress, and the shoes, and the white silk scarf, probably no one would have dared call her a whore; everyone would have been first to say hello to her.

I didn't know where we were going, but it made absolutely no difference to me; I was willing to walk the whole day long. The world was no longer indifferent, cruel—everyone we met looked at us affably and was first to say hello to Merdzhan. I wanted us to go on walking forever, I wanted there to be as many people as possible in the town and for all of them to come our way: such wonderful people!

I especially remember a woman in a white apron. She stood in the doorway of some building and smiled at us, at Merdzhan and me. She had white, white hands, and when Merdzhan and I went in, she patted my head with her white hands. Then the woman straightened the tablecloth on one of the tables—there were many of them—and we sat down. There was a jar of water on our table in which stood a few faded sprays of jasmine; there were no flowers on the other tables. Merdzhan pulled the bread out from under her headscarf and laid it on the table alongside the bunch of keys; the woman broke the bread into pieces with her white hands and laid them in a dish. Then she went to get some food, and Merdzhan started to read the letter.

How could I possibly have thought my aunt's letter was about bread?! Mind you, it wasn't my fault: as a matter of fact, we had no more than a kilo of flour left. But what did bread matter when Sadaf and Aunt Nabat hadn't said hello to us since winter, when Yakub dug up our kitchen garden, and when my aunt was prepared to give it all up and flee, if only so that she didn't have to see that painstakingly dug up earth? Well, of course, she'd been thinking about where we could go the night she walked around the yard until dark, having seen the window glass installed. I grasped this in an instant, even before Merdzhan lifted her eyes from the letter. "What's the problem?" said Merdzhan. "Come live with me, and that'll be that."

She didn't ask me any questions about it; she was only interested in how things were at the collective farm. "Some kind of collective farm now, ha!" I said, repeating someone's words.

I long ago forgot what we ate in the restaurant, but I've always remembered the woman with the white hands, her smile, and the kindly touch of her palm—she patted my head again when we left. And I still remember the street in front of the bazaar: more exactly, not the street itself, but the fact that it had suddenly changed. All the sounds had died down, and the radio sang loudly in the quiet. The fellows who an hour earlier had been conducting a spirited trade in fresh herbs and cigarettes had fallen silent and were sitting on the walkway; even those who'd dawdled the whole day along the irrigation canal had quieted down, as if they'd settled down to some task. And the shoeshine man no longer made noise with his brushes; he was sitting, leaning his elbow on his board and listening to the radio's song, sadly shaking his head. I remember the barber in his white coat: the old man was walking toward the restroom with a pitcher for washing, and you could hear how his sandals shuffled along the asphalt.

Then Yakub bought a half-kilo of mutton for my aunt and me and also something else, I don't remember what. On the other hand, I remember everything he said while we were returning to the village extremely well. First of all, Yakub ordered me not to tell my aunt about the bucket. We were men, and there was no reason for women to stick their noses into men's affairs; they didn't understand anything anyway. You had to have a firm hand with women, they had brains like chickens. And thrashing, you absolutely had to thrash them; otherwise, they'd grow completely stupid. That was another thing my father had taught him. Yakub talked a lot, and he attributed almost everything he said to my father; in confirmation, he'd point to some shrub or stone. I could no longer glance around without shivering—it turned out, according to Yakub, that my father had taught him to torment women under almost every bush. Under that tall medlar he'd told Yakub that if his wife gave birth to a useless girl, he'd smother that girl then and there. And when my mother died, and my father and Yakub walked to the bazaar the next morning, my father had thrown himself on the ground near that flat stone over there and beaten his head against it. It didn't surprise me that a man "as strong as a bull" could burst into tears and beat his head against a stone. What was hard to understand: how he could grieve so deeply if a woman was, in fact, so much like a chicken... Then it suddenly popped into my head that my mother had died of fright—she heard that they wanted to smother the baby, and she died. I thought about my mother, whom I'd never seen, all the way to the village; I was very sorry for her, and for some reason it seemed to me that she'd looked like that woman from the cafeteria. I walked and mentally kissed her white, white hands.

* * *

Several days later my aunt and I snuck out of our house at dawn and hung the lock on the door; we took with us only my schoolbooks and what flour we had left. My aunt had also prepared the samovar and the blankets and pillows. The evening before she'd shaken the ashes from the samovar and tied up the bedding with a cord, double-tight: everything would be ready. She'd come back and collect it later.

Everyone was asleep when we locked the door. The stars hadn't yet faded out. A dull crescent moon hung in the middle of the sky like a dry crust, and in the walnut tree shrouded in grayish gloom, the crow was still dreaming.

The water from the spring was flowing idly along—Sadaf hadn't gotten up yet. *Soon she'll arrive, spread out her dishes near the spring, scrape some dry clay from the wall, pick up a tuft of grass, and begin scrubbing her bowls and pots with all her might. Then she'll fill both pails to the top, put the clean dishes inside, and drag them home; the iron handles of the buckets will bite into her thin-fleshed, bluish palms. Tomorrow, the day after tomorrow, or perhaps even now, this very morning, spreading out her dishes by the water or polishing the giant copper samovar until it shines, Sadaf will suddenly find out that my aunt and I have left the village and understand that we weren't intending to steal Yakub from her.*

Today, tomorrow, or perhaps the day after tomorrow when Teacher Tovuz goes out on a walk, strolling slowly along the street, full of dignity because she's a teacher and because she smokes Kazbek cigarettes, someone will tell her that my aunt and I have left the village, and it will be clear to the teacher that Yakub hasn't taken Aunt Medina as his wife.

Teacher Tovuz will stop in the middle of the road and thoughtfully take her wrinkled chin in her bony hands with their swollen veins: a thick, gold ring will gleam on her thin, dry finger. Then she'll look at her watch. She'll have to look, although it won't be possible to know from the watch when my aunt and I left the village or why we went. Then Tovuz will sit down somewhere on a step or a clean stone, and her snow-white petticoat will inevitably peek out from beneath her dark-blue dress. The teacher will smoke a Kazbek cigarette and start to talk about how Aunt Medina was a student in the school, and as the subject has come up, she'll surely mention that if that girl hadn't left school, she'd be in the Supreme Soviet by now. She'll also remember me and repeat what she's always said: "There aren't any educated people in his family, but that boy will go far."

When it starts to get dark, Aunt Nabat will throw on the new, satin chador she sewed after Yakub's return and head for the big walnut tree under which women like her—old women in chadors—gather every day at this time to chat. She'll come out and spot the lock on our door; it will hang there today, tomorrow, and the day after tomorrow... And Aunt Nabat will understand that we've gone, gone for good. Then she'll be sorry she didn't speak to Aunt Medina and didn't want to say hello to me. And sitting with the old women under the walnut tree, now she'll lavish praise on Aunt Medina every night. First of all, it will turn out that the road to heaven is destined for my aunt: just think, raising someone else's child as if he were her own! Then it will become clear that Medina is pure and without sin. Aunt Nabat will talk for a long time, in great detail, about that. Naturally, she won't care to remember that her son has been out of his mind about Medina for over ten years; on the contrary, she'll resolutely deny that. "Those are all fairy tales," she'll say, "People make them up because they've got nothing better to do. So what, he put in window glass! He was born that way: he can't stop helping people." If the conversation turns to how Yakub keeps kicking his wife out of the house, Aunt Nabat will wave her hand. "It will work itself out," she'll say. "Yakub's a tetchy man, what can I say, and Sadaf's a little sluggish... It's nothing: these things happen in families..."

But no matter how much she praises, no matter how much the old woman defends Aunt Medina, the majority of the women will condemn her all the same. How could it be otherwise? She didn't harvest the mulberry trees—the cherries were left to the birds. Not only did she ruin her husband's home—and what a house it was!—now she wants to destroy her own family nest... The neighbor women will pick over the bones of Aunt Medina for a long while yet under the old walnut tree.

But it's empty under the walnut tree right now; Pamir brand cigarette butts float in the now-silent irrigation canal, the ones Aunt Nabat blew out of the cigarette holder while sitting here last night with her companions. *The herd hasn't been driven out yet, and the hieroglyphs under the plane tree are untouched. Here and there dogs bark a little, gently, and among the gruff voices of the dogs, I distinctly hear the squeaky yap of a puppy. Safar will soon get up, and the puppy, wagging his happy little tail, will chase after the lambs along the slope of the mountain. Then Grandfather Aslan, or maybe not him but Aunt Khadidzha and Yakub will pass with their shovels on their shoulders, going toward the mill to release the water: with a hum, the water will surge into the irrigation canal and take the Pamir butts with it. Then my crow will wake up and, perching on the wires, begin to caw loudly and insistently. And I won't come out. Not today, not tomorrow, not the day after tomorrow. And then the crow will understand that I'm not here anymore, which is very bad for her. With whom will she converse, at whom will she shriek that rain is coming, with whom will she rejoice when the sun peers out after the rain and it becomes possible to fly away from her nest? And in general, how will she get along without me? For years I've protected her nest from the boys. Who will chase away the dogs and cats when the chicks fledge and the time comes to teach them to fly? Who will wander into any kind of mud to rescue a bewildered fledgling?*

In the endless, gloomy, pre-dawn steppe, there were now just the two of us: my aunt and me. A large, flat stone lay like a gray shadow beside the road: the one beside which my father had wept. The medlar bush also seemed to me to be an ominous shadow. It seemed to me that it, the bush, had once smothered a teeny, tiny baby girl.

I was pleased that there were just the two of us in this endless expanse: my aunt and me. And all the same, I wanted very much to cry: for some reason I thought Yakub would also want to cry when, jumping over the fence, he saw the lock on our door. He'd sit in the middle of the yard between the beds he'd planted with cucumbers and potatoes and cry. It was very simple, really. If my father, "sturdy as a Nar camel," was able to weep and beat his head against a stone, how could Yakub be any stronger?

I carried the bundle with the flour. My schoolbooks, wrapped in old muslin, were in my aunt's arms. Today my aunt had put on pretty, light shoes; back during the war when my aunt worked at the factory, she and Merdzhan had come home one evening in identical, new shoes. Merdzhan quickly wore hers out—they didn't last long in daily wear on the stones—but my aunt hid her shoes in the trunk, as if she'd wanted to save them for this very day.

My aunt looked elegant and happy in her new shoes, but most probably she didn't feel that way. My aunt sensed that I was just about to burst into tears, and she tried to rouse me, distract me from heavy thoughts. Or perhaps she herself also wanted to cry, and so as not to dissolve into tears, she first chattered happily, then began to sing, then, clapping me on the shoulder, pressed forward, laughing. My aunt said things were much better in town than in the village: there were factories there, and everyone who worked was paid a salary each month. Workers bought their kids not just clothes but even shoes. I wouldn't be bored in town—Merdzhan had a radio, a person could listen to songs all day long. Or you could go out on the street: a plane tree grew there, exactly the same kind as we had at home. And there was a pomegranate tree in Merdzhan's yard, now it was all in bloom: the flowers were the reddest red. And then small pomegranates would appear on it, and then she'd buy me new schoolbooks, and I'd go to school. There were outstanding teachers in town schools!

And my aunt's voice when she talked about all these things was such that it seemed she was singing. She was humming, in fact, drawing something out in a tremulous, slightly shaking voice. And I knew what her song was about, although it was a song without words... Or maybe she wasn't singing and wasn't comforting me, maybe it was just her own tale? And she wasn't telling it to me but to the steppe, and the medlar bush by the road, and the flat, gray stone, and the crust of the dull moon. Once upon a time... Once upon a time...

2

Once upon a time there was a yard. The yard was large and dark. It was fenced in by a high wall and saw little sunlight, and the earth there was damp and muddy. Not even ants could be found in that yard. And grass didn't grow in the yard: there wasn't even anything prickly. There was a lone pomegranate tree, but the tree pined away in melancholy. It yearned

*for its brothers who spread their branches at will on the mountain slopes
and feasted their eyes on the sky above, drank sweet spring water, and
reveled in the sunlight.*

To enter the yard, it was necessary to go through a low, narrow
door. You opened it and found yourself in a covered gallery under
which water flowed deep down in the earth. It flowed and flowed, all
the way to the mosque. There was a well at the mosque. That's where
people washed dishes, did laundry, and cut off the heads of chickens.
The ground there was drenched in blood and thickly covered in
feathers.

It was a two-story building, with two iwans running lengthwise
along the entire structure. The best rooms opened out onto the upper
iwan; below, tiny, dingy, dark rooms could be seen between the thick,
soot-covered columns that supported the upper iwan. Two of these
were empty—even the doors had been removed—but people lived in
the other two: Merdzhan, my aunt, and I in one of them, and in the
other, at the very end of the iwan, a lone fellow by the name of Gubat.
He had a swarthy face, and one leg was shorter than the other. Gubat
said he was a groom and that he looked after the military commander's
stallion. He said the stallion was buck wild, wouldn't let anyone but the
commander and Gubat come near, but Merdzhan said Gubat wasn't a
groom at all, simply the janitor—he swept the yard at the recruitment
center.

Directly opposite our tiny room was a wooden staircase leading
to the upper iwan. Each day two women climbed up and down it: one
heavily and slowly and the other at a run, skipping.

The woman who climbed slowly was named Grandmother
Baykhanum: before, she'd had four sons, but not one of them returned
from the war. Grandmother Baykhanum constantly conversed with
God, and so as not to interrupt that conversation, she talked with
no one else. Grandmother Baykhanum spoke with Allah when she
came down the staircase and when she climbed up it; each morning
she carried something out of the building to donate in the name of
Allah. Every morning and every evening Grandmother Baykhanum
performed her prayers on the iwan and then stood for a long time,
fixing her eyes on the sky and speaking with Allah in a whisper.

Each morning the girl named Surat ran happily down the stairs and went to work at the district committee of the Communist Party. She returned earlier than everyone else, and the floorboards on the upper iwan immediately started to creak happily. Surat walked around the iwan in elegant, white shoes, singing a little song. Falling silent, she'd munch on something, clear her throat, and start crooning again. Surat sang because she'd received a letter from her fiancé and because one of these days her fiancé was supposed to come back from the Far East. Surat kept the letter from the Far East in the small pocket of her dark-blue jacket, and it was always with her, both in the morning when she came down the staircase and in the evening when she ran up it.

In the evening lamps were lit in the rooms—two upstairs, two downstairs—and four kerosene stoves smoked on the iwans in front of the doors; there was no firewood at all for the fireplace or coal for the samovar in town. After dinner Surat came downstairs to visit us, and the wooden stairs chirped happily beneath her feet. Surat came to talk about her fiancé, and each evening she read my aunt and Merdzhan his letters and showed them photos. The photos were always the same ones, and the same person looked out of them. Each evening Surat enumerated the stars on his shoulder marks and told the story of how they'd met. I already knew that story by heart, and as soon as Surat set about telling it, I immediately saw the train barreling down the black rails in the darkness, whistling, the very train in which she was traveling to Baku for a conference. An army conscript was traveling on the same train as Surat; they were sitting next to the window, facing one another. He didn't say a single word to her the whole day, didn't even glance at her once. But when evening fell, Surat, lifting her head by chance, suddenly discovered that the fellow wasn't just looking out the window but examining her reflection. The train traveled on, stopped, picked up speed again, and as before, the fellow fixed his eyes on the window. Night fell, everyone slept, but he didn't sleep. Surat didn't sleep either: her Communist Party membership card lay in her suitcase, and it was impossible for anyone who had a Party card in their suitcase to sleep—the times then were unsettled. Surat waited and waited to see whether her neighbor would say anything, if he'd speak, but he was silent. Finally, when it was past midnight, Surat couldn't help herself: she chuckled. The fellow took his eyes off the window and looked timidly at her. They smiled at one another. They sat for a while and then smiled at one another again. The fellow still didn't say anything. At dawn soldiers appeared in the car, checked documents, and when they left, the fellow picked up her passport. Surat also looked at his passport. The fellow found a scrap of paper, wrote something, and handed it to her. "I'll always carry your image in my heart" was written on the small paper.

When Surat said these words, teardrops glistened in her eyes; she pulled a tiny, little handkerchief from her pocket and wiped her eyes.

Then there was a stop: they got off the train, bought candy. At another stop the fellow somewhere managed to procure a scarf with red roses and gave it to her. Then the train stopped for good—for some reason I couldn't imagine that train at a standstill—and they spent all day together in Baku. They strolled along some kind of embankment, walked around some streets—I instantly forgot all that, but the train barreling down the black rails, the dark window, and Surat reflected in the glass—that's etched forever into my soul. The fellow left for the front, the war, he wrote Surat from far-away cities—all that was interesting, but it lived in my thoughts only while Surat was telling about it. As soon as she fell silent, I again saw the dark window, the young fellow looking at her reflection, and the train: whistling happily, it barreled down the black rails into the dark.

Talking about her fiancé, Surat couldn't sit still; she'd get up, sit down, walk around the sheet of canvas Merdzhan used in place of a palas carpet. Only my aunt and I listened; as for Merdzhan, these stories didn't touch her at all, and she thought nothing of getting up and turning on the radio at the most interesting part of the story. Sometimes she even interrupted Surat and started talking about something different, or she suddenly laughed at the wrong time. However, most of the time Merdzhan simply sat by the wall, legs stretched out. Spitting a little on her fingers, she calmly counted up the day's proceeds—tomorrow she'd have to deposit them in the bank.

When Surat left, taking the letters and photos with her, we put out the light. The door remained open during the night, the room was already stuffy; I lay down near my aunt and fixed my eyes on the wall across the yard. Surat didn't immediately go to bed, and the shadow of her body, illuminated by the electric light bulb, moved around for

115

a long time on the high wall that surrounded our yard. I watched how beautifully she moved, and it started to seem to me that the woman on the wall wasn't Surat but Gulchoehra from the film *The Cloth Peddler*. Just like Gulchoehra, she lifted up her hands, tossed back her head, sang; most importantly, even her face looked like Gulchoehra's. Sometimes the sight so engrossed me that I expected Asgar to appear: soon, soon he had to show up, the happy cloth peddler—he'd toss his bundle of goods into the yard, sit on the wall, and start to sing. But happy Asgar didn't appear, and Surat lay down to sleep. She slowly pulled off the green dress she wore at home and draped it on the chair; at those moments I watched her shadow especially intently, although I knew I ought to close my eyes. I very much wanted to know what she wore under her beautiful dresses. But the light went out—the "film" had come to an end. And although I never managed to find out what she wore under her dress, I felt relieved: *It isn't a good thing that Surat sings—Grandmother Baykhanum can hear. The old woman really doesn't even want to look at her, all because Surat sings so much and runs so happily down the stairs.*

As soon as Surat put out the light and her shadow disappeared from the wall, the loud creak of bed springs could be heard from the opposite end of the iwan—that was Gubat, tossing and turning in his iron cot. Sometimes he'd suddenly bound up in the middle of the night, and limping on his short leg, wearing just his underwear, he'd set about chasing away the cats that congregated in our yard from all over the street: they crawled under the door and, making themselves comfortable in the middle of the yard, fought and yelled like mad things. Gubat went to bed late because he got up late, sometimes loafing around in bed until almost noon. At first I didn't know that Gubat, lying on his squeaky cot in the darkness, also watched the wall, and I was very surprised when he told me about it. I was especially struck by the fact that he also called the shadow moving on the wall a "film." I didn't ask what kind of film he was looking at on our wall, but I felt that in watching the girl's shadow, Gubat saw a great deal more than I did. Sometimes he called out quietly to me after the "film," but I didn't answer: I wanted Gubat to think I was sleeping. All the same, in the morning he compelled me to confess that I'd watched.

During the day Gubat and I were the only two at home. Getting out of bed, he'd put the kettle on the kerosene stove and, limping, begin to walk moodily around the iwan. Sometimes he'd strike up Asgar's song, the same one the cloth peddler sings at the beginning of the film, strolling around the flowering garden.

"Hey, Sadyk," he'd shout, seeing me on the iwan, "how do you say 'churek' in Russian?"

"'Bread.'"

"That's right, good boy!"

He was silent for a little while, stirring the kettle with a spoon.

"And how do you say 'kashik' in Russian?"

"'Spoon!'"

"Good boy."

Again he'd fall silent, stirring the kasha.

"And how do you say 'kechi'?"

"'Kechi'? I don't know."

"'Goot!'" (he meant "goat").

Gubat said the words he knew in Russian that I didn't know with special pride, and he even stopped stirring the khashil.

I kept waiting, thinking he'd surely ask how to say "khashil" in Russian, but for some reason Gubat didn't ask, although he cooked that particular kind of flour kasha every day. Passing by, Grandmother Baykhanum would sometimes hand Gubat a lump of butter wrapped in lavash; on those days, Gubat ate khashil with butter. Most of the time, however, his khashil was without.

Gubat's room contained just a large, empty trunk. All his remaining property—the kerosene stove, the sack he laid out on the floor while sitting near the stove, and the iron bedstead with bedding—were always to be found on the iwan. Gubat's blanket was quite new, and his mattress was in good shape too. He'd shown me his bedding the very first day. As soon as Merdzhan took my aunt off to find work, Gubat called me over and turned the mattress from one side to the other several times for me to see. It turned out that Merdzhan had called him "lice-ridden"—he didn't even speak to her, would never in his life say another word to her! How would he have gotten lice, anyway? If she wanted to know, even during the war, when those vile creatures ran all over people like ants on grass, he'd never removed a single one from himself! One thing was for sure, he had enough soap—every week they gave out a new piece! He wasn't looking after just anyone's horse: it belonged to the military commander.

And exactly as if to spite Merdzhan, every week Gubat trudged to the well at night and washed everything he'd worn, even his wool uniform jacket. And when his grayish underwear hung from the clothesline between the columns and water streamed from them, everyone knew that Gubat was lying naked under the blanket: today he wouldn't be chasing off any cats.

Having fortified himself with khashil, Gubat uttered, "Thank God!" with feeling and got up. "Well," he'd say, looking inquiringly at me, "now I've got to go feed the horse, haven't I?" Gubat was sorry to leave me alone—he knew I'd be bored.

Gubat went off, I poured myself some tea—Aunt Medina left it on the kerosene stove, turning down the heat under the teapot—picked up the piece of white bread that Merdzhan brought me every evening, dropped a piece of sugar into the glass, and set about eating breakfast. Having eaten, I turned on the radio and sat down on the iwan in front of the door. Sometimes I'd start leafing through my textbooks, although I knew every page by heart—I didn't have anything else to do... That's when I started composing the tale about the pomegranate tree and writing it in the previous year's notebook. There turned out to be very few blank pages left, and they quickly ran out. But the tale still continued.

And so, Aunt Medina and I entered that yard. She'd just kissed Merdzhan in the bread shop; we'd just walked along the main street. Just like last time, the keys again jangled in Merdzhan's hands, and everyone we met cordially said hello to her. We'd just descended downhill along narrow, stony back streets. Interrupting one another, Merdzhan and Aunt Medina were talking about the village, the factory, the soldiers who'd been stationed with us during the war; I ran behind them and tried to convince myself that things were good here, that it was quite possible to live here. But no matter how hard I insisted, no matter how hard I tried to persuade myself, still, more than anything in the world, I wanted to go back to the village!

When we entered the yard and I saw the thick, two-meter-high walls, the dirty yard, and that pomegranate tree, everything became clear: it was impossible to either live or study here. All that had been twaddle, an absurd invention, like the red flowers that supposedly blossomed on this miserable scrub of a tree. *We'll return to the village this very day!*

Merdzhan went up to a low door painted reddish-brown and opened it. Then she put the tea kettle on the kerosene stove. I stood near the door and didn't want to enter because Merdzhan's room was low, dark, windowless; because the yard was also dark and dirty; because my aunt had deceived me—there wasn't a single flower on the pomegranate tree.

But Aunt Medina took off her elegant shoes near the door and entered that gloomy hovel as if it were perfectly normal. She even complimented the cloth over the samovar—it turned out that Merdzhan had bought it quite recently. She looked at the photos that hung on the wall, ran her hand over the dishes in the niche. On top of that, Aunt Medina went up to the mirror and began to twirl around in front of it; she straightened her hair, smoothed her eyebrows with a finger, even turned her back to it, trying to examine her back over her shoulder.

Then we drank tea on the clean, gray canvas that Merdzhan spread out in place of a palas. I sat there and thought: "When in the world are we going home?" Merdzhan and Aunt Medina were discussing how to speed up the process for being hired at the factory, how Merdzhan would take her to get a job this very day, but I still didn't lose hope of going back. Nothing in the village frightened me anymore: *let Yakub come visit every single day, let the neighbors say whatever they want, let Sadaf refuse to say hello to us—just let it happen! Because our house stands on the mountain, and there's a garden behind it and roses in front of it! And the berries on the mulberry tree have already begun to turn white, and the black cherry is swollen with sap. So he put in glass and dug up the kitchen garden, but the house is really ours, and nowhere else in the world is there such a house!*

My aunt didn't notice anything; she chatted animatedly, drank tea with pleasure, blew loudly on the saucer, but all the same, I didn't believe we'd stay. It even seemed to me that my aunt was so cheerful precisely because we had our own home and didn't need to stay at Merdzhan's, where there was such a dirty yard, such high walls, and not a single flower on the pomegranate tree—just dusty, gray leaves. *We can return home this very day: we'll take the lock off the door, I'll immediately climb up to get cherries, and my aunt will scale the wall and pick mulberries.*

Finishing her tea, my aunt again twirled a little in front of the mirror, again looked at the photos, and again praised the cloth over the samovar. Then she went out onto the iwan, and she returned very satisfied. I understood that we were staying, that we were going to live here in Merdzhan's half-dark room or some other cubbyhole: it was time to tidy up a bit and get settled.

But the tidying up and getting settled didn't happen; Merdzhan wouldn't permit us to take up residence anywhere except with her. She wouldn't let my aunt go back for our things—a blanket and pillows could be found, for heaven's sake. Then my aunt and Merdzhan went off to the canning factory, leaving me in the room. They returned fairly quickly, laughing the whole time because they'd been lucky enough to put one over on some "blockhead among blockheads" and get my aunt a job. Merdzhan said that in such cases you just couldn't avoid using cunning, and that was generally the only way to deal with men. And in the evening when they put out the light, she told Aunt Medina a long story about how she'd gotten work as a shop assistant. There was also a "blockhead among blockheads" in her story—the director of the district executive committee's trade organization. He gave her the runaround for an entire month—he kept wanting her to come in at night. She got fed up with that rigamarole, threw up her hands in disgust, got all dolled up as if she were going to a wedding, and appeared before him. Well, she amused her heart a bit, played such a trick on him, the darling—today's nonsense was nothing compared to that! Of course, I was unable to comprehend exactly what nonsense Merdzhan had in mind, but I was more concerned with something else: if the director of the district executive committee's trade organization was a liar and a blockhead among blockheads, then why did she send him four kilos of white bread every day? Merdzhan told the story of how she'd gotten around the director of the district executive committee's trade organization, and Aunt Medina listened and laughed so lightheartedly, so easily, that it was as if neither this vile, stuffy, little room nor the light-filled home we'd abandoned existed.

That night my aunt and Merdzhan discussed men for a long time: the ones who were blockheads among blockheads and the ones who weren't blockheads. Merdzhan told my aunt that she'd already received several marriage proposals—because of the bread, suitors would just turn up. But all these bridegrooms were blockheads among blockheads—if only one of them had resembled a man! Merdzhan said Gubat was no better than the others, although he'd hung around her before the bread. Not a word was said about Yakub, but I myself had determined without a moment's hesitation that he was a blockhead among blockheads. That evening I came to a firm conclusion: every woman has her own song, like that of my aunt. That song comes from childhood, it lives in a woman's heart from her school years, and when it comes time to get married, women suddenly remember it. They remember it and consequently don't want to marry a Mukush, a Yakub, or even a Gubat.

I don't know how many days I'd have languished in that dark yard if my aunt hadn't declared upon returning from work one evening that starting the next day, she'd take me with her. I didn't know when we'd left the village or how many times the sun had risen and set since then, but by that evening when my aunt announced that now I wouldn't fall into melancholy, I could say with complete honesty that I hadn't missed it for some time. I didn't think about the village anymore, didn't daydream about climbing the wall and waiting until Yakub appeared so I could split his head open with a stone. I sat quietly near the door and waited until my aunt returned from work. I also waited for Gubat; he'd tell me about the military commander's stallion and about what had happened that day at the bazaar. Then Surat arrived; she'd invariably smooth my head, gently tweak my nose, and run quickly up the stairs, laughing. It was also interesting to wait for Grandmother Baykhanum; she'd climb up to the upper iwan, unfold the prayer rug with the accessories for prayer, and turning her face to the sky, talk with God for a long time.

Aunt Medina declared that starting tomorrow, I'd spend the day in the small orchard opposite the factory: the orchard was very pretty, and it was next to the highway where cars went back and forth; anyway, it wasn't so boring. And there was a kindergarten nearby, they took the kids on walks in the orchard: I could enjoy myself with them. And during the lunch break, she'd bring me food from the cafeteria; there in the orchard, you could even eat. At the very least, the food wouldn't stick in her throat, knowing there was a hungry child at home. My aunt was satisfied, but I wasn't particularly happy; I was very much afraid it would turn out, once again, that there was no orchard, no kids. In fact, in the tale about the pomegranate tree that I'd written on the pages torn out of my notebook, an aunt by the name of Medina had already lied once to a boy by the name of Sadyk: she'd said that the pomegranate tree would be covered in flowers, and there hadn't been any flowers. Sadyk had taken it badly and run off into the mountains, where the pomegranate trees really were covered in scarlet flowers, and Sadyk hid from his aunt in their flowering branches. She traveled over all the mountains looking for Sadyk, but she never found him—the pomegranate trees didn't tell her where he was hiding. Let her cry: next time she wouldn't lie.

But there was an orchard. And there were trees: peach trees and almonds and walnuts. Although all the young fruit had been plucked from the almond trees and the branches broken, no one had touched the other trees yet—you wouldn't eat unripe peaches or walnuts. The canning factory was on the edge of town. The wide asphalt street that extended from the bazaar—more precisely, from the garden behind the bazaar, where a bronze Lenin stood, surrounded by young pine trees—changed into the highway here by the factory and ran down to the train station. The factory was fenced in with a long, wooden fence, and where the fence ended, the road along which cars drove to our village branched off from the highway.

The factory wall was so high that all I could see from the orchard was a large, black smokestack. And there was another one, very thin; right before the lunch break, this smokestack began to whistle loudly like the steam engines whistled at the train station, and clouds of thick, white steam poured out of it. The big gates opened, and a crowd of women in white lab coats flooded the street. Instead of shoes, they wore wooden sandals with straps, and as soon as the women workers went out onto the asphalt, nothing could be heard except the clatter of wooden soles. Coming out of the gates, the women split up into groups: some went into the orchard to lounge on the warm grass, while others hurried to the tearoom, sat down at the tables there, unfolded bundles of food, and set about eating.

Finally my aunt appeared at the gates. She smiled at me and covered the bowl of food with the end of her gauze head covering. Each day a short, scrawny person standing near the gates would look in my aunt's bowl; my aunt said that was his job. We'd sit down somewhere under a tree and eat the soup with pleasure. Then my aunt gave me money so I could go to the tearoom a bit later. She herself was never able to drink tea—as soon as we finished eating, the long smokestack would begin its extended whistle, and tucking the empty bowl under her scarf, Aunt Medina hurried toward the gates. Now, at the end of the break, the girls' wooden soles clattered even more loudly, more abruptly; the orchard emptied, the factory gates closed. The tearoom also emptied out, but I didn't go inside to drink tea—I was saving up the money.

I dawdled around in the orchard opposite the factory right up until evening, until the end of the workday. Along the other side of the highway, the short, thin person at the factory gates cooled his heels with nothing to do. He was obliged to look in my aunt's bowl, I was obliged to sit in the orchard and not budge from my spot. And I really didn't go anywhere, except that I hid whenever cars from our village sped past. I didn't want to be seen; I looked pretty pathetic here by the road.

Off in the distance, behind the station, trains often passed through. I looked after them and thought about the train on which Surat had traveled to Baku; for some reason it seemed to me that that train was barreling somewhere along the black rails, whistling happily, carrying Surat's blurry reflection with it into the dark. *And maybe Gubat really is a groom, and maybe it's true that, besides him and the military commander, no one can approach the stallion. And by the way, where is the district executive committee's trade organization, and who is he, that person who wanted to drag Merdzhan into his office? And why does she send him white bread every day, four whole kilos of it? I wonder if the cherry tree has stopped producing cherries back in the village or whether there are still some left. The baby crows have probably already hatched. And how are things back there in our kitchen garden? How many cucumbers and tomatoes were there, all of them harvested long ago? Sadaf is most likely with her father, or perhaps she's returned. They drive her back and forth, back and forth: husband to father, father to husband...*

I sat in the small orchard and thought. Over the course of the day, I managed to think about so many things that I was never bored, and I didn't notice how the day passed. The whistle whistled, and the women came out into the street; they weren't wearing smocks now, but those who didn't have other shoes still wore the wooden sandals with straps. We'd pass near the bazaar, then near the statue of Lenin, turn into a narrow side street, and then into another. In the mornings we made our way in the opposite direction.

One day while making our way along the bazaar square in the morning, I asked my aunt to leave me there, near the bazaar. She agreed, simply cautioning me that I had to be in my place when the whistle sounded. And also: if I should happen to suddenly meet Yakub, under no circumstances was I to tell him where we lived.

I didn't meet Yakub at the bazaar, and I didn't have the chance to keep our address secret from him—Yakub turned up right on our doorstep.

My aunt and I had just gotten home; Merdzhan hadn't yet returned from work. Humming a little song under her breath, Surat was cooking something tasty, as usual, and the whole yard was filled with the aroma rising from her pot. Gubat was also making dinner for himself. Piling potatoes to the brim of that same kettle in which he made khashil in the morning, Gubat put it on the kerosene stove and walked around the iwan, limping: by the way, he didn't put a foot beyond the column that marked the boundary since he'd quarreled with Merdzhan. Gubat and Aunt Medina were talking about the war, about how we'd all been reduced to starving; Gubat listed all the things he'd sold during the war, and my aunt recounted how she'd exchanged half a house for bread. Bending his head as if the ceiling were too low for his height, Yakub approached us. Without turning her head, my aunt continued telling Gubat about how she'd surrendered the rafters to Khamza, the bread cutter; it seemed she hadn't noticed our guest. Gubat didn't understand why she was doing that; he stood for a minute behind the kerosene stove and then disappeared into his little room.

Yakub stopped opposite the door, looking around for a place to sit; there was no such thing on the iwan, and my aunt made no move to offer him a stool. Yakub had a package of gingerbread cookies in his hands; cookies spilled from the torn packet, and he didn't know what to do with it. My aunt stood with her head turned away; I hung my head, scowled, and firmly resolved not to say a word to Yakub. He carefully laid the cookies at the base of the column and coughed several times. Then he looked angrily at me, at my aunt, at the stools in Merdzhan's room, and said very loudly:

"I've come for you!"

My aunt stood silently by the column.

"I've come for you," Yakub repeated.

My aunt lifted her head and looked him straight in the eye; it seemed to me that now she'd say, "Get out of my sight!" Yakub probably thought the same thing.

But my aunt didn't say, "Get out of my sight!"

"For us?" she asked. "Was it worth putting yourself out?"

"What do you mean, 'putting myself out'?! Nadzhaf would've done anything for someone close to him, and if I'm anxious about his sister, that's 'putting myself out'? Thank God, not every relative is in the grave—Nadzhaf's sister shouldn't be living like a vagabond in a strange yard!"

Bending his thick, red neck, Yakub looked at the potatoes boiling in Gubat's kettle. My aunt also glanced at the potatoes, then at Yakub, and I wanted very badly for her to give him what for, right this minute.

"Go away, Yakub," said Aunt Medina. "Go away. People here are no worse than you are."

"So what, if they're no worse? Even if they're better, I can't allow the sister of my friend, my brother, to live God knows where! To give up the house—the branches in the garden are close to breaking with fruit—and work for kopecks in a factory! Nothing to eat? Step into the storehouse and take whatever your heart desires! Thank God, the keys are in our hands! And everyone would calm down, they'd know that Nadzhaf's honor had been preserved!"

"And who asked you to preserve Nadzhaf's honor?" asked my aunt with a curl of her lip. "If you're so attentive, take care of your own wife—all you know how to do is give black eyes! And as to the garden and the kitchen garden—they're of no use to me. Plant something yourself, sell it, eat it—I won't say a word. You can have the house, too—tear it down even! But leave me in peace, Yakub—nothing will ever happen between the two of us!"

"Why? What wrong have I done you?"

"You haven't done me any wrong. But I don't need a thing from you, good or bad!"

"I won't leave you here, understand?"

"You? I don't even know you!"

"But I, on the other hand, know your hostess very well!"

"You know her? Compared to you, she's a pure angel!"

"I'll say! Her purity is known throughout the region!"

"Are you listening to gossip? Or have you seen this with your own eyes?"

"I've got ears!"

I lifted my head and looked at his ears: he did indeed have ears, how had I not noticed them before? My aunt moved away from the column, picked up the bucket, poured water from it into the teapot on the kerosene stove, and stood in front of Yakub with the bucket in her hand.

"Those ears of yours will soon hear similar things about me too," said Aunt Medina. "And now get out of my sight! No one invited you here!"

Not bothering to use the steps, my aunt jumped down into the yard right there, close to Yakub, and went off to the well, loudly clanking the bucket. Yakub stood there for a few seconds, looking around in bewilderment, then turned sharply and paced quickly across the yard. And when my aunt was no longer visible, he cracked open the door to the street, stuck his head through, and shouted:

"All the same, I'll finish off this creep! No one in our family has ever tolerated dishonor!"

The door banged shut behind Yakub, and it opened again immediately afterwards—Merdzhan appeared in the yard. When my aunt brought the water, Surat, leaning over the railing, asked who in the world the jerk was, the one who'd been shouting. My aunt couldn't answer because Merdzhan, removing the scarf from her head, was saying that such a fellow had just come out of our yard—one to die for! Take off his charyki and put on a tie—he'd clean up better than a government minister! Surat said she'd chase that kind of minister into a corner with a stick to his head so that he'd learn how to talk to women. As usual, they started quarreling: Merdzhan insisted that rudeness wasn't the worst fault a man could have, but Surat argued that he couldn't be a man if he didn't respect women. My aunt didn't take part in the argument; she said only that Yakub was a very distant relative, that you couldn't find a worse man in the village, and that if Merdzhan had seen his wife, whom he'd worn to a shred, she'd be saying something else.

The argument about Yakub didn't last long, but his gingerbread cookies lay near the column for a long time afterwards. Gubat didn't ask anything about him, and only after three days or so, when we were alone, did he finally say, chuckling:

"That fellow from your town—what a jerk! Did you notice—he didn't even say hello when he walked in!"

A few days later Yakub appeared near the bazaar. His shadow fell over me, and he thrust a paper torn from a notebook into my hand.

"Give this to your aunt!" he said. And he added angrily: "You're lazing around, you good-for-nothing! You'd do better to sell sunflower seeds!"

I didn't give my aunt the letter; it said that she'd exchanged our family for a lame cripple. Gubat did, of course, limp—one leg was shorter than the other—but everyone knew Gubat loved Merdzhan and that Aunt Medina meant nothing to him. Yakub wrote that he'd support my aunt like a shah's wife, that he could support five wives like shahs' wives. In fact, Sadaf, whom he'd worn to a shred, was also a shah's wife: she had "two dozen unworn dresses, and scarves by the pile lying in her trunk." And then the letter said that the house and garden all belonged to Sadyk, that my aunt had squandered her own home during the war. How could I give my aunt that letter? I read it to the end, tore it into tiny pieces, threw the pieces into the irrigation canal, and observed with pleasure how the water carried the paper away.

But Yakub was right about sunflower seeds. That same day I took the change I'd saved up, having stashed what my aunt gave me for the tearoom in a tin, added three brand-new ruble notes that Merdzhan had given me, and bought a cracked, chipped glass from the owner of the tearoom. I didn't have a sack, but I found a large tin can in the trash heap behind the factory.

For several days I hid my trading operation from my aunt—I was always in my place at the sound of the whistle, and I left the can of sunflower seeds near the booth, under the watchful eye of the shoemaker, Uncle Selim. But it wasn't possible to keep going that way for long—my aunt found out about the sunflower seeds. She found out and didn't get angry; she said it was nothing—at the very least, the child had something to do. She even sewed me a small bag; I poured the sunflower seeds into it and threw the tin can back on the trash heap from which it had come.

Let it go, Sadyk, no need to be sad: forget your village! Look how good things are around you: the sun has just barely laid itself across the road, no one has stepped on it yet, there's no trash anywhere around, and the water in the irrigation canal is clean, clear.

And just listen to the silence: you really love it when it's quiet. Of course, that woman is yelling at the top of her lungs, but don't pay any attention. Let her yell her head off: "Hands up, legs apart! Breathe deeper!" Hands up, legs apart—that's not important for you, but breathing deeper—that's a good thing! Breathe, Sadyk, breathe while you can: see, the asphalt is also trying to breathe deeper...

The shops are still locked up: the grocery shop, the kerosene shop, the shop where they sell manufactured goods. But the tearoom is already open, the waterboys are lugging water. They carry it on strong poles, four buckets at a time; the buckets rock back and forth, back and forth. The waterboys put down the buckets by the doorway, straighten up, and throw back their shoulders, trying to suck in more air.

The giant, copper samovar that stands in front of the tearoom is still breathing gently. Soon the first customers will appear, and it will come to a boil, gasping. Look, Sadyk, if you stand here gaping too long, you'll lose your chance—others will grab all the good sunflower seeds: they'll leave you high and dry!

The sunshine is sneaking up on Uncle Selim's booth. Soon he himself will appear. Well, Sadyk, tell me, why are you moping around when you've got a friend like that? And if Uncle Selim earns enough to buy meat today, he'll tell jokes from morning till night. What stories he'll tell, each one funnier than the last! And if Uncle Selim has meat for dinner, then tomorrow without fail he'll bring the bones wrapped in a rag and give them to the black cur. "That's right, hound," Uncle Selim will say, petting the dog. "The thing is, you really should have barked!"

The dogs have long since collected around the bake shop. Three of them are ordinary street moochers; Uncle Selim doesn't care for them, although he doesn't dislike them nearly as much as the butcher, Ali, who drove the black cur into the street. The butcher had traded with a shepherd for that dog, given a sheep in exchange for him, but when thieves broke into his house and stole a carpet, the dog didn't even attempt to bark. So Ali drove the dog away.

Here comes Ali, pulling a well-fed, red cow behind him with a rope. Now he'll lead her to the far end of the bazaar under the walnut tree, tie up her feet, tip her over, and a fountain of blood will spurt from the cow's throat. As red as can be. Then Ali will cut the cow into pieces and sell her meat. And if Uncle Selim does well today, he'll buy a half-kilo of that meat. And tomorrow the black cur will gnaw on the bones. A puddle of thick, black blood will stand under the walnut tree for a long time—all that's left of the red cow.

The bazaar gradually comes to life; people bring in fruit, vegetables, herbs. They drag in their goods in buckets and in khurdzhin bags thrown over their shoulders. Now Saftar will appear with his small bench. He'll sit down, lay out his brushes, and start waiting patiently. One after another trucks will start to drive up to the bazaar, rumbling, and the collective farm chairmen will slowly climb down from the cabs. As a matter of course, every chairman will come up to Saftar and put a foot on his bench, and Saftar, gently knocking his brushes together from time to time, will clean the dusty, black boots until they shine.

The more shoes he cleans, the more money he makes. If he does well in the morning, Saftar will run around the bazaar and fetch two large pieces of lavash, fifty grams of honey, fifty grams of butter, and wash his wax-smeared hands in the irrigation canal for a long time. And only after this will he sit down to eat. If Saftar doesn't do well and has to satisfy himself with bread and salt, he won't even bother to wash his hands.

Would you want Saftar to always eat honey and butter for breakfast, Sadyk? And would you want Uncle Selim to have meat every night so that he can bring the bones to the black cur in the morning? That would be marvelous, of course. But never mind: even if Saftar doesn't do well today, you needn't be upset. The days aren't all alike: tomorrow he may very well wash his wax-smeared hands in the irrigation canal again. And the same for Uncle Selim: if he doesn't have enough money for meat today, he'll have enough tomorrow. So don't be upset, Sadyk, there's nothing to get upset about here...

The dogs have already moved away from the bake shop; they're running here to the bazaar. Good grief, why are you always so sad, hound? Do you miss your native mountains? Or are you ashamed to run around the streets with the moochers? How meek you are! You really must hate the butcher: he lured you away from the mountains and then drove you out onto the street! If you'd only bitten him the way you should have, let him find out what happens when you kick a dog and blame him all the time for a cursed carpet!

It's nothing, Sadyk, it's not so bad: soon Gubat will lead the military commander's stallion to the blacksmith, or maybe he'll just drop by to see you, to sit beside you and watch the bread shop. You'll offer him some sunflower seeds, but Gubat won't touch them. "Goods are for selling," he'll say firmly. At the same time, if a buyer approaches, Gubat will fill the glass with sunflower seeds with pleasure. If only all the buyers would come while Gubat is sitting here! Gubat hands you a ruble after taking it from the buyer, and from his face you'd think he was giving you a thousand rubles. And you wish with all your heart that Merdzhan would glance out of *the shop, even better, walk through the bazaar. You wouldn't mind if she walked by you a hundred times a day; she'll take a handful of sunflower seeds from the sack and go off to enjoy herself, spitting out the hulls. She's wearing a white scarf, a yellow silk dress, and the keys are in her hands: jangle, jangle. And let Butcher Ali watch her, bare his yellow teeth, and bow humbly to her, the way he bows to people wearing hats and ties. Is it really possible to mope around when you see time and again how that hulk bows and scrapes in front of Merdzhan?*

Knock it off, Sadyk, forget about it. Soon the whistle will sound, you'll hoist the small bag of sunflower seeds onto your shoulder and hurry to the factory gates. You'll sit under a tree with your aunt, she'll crumble some bread into the soup, and you'll eat; you'll finish off the soup and bread. Then you'll settle in again near Uncle Selim's booth, and he'll patch up shoes and tell you and the black cur stories about his youth. And then you and the black cur will be far, far away in the mountains; there are lots of pomegranate trees there, they drink spring water and flower scarlet. The black cur will do battle with giant wolves, and you'll feed him fresh meat. Each week you'll send Uncle Selim a ram, so he'll always be happy. And if you travel to town, you'll undoubtedly be wearing tall, black boots; that day Saftar will be able to earn even more. You'll take care of Butcher Ali as easy as pie: you'll go up to him and, with a single blow, topple him to the ground covered in cows' blood and kick him for a long time with your boots. The idlers dawdling along the irrigation canal will also get theirs, you'll boot their backsides into the irrigation canal: that'll teach them to ogle the bare-legged girls from the orphanage! And then your big day will arrive: stomping your black boots, you'll slowly climb the white staircase, open that same door through which the blockhead among blockheads wanted to drag Merdzhan, and you'll kill that blockhead among blockheads. Now you've figured out why Merdzhan sends him four kilos of white bread every day...

Now the evenings in our yard passed much more happily. Now I had my own money, and every time Merdzhan sat down to count up the day's proceeds, I sat down near her.

I exchanged my crumpled, dirty rubles with Merdzhan for spotless, new ones. I didn't want to change my rubles into ten-, much less thirty-ruble notes, because then I'd only have a few pieces of paper—this way,

I had a whole stack. Each day I added just a little to it, but I counted all my money afresh, and I did it slowly, laying out the papers—each one separate from the others—with relish; it seemed like more money that way.

I stacked up and spread out the rubles, and Aunt Medina sat opposite me by the wall and didn't take her eyes off me. Either she was pleased to see that I'd finally found something to occupy me or she was thinking her own thoughts as she looked at me. Lately she'd been thinking a great deal, sitting just this way and leaning against the wall, her eyes tired and happy.

Maybe it was because Yakub had finally left her in peace, although it was difficult to believe this. But that's the way it was—it had been enough for my aunt to walk near the bazaar without stockings for Yakub to leave her alone. A few days later he caught me on the square, berated me for a long time for having allowed such shameless behavior, and in the end called me a woman and spat in my face. Of course, he had no way of knowing that Aunt Medina simply had none to put on, that the stockings Merdzhan had given her had worn out long ago, and that Merdzhan had promised without fail to get stockings for the two of them just as soon as they appeared in the warehouse. It was entirely possible that stockings would soon be brought and that my aunt would appear on the street in new ones, but Yakub really had no way of knowing that. Yakub was done with us—I understood that when he called me a woman and spat in my face. Later he even sent word to my aunt through some people that he no longer considered himself our relative.

But perhaps my aunt isn't thinking of Yakub at all, but about the Russian? Several days before my aunt had whispered about him with Merdzhan for a long time after she put out the light. The cleaning lady in the office had gotten sick, and that Russian, the factory's head mechanic, had asked my aunt to clean up his apartment. My aunt talked excitedly about this: first, he'd entrusted the keys of his apartment to her alone; second, he was such an honorable person—he didn't once open the door while she was cleaning. But there was more! While dusting, my aunt had knocked a mirror onto the floor, a large, beautiful mirror in a wooden frame: it broke. And just think, seeing my aunt in the office the next day, that man hadn't reproached her with a single word; on the contrary, he even smiled at her. The cleaning lady had long since returned to work, but each day he gave my aunt his keys. And all so that she wouldn't think he was angry. "Well, tell me, Merdzhan, who among our people would behave in such a way?"

Merdzhan mutters something sleepily; it seems to me that she isn't listening, she's thinking about something else. But I'm thinking about this: I remember how my grandmother once knocked over a glass while pouring my father's tea. The glass broke, my father yelled at her a long time without getting up from the palas, and my frail, old grandmother who'd never possessed shoes because she didn't earn any money looked at him silently and blinked her eyes in fright. I can see her eyes even now. And Mukush's sharp chin. How furious he'd been when my aunt broke a bowl! Mukush was afraid to shout at my aunt, he knew she'd break a second, and a third, and a fourth bowl; he just breathed heavily, and his chin shook with rage. And Sadaf, who lives "like a shah's wife"? Will they really forgive her if she breaks a teacup? Perhaps they'll forgive one broken teacup, but a second one will certainly earn a black eye. I've seen all that, and I'd very much like to see the mirror—the big, beautiful mirror my aunt broke—and that Russian who smiled instead of swearing at her. But my aunt doesn't need to spend evening after evening thinking about him, although why she shouldn't do that, I don't know. Most likely because vodka is a god for Russians; after all, Yakub says that for the sake of that disgusting thing, they're prepared to walk on their hind legs in front of anyone. And Gubat said, too, that they don't practice circumcision...

Gubat and Merdzhan made peace. The boundary column lost its former significance, and Gubat came over to chat with us every day after dinner. But that's just a manner of speaking, "to chat": in front of Merdzhan he didn't dare open his mouth. He'd sit silent for some time, sit silent and then leave without having said a word. Sometimes Gubat had a drink for courage before coming to us, and then he deliberately clanked the stool, talked loudly, even lit a cigarette, although he couldn't bear tobacco—he thought Merdzhan appreciated swagger in a man. Once, emboldened by frustration, he suddenly shouted to Surat, so loudly that it carried through the whole yard:

"Hey, Women's Department, why aren't you doing your job? You should marry Merdzhan to me!"

At first Merdzhan pretended not to hear, but then she turned to Gubat and from a distance gave him the middle finger.

"Did you see that?"

By then Gubat had nothing to lose.

"Damn it all—you'll be mine, all the same!"

"All my life I've dreamed about a lame man!"

"A lame man is half the trouble!" Gubat shouted, having apparently decided not to be offended. "Others have intact legs, but their noggins don't work!" And he confidently added: "You don't have anyone to marry: I'll get you in the end!"

From time to time Gubat embarked on these conversations, but always from afar, moving away to a decent distance. As soon as he drew near Merdzhan, his tongue immediately grew numb. And everything went on as it had before: Surat talked about her fiancé in the evenings, and Gubat and I watched the "film." Now Surat was talking more and more about the wedding, and I wanted the wedding to be in our yard. But what about Grandmother Baykhanum? None of her sons had returned from the war after all. But maybe there was no need for a wedding. No zurna, no drums... As a matter of fact, Aunt Medina had been given to Mukush to the loud wailing of the zurna, and nothing good had come of that.

Arriving at my spot in the bazaar one morning, I found out from Uncle Selim that a particular first lieutenant had returned from the army the day before. Then Gubat appeared and reported that the demobilized lieutenant wasn't just anybody, but the fiancé of our Surat. It turned out that Gubat knew the fellow, even knew where he lived. He showed me a handsome house in the very center of town and said, eyes shining excitedly, that any day now our Surat would be brought to that house accompanied by music, and then her hubby would "settle up" with her. Eyes fixed on the door of the bread shop, Gubat described in detail what a handsome fiancé our Surat had: broad-shouldered, well-proportioned. Then he started describing the wedding night, how the newlyweds would be led off to the bedroom, and women in red dresses would stand by the door and wait for when the groom "settled up" with the bride... Gubat clapped me on the shoulder and said with regret:

"Yes, brother, our 'film' has ended!"

I couldn't wait to see Surat's happy face, and I walked home without waiting for the bazaar to close. However, Surat wasn't at home; we didn't see the "film" that evening. There was no film the next day, either; I didn't see Surat either in the morning or at night. For four days in a row she came home much later than usual and silently climbed up to her room.

In the morning she came downstairs just as quietly, and she immediately ran off somewhere. All this time she said not a word to anyone, just banged the wicket gait loudly both when she left and when she returned home. Finally, sometime in the evening, I think on the fifth day, Surat came into our room without a sound, like a shadow. She stood a long time in front of the mirror looking at her own face, as if she were first getting out of bed after a terrible illness. She wiped her reddish, swollen eyes with her scarf, smoothed her eyebrows, touched her lips with a finger, and only after that did she look at my aunt.

"They've addled his brain," Surat said very quietly and sat down on the floor by the wall just like my aunt, leaning back against it.

And beneath her elegant, silk dress, I suddenly saw ordinary, blue pantaloons. The same kind of pantaloons women wore in our village. I'd often seen that kind of pantaloon when women bent over the irrigation canal rinsing the dishes. And Surat seemed to me to be a most ordinary, most unremarkable woman: there was nothing mysterious about her at all. The train that carried Surat to the women's conference in Baku had stopped, and on the tracks where it had barreled along for so many years, whistling happily, everything suddenly grew very quiet.

And then in the dead silence of the room, the anxious hum of a bumblebee could be heard; it had flown in somehow or other and now just couldn't find its way out. Surat began to cry, and she started to talk about how the mother and sisters of her fiancé had slandered her in front of him. The mother declared that a respectable girl wouldn't have gone to work at the district committee. The younger sister said that if

135

Surat had been worth anything at all, she'd have been married long ago. And the elder sister, that witch, that snake, that wizened old monkey—she worked as a cashier in the bathhouse—spun a tale that she'd seen Surat going to the bathhouse with men. She herself, she said, had given Surat the ticket with her own hands. And the fellow also had an aunt who needed to provide for her daughter; she also had plenty to say…

When Surat climbed the stairs to her room, as slowly as she'd come down them, Merdzhan declared that all her stories were nonsense: the problem lay elsewhere entirely. The previous summer Surat had traveled with performers from the House of Culture to swim in Lake Sevan. Why did she need to travel so far? Be that as it may, the main thing was that people said she'd gone drinking with men and behaved inappropriately. Apparently they'd even wanted to expel her from the district committee, but they took pity on her—she was an orphan. As soon as her fiancé arrived, they instantly reported it all to him—his buddy worked for the district committee—and, well, he immediately cast her off, telling people, "I don't even know her."

There was a "film" that night, but it didn't look a thing like *The Cloth Peddler*. And Surat was no longer Gulchoehra but a most ordinary woman who wore ordinary, blue pantaloons. And she cried for a very long time, standing by the window.

Surat cried by her window for many days. Then Gubat said that our Surat's betrothed was marrying his cousin, and Merdzhan brought another bit of news—Surat's fiancé had been named chair of the town council. That night I went into an elegant flower garden in my big, black boots, climbed to the second story of the beautiful, two-story building called the town council, seized the blockhead among blockheads by the collar, and flung him out into the street. The "film" had ended, but the dark shadow of Surat remained on the wall forever.

One morning when I was hurrying to the bazaar to get my hands on the better-quality sunflower seeds, Gubat called me over.

"Did you watch last night?" he asked, sitting up on his squeaky bed.

"No," I answered. "I don't watch anymore."

This time Gubat believed me. He drew me to him and whispered:

"Last night I didn't sleep the whole night... They had the wedding, the girl almost killed herself. She wanted to strangle herself with her scarf!"

He yawned and lay back down.

"I'm not going to watch anymore either," he said and turned over, angrily dragging the blanket over his head. I knew Gubat was telling the truth.

3

Long before the start of the school year, my aunt walked to the village, brought back a certificate showing I'd completed the fifth grade, and delivered it to School #1. The school was located not far from the center of town, along the road from the bazaar to the factory. Directly behind it rose a high, white wall, which surrounded the orphanage.

My aunt forbade me to sell sunflower seeds for the four days leading up to the start of the school year. I was bored to death; I hung around the bazaar, wandered around the factory, and because I had nothing better to do, I went several times to look at the beautiful, rich home that Gubat had pointed out to me. The very same fellow whose eyes had once been riveted on Surat's reflection in the train window and had then written her the note that read "I'll always carry your image in my heart" lived in that house; now he was the "town council," known to the whole town as Comrade Dzhalilov.

Ever since first grade I'd considered the first day of September a holiday, a big holiday, just like Nowruz-Bayram. The only difference was that the entire village prepares for Nowruz-Bayram: they wash, clean, do laundry. Before the start of the school year, the pre-holiday fever swept over just Aunt Medina; in any case, I never heard the phrase "September holiday" from anyone besides her. The last night of August she always bathed me; dressed me in clean, freshly mended pantaloons and an immaculately clean shirt; and sitting me on the big, flat stone, painstakingly trimmed my finger and toenails. Then my aunt picked up a long pole and walked around striking the quince or the peach tree so that I'd have something for school tomorrow: I was forbidden to clamber among the trees on this day—God forbid that I should stain or tear my shirt!

On the last night of August my aunt obtained permission to leave work early. She heated water on the kerosene stove and, eyes shining happily, set about laundering my pantaloons and shirt. They dried out toward evening, and my aunt persuaded Gubat to take me to the bathhouse.

Looking in the mirror in the morning, I was pleased with my appearance. My pantaloons were exceptionally skillfully patched. My shirt wasn't just clean—it was ironed, the first time in my life that I'd worn an ironed shirt. Merdzhan stuffed four gingerbread cookies and a handful of candy into my bag and said that I looked quite dapper today. Gubat glanced out from under his blanket and waved at me. "Good lucky!" he shouted in his rough-and-ready Russian.

The school doors, the ones overlooking the bazaar, were flung wide open, and the whole street was jammed with schoolchildren. The black cur sat near Uncle Selim's booth and looked at the crowd of children with endless wonder. The radio atop the tall building with the star talked loudly about school and, as if to hurry the kids, played happy music from time to time.

Pressing an old ankle boot between his knees, Uncle Selim fitted a patch and explained to the black cur what school is and why kids go there. I hurriedly fed the cur two gingerbread cookies, and while the cur chewed them, Uncle Selim was able to bless me and exhort me to study hard. In the doorway I turned around, looked at Uncle Selim, and understood that now he was telling the cur about me.

Each morning as soon as the canning factory whistle blew, a teacher wearing a red armband went up to the school bell hanging on the iwan; immediately after our bell rang, the bell rang in the courtyard of the orphanage. The teachers picked up the class registers and walked down the steps from the upper iwan one after another; only the school director, Firyuza-khanum, remained there. She stood, leaning her elbows on the railing, and waited while the lessons began; her smooth hair shone, her rosy face glistened as if she'd just bathed, and the polite smile rarely left her lips.

If some out-of-breath boy came running up after the bell, Firyuza-khanum admonished him that this had to be the very last time and sent the latecomer to class. Then she left, and until the bell rang to change classes, the upper iwan remained empty.

My name came last in the class register, and the desk I chose for myself was also the last one. If I'd wanted, I could have sat a little closer to the front, but I didn't care—the only desk in the whole classroom that attracted me was the one in which a girl by the name of Khakikat sat, but the place next to her was occupied. Khazer, who sat next to Khakikat, was the top pupil, and I immediately understood that I wouldn't be able to surpass him in a single subject. All the teachers smiled at Khazer, and he was terribly conceited. I could have made peace with the fact that Khazer was the top pupil, but to cede the smiles of the teachers to someone else, smiles that for so many years had been my only—and fully deserved—honor: that was more than I could bear.

It could never have satisfied me for long—to sit at the back desk and remember the front desk at my old school, and my old teachers, and how they'd smiled at me in school, on the iwan, and in the street. All that fall I frightened Aunt Medina with my gloomy look when I came home from school. I just might have abandoned my studies, but one day Firyuza-khanum came into our classroom. We'd just finished a dictation. Firyuza-khanum walked up to my desk, looked at my notebook, and went forward, looking at all the notebooks. Then she returned to me.

"What's your name?"

"Sadyk."

"Well then, Sadyk, show me your notebook."

She took the notebook, opened it to the place where today's dictation had been written out, and showed it to the whole class.

"Do you see this, children? Sadyk will be one of our school's best pupils."

She laid the notebook on the desk and patted my head. As soon as Firyuza-khanum left, the kids rose halfway in their seats, as if in unison, and turned toward me.

A few days passed. Seyyad-muallim, the algebra teacher as well as our homeroom teacher—a tall, round-shouldered man—brought a stack of notebooks to class.

"Sadyk!" he called to me.

I stood up. Seyyad-muallim asked me the name of my previous math teacher, and then he said I'd completed the homework better than anyone: both the word problems and the numerical problems had been done flawlessly, without a single mistake. During the break the kids surrounded me; even the haughty Khazer now recognized that I was a person.

Before the end of the first quarter, I received the thing that I'd in no way wanted to cede to Khazer, and I generously forgave him all his other successes and his cockiness. I only found out much later, in winter, that Khazer was so well-dressed and put on airs not because his father was a tailor, able to sew him clothes, and not because he had top grades in all his subjects, but because he was the brother of the "town council," Dzhalilov. The teachers called Khazer by his last name several times a day, saying the name loudly, but only when Khazer showed me his beautiful home did I figure things out.

One day after school Khazer drew me aside and proposed heading over to "a certain place." To do that, he told me, it was first necessary to buy some walnuts at the market. Then we'd walk past the school, toward the wall of the orphanage. There were gates there, and under the gates was a small gap: Khazer would whistle, and Aysha, a girl from the orphanage, would crawl through the hole. We'd give Aysha the walnuts, and she'd let us feel her up.

We bought some walnuts at the bazaar, walked around the orphanage, Khazer whistled, and a girl really did appear in the gap under the gates. The girl was thickset, stocky, but she crawled nimbly through, like a cat. Seeing me, she froze in surprise: first she turned white, then she blushed all over. But Khazer didn't skip a beat; he grabbed the girl by the hand, thrust the walnuts at her, and started fondling her. Finally letting Aysha go, he called me. I couldn't move a muscle. The girl waited a little while, fastening eyes round with fear on me; then she turned and ducked back into the hole under the gates.

At first Khazer made fun of me, but seeing how shocked I was, he asked in a businesslike manner:

"What are you afraid of? No one comes here! Come back tomorrow?"

"No," I answered. "I won't come back tomorrow."

But the next day I went again to the gap, and the day after that too. We bought walnuts with my money, but I didn't once work up the courage to move close to Aysha.

I myself couldn't understand how it happened: without even thinking, I'd squandered my beautiful, brand-new rubles, accumulated through such hard work, on walnuts. I sat at my desk in the back, looked at the rare poplar trees rising over the white wall of the orphanage, saw Aysha's frightened eyes in front of me, and thought of only one thing: why hadn't people planted walnut trees instead of poplars in front of the orphanage? I knew Khazer thought I was an idiot when I squandered my beautiful, brand-new rubles to fill the pocket of his smart jacket with walnuts, and also when I skulked by the orphanage wall, waiting impatiently for the time when Aysha, quaking with fear, would duck back into the gap. Each time Khazer made fun of me and called me a fool, but I didn't answer; I was thinking about Aysha, how she was now sitting somewhere in a corner hastily munching the walnuts we'd brought her.

How I wished Aysha could eat walnuts every day! I wanted this even more than I wanted Uncle Selim to always have mutton for dinner or Saftar, the shoeshine man, to eat lepyoshka with honey every day at the bazaar.

After saying goodbye to Khazer, I didn't immediately go home, but hung around for a long time near the bazaar; I played with the black cur, chatted with Uncle Selim. I saw Comrade Dzhalilov a few times. He didn't wear a hat: his thick, black hair was neatly combed back. If someone greeted him, he nodded his head unhurriedly in return; he never said hello to anyone else first.

And I often saw yet another person near the bazaar. This wasn't even a person, but half a person, a stump. The disabled man would sit on his board near the gates of the bazaar for whole days without moving, coming to life only when the kids from the kindergarten appeared on the street. Seeing the kids, he'd seize two small pieces of wood and thunk them along the asphalt, trundling happily after the kids. His strength would quickly desert him; he always stopped in exactly the same place—near a poplar that had been cut down—and sat there for a long time looking at the gaggle of kids climbing higher up the street. Then he'd turn around and go back to his former place. And the whole day he kept glancing at the kindergarten into which the kids had disappeared until they appeared on the road again.

* * *

Autumn came to an end. Only here in town, there wasn't anything to end. The last leaves fell from the broken branches of the mulberry tree; the walnut tree behind the bazaar was stripped bare, and its few branches stuck out in different directions. The trunks of the poplars behind the orphanage wall turned white, resembling skeletons.

One day in arithmetic class, glancing by force of habit at the bare poplars, I froze—the tall figure of Yakub was walking along the iwan. He approached, pressed his forehead to the glass, looked into the classroom, and pleased to see me, swung around toward the door. Without waiting for him to knock, I asked permission from the teacher and slipped out into the hallway.

We walked silently into the yard; by the gates, I stopped. Yakub stuck his hand into his pocket, pulled out a stack of money, and without explaining anything to me, asked:

"Forty kilos of potatoes at three rubles each—how much is that?"

"A hundred and twenty rubles."

Yakub counted out the money.

"Correct. Twelve kilos of onions at four rubles each?"

"Forty-eight rubles."

"Good. Add forty-eight to a hundred and twenty."

"A hundred and sixty-eight," I answered immediately, seeing that Yakub was pleased with how quickly I could calculate.

"Correct. Now add another hundred and fifty rubles—that's for the cucumbers and tomatoes."

"Three hundred and eighteen rubles."

"You're really good with numbers! How much did you say that was?"

"Three hundred and eighteen."

"What's left?"

"I don't know."

"Well, let me tell you! I sold your apricots—that money went to the walls. I sealed all the walls. I collected a sack of walnuts—they're all whole, I didn't touch a single nut. I'll sell them, fix up the gutters and the roof that needs to be mended. There weren't any pears this year. Anything else?"

"Nothing," I said, looking in surprise at the money he'd given me. There wasn't anything else.

"Put the money away! Put it in your pocket!" And as I put the money in my pocket, he added, "Don't give anyone a single kopeck. Do you hear? Buy a new jacket and pantaloons."

"Okay."

Yakub looked me over silently: jacket, pants, galoshes. Then he turned and started walking toward the bazaar. But suddenly he came back, pulled a handful of walnuts and dried berries from his pocket, and poured them into my pocket.

"So you're in school?" he asked.

"I am."

"Well then, go study!"

Satisfied, I ran back to class; the money rustled in one pocket, and the other pocket was stuffed with walnuts and mulberries. This happened not long before the school holidays. I didn't see Aysha now—Khazer had gone away with his brother to Baku.

It began to get cold. One morning Surat appeared in the yard in a pretty, green coat. Gubat dragged his bed into his room. Then snow fell, and with it, a heavy, soft silence lay over the yard.

The square in front of the bazaar gradually emptied out. Uncle Selim's booth disappeared. Saftar was also nowhere to be seen. Butcher Ali moved inside the bazaar under the roof; the block on which he chopped meat also moved there. Qatiq and cigarettes were sold only in the tearooms now, and the square in front of the bazaar now belonged to the kids, who spent whole days romping on the ice.

The radio on the tall building was completely covered in snow, but all winter it spoke to itself in a raspy, cold voice. Snowdrifts lay over the walls that fenced in the orphanage on all four sides; I didn't see Aysha all winter, as if she were also hidden under a thick layer of snow.

Not once did Khazer mention Aysha. Looking smart in warm, wool mittens, a red scarf, and shiny, black boots, he spent whole days skating on the ice in front of the bazaar, and I looked at him and thought that it was as easy for him to forget Aysha as it was to earn top grades or run across the ice.

I didn't forget Aysha, didn't forget her eyes, the way her eyes resembled those of the black cur, who now spent the nights with his pitiful friends behind the steamshop or by the warm wall of the bakery. As soon as it smelled of spring and the snow on the wall surrounding the orphanage began to darken, I was the one to remind Khazer about Aysha. Again we went to the store, again we bought walnuts and gingerbread cookies with my money, and again I waited for Khazer by the white wall, and then I was tormented day and night by the thought that it was I who had reminded him about Aysha.

That spring it was quiet in our yard, as it had been during the winter. Gubat again took offense at Merdzhan over something, but now he not only didn't want to talk to her, he didn't want to talk to any of us. He returned home late at night and immediately went to his room; he didn't even drag his bed out onto the iwan. In the morning Gubat got up when everyone was already at work and, after a hasty meal, left for the military commander's horse. Merdzhan also went around gloomily, not looking like herself. For several days already she'd lain down in bed after returning from work and gotten up only in the morning when it was time to open the shop. I felt that Merdzhan and my aunt were hiding something from me because they didn't talk to one another, not even when they lay down to sleep. Only once did I happen to hear a snippet of conversation: my aunt was telling Merdzhan about Seyyad, my teacher, about how he'd accompanied her all the way to the square where the Lenin monument stood. He'd started by complimenting my talents, and then he said that he'd like to become Sadyk's father if, of course, she agreed.

I couldn't understand whether my aunt had agreed or not. She spoke highly of my teacher in a gentle voice, but at the same time she stubbornly avoided meeting him; she even walked to work by way of the bathhouse now, although it was a much longer route. Aunt Medina developed a passion for reading; Surat brought her one book after another. And Merdzhan lay in bed all evening as before; she slept, or simply lay there and thought, staring up at the ceiling.

But one night Merdzhan suddenly jerked out of bed.

"To hell with it!" she said loudly. "I'll marry him, come what may! Even if he's a butcher, at least he's a man!"

She quickly put on her jacket, carelessly tied her scarf, glanced at herself in the mirror, and darted out into the yard. I looked after her and couldn't collect my wits from fear: *Which butcher? Surely it can't be Butcher Ali?!*

In the morning when I was leaving for school, Aunt Medina whispered to me that I should come back home a little later today—people were coming to arrange a match for Merdzhan. Why was she talking so cautiously, as if she were afraid of something? *She surely doesn't know that I hate Ali—I've never told her about the black cur he drove out into the street, or that every time he sees the cur, he scolds him for the carpet the thieves made off with. Why is my aunt hiding the fact that Merdzhan is preparing to marry the butcher from me?*

The whole way to school I reflected bitterly on this, and I finally came to the realization that the issue wasn't the butcher, but Gubat. *My aunt knows that I want more than anything for Merdzhan to marry him. So she's afraid I'll foolishly tell Gubat everything and that he'll make a scene, which would be pointless—Merdzhan knows what she needs to do. But if that's the case, why did my aunt say anything in the first place? Couldn't I just hightail it over to Gubat at military headquarters during a school break? No, something else is going on here...*

I didn't usually go straight home from school. Having visited the gap in the wall, I'd wander around the bazaar for a long time afterwards, or gaze at the trains shuttling back and forth between the train station and the canning factory. Today I immediately threw myself into finding Gubat. I understood that I was committing a betrayal, but Merdzhan was going to marry the butcher! I walked all around the bazaar, visited all the tearooms, looked into the yard at military headquarters. Gubat had disappeared from the face of the earth.

I spotted him at last by our building. Sitting on the military commander's buck-wild stallion, Gubat had ridden to our doorway and was trying to ride through into the yard. The horse whinnied, reared, hit the boards of the door with the horseshoes on his front hooves. *What is Gubat doing? The horse really can't go through that door!*

Men crowded around. Afraid of the unruly stallion, women didn't come close, but the roofs were bursting with them. Boys swarmed up trees. Everyone was shouting.

"He's drunk!"

"Are you kidding? No drunk could keep his seat on a horse like that! Looks like he's nailed in place!"

"But his eyes are humongous! Of course, he's drunk, there's no mystery about it!"

"Oy, now he's going to break the door!"

But only the women shouted that way. The fellows were in raptures over Gubat.

"Way to go!" they shouted. "Hold tighter!"

"A regular Budenny!"

"What do you mean, Budenny—a Chapayev!"

"No, a Koroghlu! Just look at the horse—it's Kirat, all right!"

"Hey, Gubat, get out of here! The butcher's coming!"

"Ali's coming!"

"Ali!"

Butcher Ali walked calmly up to the horse, grabbed his bridle, and leaped. I didn't understand what was happening, but the next moment Gubat lay face down on the ground, and with a loud whinny, the stallion was tearing along the street. The butcher started kicking Gubat. I screamed with all my might, snatched up a giant stone, and rushed at the butcher. But then Aunt Medina came out of the wicket gate, and the stone fell from my hand.

The butcher cursed for a long time, chasing away the crowd. Then he left. Gubat, my aunt, and I remained on the street. She squatted down and lifted his head, her hand beneath it. Gubat's face was covered in blood.

Two fellows lifted Gubat and carried him into the building. It sticks in my mind that the samovar was boiling on the iwan, the big, white samovar that always stood on Merdzhan's table. Then three women wearing chadors came out of Merdzhan's room. Merdzhan peeped out, looked around the yard in fright, and shut herself in her room once more.

They laid Gubat on his bed. My aunt moistened gauze with hot water from the samovar and washed the blood from his face. Gubat didn't open his eyes until the lamp was lit in the evening. And everyone was silent in our yard until then.

Aunt Medina went out into the yard several times to cry. Surat also started crying when she saw Gubat. Only I didn't cry. But in the evening when Gubat opened his eyes and smiled, I couldn't hold back. I cried for a long time; Surat and Aunt Medina were unable to soothe me.

My aunt brought noodle soup and began feeding Gubat, carefully lifting the spoon toward his torn lips. Surat was sitting there, too, on the old trunk.

"We'll find someone much better than that for our Gubat to marry!" said Surat.

Gubat smiled. Why was he smiling? Had she said something funny? *Or is it pleasant for him to have his head supported by my aunt's hand? Or maybe he's happy he's still alive?*

It was past midnight and long past time for me to go to sleep, but no matter how my aunt tried to persuade me, I wouldn't agree to go into Merdzhan's room. Then, following Surat's lead, she started repeating that she'd marry Gubat to a wonderful girl, clever and beautiful. Then she said that Ali had behaved badly, but Gubat was also in the wrong: it was necessary to forget and make peace— what had happened was over and done with. Gubat would have to make peace with Merdzhan, and the three of them together—she, Merdzhan, and Surat—would find Gubat a bride. She herself would cook each and every dish for the wedding! I didn't believe it: I understood too well that this was a tale, one of her beautiful tales, like the one about the pomegranate tree.

No, Aunt, I won't go into Merdzhan's room ever again. You yourself once said that my father's blood was in me and that someday it would show itself. Yes, Aunt, I'll be just like my father: just as stubborn, just as evil, and just as strong. I have to become like that; my father would have grabbed Ali by the throat, flung him to the ground, and kicked him for a long time with his black boots... I won't go into Merdzhan's room!

Merdzhan doesn't exist for me anymore. Butcher Ali exists. The black cur exists. The gap under the orphanage gates exists. Gubat with his bloody, beaten face and the big stone I had to throw aside exist. Go ahead, Aunt, lie down to sleep! Go and lie down next to Merdzhan, although you hate Butcher Ali as much as I do.

Aunt Medina had to bring the blanket and pillow and lay out my bed near Gubat. Gubat slept deeply; only once did he cry out suddenly in his sleep. What had he dreamed? All night long I saw only one thing—the stone I'd lifted from the ground, the one that my aunt hadn't let me use to smash the butcher's head. Somehow or other that same stone later turned up near the school: I seized it, drew back my arm, and launched it at Khazer. Khazer let out a quiet yell and crumpled to the ground.

I don't know how the stone with which I cut open Khazer's head came into my hand. I only know that I'd seen a different stone, seen it since the morning—in all my classes, in all my breaks.

"Got any money?" Khazer had asked with a poisonous smile as we left school. Today, too, he wanted me to go with him and stand there near the gap.

"I've got money," I answered, "but you won't lay another finger on that girl."

"Ha! See this?" Khazer showed me a three-ruble note.

"All the same, you won't lay a finger on her!"

He burst out laughing and slapped his knees.

"Aren't you clever! What, are you sweet on that whore?"

"Your mother's a whore!"

"Wha-at?!"

"Your mother's a whore! Are we clear? And your sister! And your grandmother! Your whole family are whores!!!"

Khazer aimed for my nose, but I ducked, and his fist grazed my forehead. If I hadn't ducked, and if Khazer hadn't run away, it's possible that I wouldn't have picked up that stone from the ground.

Then we found ourselves in the office of the school director. They laid Khazer on the sofa. They closed the door. As if in a fog, I saw one of the teachers light a handkerchief on fire—it was necessary to cover the wound with ashes. Two teachers held me by the arms; one of them, Seyyad-muallim, laid his hand on my forehead. "Don't be afraid, boy, don't shake," he said softly.

"Just think: both of them excellent students, the best students..."

The words sounded muffled, as if from a great distance.

Firyuza-khanum raged around the office; now and again she walked to the window and, pulling back the window sheer, looked out at the street. She didn't seem pretty at all now. Her face was hard, as if made of stone; her eyes flashed cold and sharp, as if they were pieces of glass.

Firyuza-khanum wiped Khazer's tears with her own scarf. She sat next to him, put her arm around his shoulders, and began gently, tenderly repeating, as if she were singing a lullaby:

"Khazer's a splendid boy, Khazer's a clever boy..."

Then she got up off the sofa, and her face again became hard and cold, like stone.

"Send for his aunt!" she said. And she added, turning toward me: "I cannot keep a boy like this. Let him study in his own village."

I bolted for the door.

It was bright on the street, and the air was light, as light as could be—you could fly like a bird when the air was that way. I ran to the river. There beyond the river was the road that led to our village. *Goodbye, black cur! Goodbye, Uncle Selim! And goodbye, Aysha! I waited so long, I wanted so badly for you to shove Khazer away, to slap his face just once! You didn't do that, and you'll never do it! There's no earthly reason for me to stay in this town! Goodbye!*

Someday I'll come find you, Aysha. You'll put on a green dress made of fine, patterned fabric. You'll put your round, white hands on my shoulders. I'll embrace you, and you'll start trembling and cling to me. And I'll start to kiss you, your forehead, your eyes, your lips, and I'll forgive you everything, Aysha, everything!

I walked to the village. *I'll go back and live by myself, by myself day and night.* But now it was day, and the sun shone brightly, and all the same, it was absolutely terrifying. I cried from fear, and my sobs echoed

149

through the gorge... *My aunt is now in Firyuza-khanum's office, and Firyuza-khanum is looking at her with those eyes made of glass. They've told my aunt that Sadyk attacked a boy, pierced his head with a stone. She doesn't believe it. Believe it, Aunt Medina! I want you to believe it, to be angry at me, and not to try to find me. There's only one thing I don't want, although I know it's unavoidable: I don't want you to cry there in front of them, I don't want you to wipe your tears with the end of your scarf as you come down the stairs!*

By the time I reached the village, it was already getting dark. It was terrifying just to look at our dark windows, so I went to Yakub's house; there, a light shone in the windows. I sat down by the fence, caught my breath, then knocked softly. No one heard. I knocked louder. Sadaf came out and opened the wicket gate. She wasn't surprised to see me; she didn't say a word, as if this was meant to be.

We climbed new, cement stairs to the iwan. Yakub wasn't home. His fat, red-cheeked sons were sitting around a big bowl and scarfing down qatiq. Sadaf started to collect the dishes. Finishing her evening prayers, Aunt Nabat came in from the neighboring room; she also wasn't surprised to see me.

"You've come back, son?" she said, simply. "Sadaf, bring him some bread."

But Sadaf was making a racket with the firewood by the stove—she'd noticed that I was shaking all over. Aunt Nabat herself brought the bread, laid it in front of me, and sat down on the trunk in the corner.

"How's your aunt, is she well?"

"She's well, thank you."

"Why did you come back?"

I said nothing. Aunt Nabat didn't ask any more questions.

"Eat, son," she said, sighing. "We've already had dinner."

Then she got up from the trunk and, trailing her long, black skirt behind her, went up to the window. She stood there looking out into the darkness. Then she sat back down on the trunk, leaned her head on her hand, and said, shaking her head:

"And Yakub was arrested. Arrested! Damn those storehouses!"

4

I dreamed I was walking away from town; the black cur ran after me, I called him the whole time—I wanted to take him with me to the village. But the three gaunt, mangy dogs trotted insistently after the black cur, and the cur didn't want to abandon his comrades: he ran a little bit, stopped, and looked back at them. I tried to drive the dogs away; I flung stones at them, and they dropped back a bit, then rushed forward again to catch up to the cur... I was sorry it was just a dream, but in fact, if I hadn't had the dream, I might never have understood that it was an impossible thing, dividing the black cur from his friends.

Yakub's fat-faced, red-cheeked boys slept deeply, lying in a row on the palas. Having thrown the black, satin chador over her head, Aunt Nabat performed her prayers in the adjoining room; small, gaunt Sadaf was boiling milk on the iwan. I looked at her enormous stomach, as big and heavy as a watermelon, and wondered why she didn't tip over, how it was possible to drag around such a belly on those tiny, thin legs.

When I opened my eyes, the yard still lay in shadow, but the dewy grass near the irrigation canal was already glistening in the sun's rays. Yakub had covered the little paths that led from the wicket gate to the iwan with cement, and he'd built a cement basin in the middle of the yard; clean, cool water overflowed the edge and streamed freely into the grass.

I couldn't believe my ears: I heard my aunt's voice in the yard. *How did she manage to get here? It's just barely light!*

"Is Sadyk with you?"

"Yes, he's here. Come inside, Medina!"

Thrusting my feet into my shoes, I darted up and raced to meet my aunt—I understood that if she didn't see me at that exact instant, her heart would burst.

Aunt Medina held the heavy bundle of my schoolbooks in her hand. Seeing me, she dropped it slowly to the ground. I took the books, my aunt exchanged a few words with Sadaf, and we went home.

My aunt didn't say a single word to me. She didn't ask anything about Khazer; she didn't say a single word to blame me for running away. She was too happy. My aunt rejoiced that I'd been found, that it was quiet all around, that the air was so clear, and that violets were already blooming along the irrigation canal.

My aunt pulled out the sliver of wood shoved into the hinges of the wicket gate in place of a lock, and we went in. The mountain rising behind the house was completely red, as if plastered over by the sun.

The road winding up the slope lay open to the sun, and looking at it, for some reason I remembered Teacher Seyyad and how he'd said to my aunt, "If you agree, Medina, let Sadyk be a son to me."

I wanted to ask Aunt Medina what they'd said to her at school, whether Merdzhan was going to marry the butcher, would Gubat get well. But I didn't ask any of that; I said something completely different:

"I'm not going back to town."

My aunt took off the rusty lock hanging on the door of our house, threw it onto the soft earth, shoved the door, and went into the entryway.

"I'm not going back either," she said.

It was bright in the room, astonishingly bright in our room. The glass that Yakub had installed was completely intact. By the wall stood a large sack of walnuts tied tightly with string. My aunt got down on her knees and started to slowly untie it.

"Aunt, you know that they arrested Yakub?"

"I know."

She untied the sack, pulled out a couple of walnuts, squeezed them in her fist. One cracked: my aunt broke it open, picked out the nut meat, and thrust it into her mouth.

"Just don't drop out of school, Sadyk," she said. "I'm going to lie down; I'm a little tired..."

Aunt Medina untied the bundle in which she'd packed up the blanket and pillows the year before and started to lay out the bed.

People and Trees

Part One

1

When Aunt Nabat's son, Yakub, the storehouse keeper, was sent to prison, it immediately grew very quiet in the village. The degree of quiet in our village really depends on what's happening on the square, and every evening Yakub had collected the boys near the mosque. For two hours or so they flailed around on the ground, and that whole time nothing could be heard in the village except the delighted howling of fans. After the wrestling, they turned to belt wrestling—and again there were shouts, noise, laughter. Yakub didn't belt wrestle, of course, because he couldn't find a partner for himself among the kids, but he directed everyone in this amusement. It's quiet on the square now because Yakub has been arrested. And near the collective farm storehouse standing at the foot of the mountain by the very edge of the village, it's also quiet now without Yakub. Except that water makes noise: breaking free from under the cliff, it rushes through the pipe under the storehouse and falls from the high, raised stone gutter into a deep reservoir. Its muffled, measured hum in some ways reminds me of Yakub's bass voice; every time I pass near there, I think of him.

And yet there wouldn't be such quiet in the village if matters were limited just to Yakub. Things don't happen that way: if people have been caught stealing, it means the accountant is involved, and the chairman. The accountant isn't important, of course, but the chairman being arrested is very noticeable—the bathhouse has been closed, and once the bathhouse is closed, life on the square in front of the mosque simply stops. The bathhouse will open when there is firewood, but where does the firewood come from if there's no chairman? This means that people will have to wait until a new chairman appears. And in his absence, a lock will hang on the bathhouse because if you leave it open, God forbid, people will get into mischief there: write obscene words, draw smutty pictures, and all kinds of disgraceful things.

Our bathhouse is closed, closed again. A new chairman has appeared, but the door remains locked, as before. And the square in front of the mosque remains quiet, as before.

After Yakub, a few more people returned from the army, three of whom I remember. One of these was Yusuf, the son of Aunt Azra. As it turned out, he didn't set foot out of the house for a whole week after his return; they said he was tired, that he was sleeping.

But even after a whole week, he evidently hadn't caught up on his sleep, and an unhappy, drowsy man appeared on the square in front of the mosque. He said hello to the old men and leaned his shoulder against the wall, hanging his head and fixing his gaze on the water babbling quietly as it ran between the flagstones. As if he'd appeared solely for that reason: to look at the water. He looked, looked, and left.

After Yusuf, Husein returned from the army. "Beanpole" Husein, as we called him. For two whole hours music played at his house, and he walked around his own iwan and talked at the top of his lungs just like Yakub, and he roared with laughter too. I'd already begun to think that now the battles on the square would begin again, and the boys would belt wrestle—in a word, that the quiet would come to an end. However, the next day I caught sight of Husein in that same spot where Yusuf had stood not long before. The most surprising thing was that Husein was leaning his shoulder against the wall in the exact same way and staring fixedly at the water. I saw him there several days in a row, even in the most intense heat, when there wasn't a soul on the square; leaning his shoulder against the wall, he stood and looked at the spring. One of those evenings, looking always in that same direction, he suddenly said loudly: "Our village is gone. Gone." I understood—

this was the end. There wouldn't be any wrestling, no belt wrestling—there wouldn't be anything. And it suddenly struck me that Husein's words were somehow inexplicably connected with the water—they'd probably also come into Yusuf's head when he looked at the water that way, but he'd just kept them to himself.

I really didn't like what the men coming home from the war said about our village. Look at Yakub! It would've been great if everyone who returned from the front had acted like he did—if they'd collected the boys on the square, organized wrestling and belt wrestling—and most of all, if there hadn't been any of those pitiful conversations. And what, exactly, had happened, what had changed in the village during the war? I couldn't understand that. When Husein, looking fixedly at the water, said what he said about our village, I also glanced at the spring: water is water, it had neither decreased nor increased. And the almond tree bending low over the spring from the neighboring garden was the same as always. And the vines twined thickly around it—nothing special had happened to them either. Except that someone had planted a thorn bush around the sweet cherry tree, fastening it to the trunk with wire. That was because of the war, of course, but thorn bushes are no big deal at all. Even the locked bathhouse—that was bad, but it had also happened before the war—I had seen it locked many times.

The third soldier who'd fought at the front was Uncle Nazar. I met him at the mill and immediately noticed his black suit—no one in our village wore those. Uncle Nazar asked whose son I was, and when I named my father, he perked up and cheerfully exclaimed, "Ah, Nadzhaf! Bulldozer Nadzhaf!" I was a little taken aback by those words and quickly started thinking about what they might mean. The miller, Uncle Musum, apparently decided that I was upset, and he began to sing a happy little song to distract me.

* * *

After that I often met Uncle Nazar near the spring. In contrast to Yusuf and Husein, he didn't lean his shoulder against the wall, and he didn't say pitiful things about our village. He'd been in different countries during the war, and he'd seen how clean the springs were there. He tried very hard to make our spring the same. Uncle Nazar sternly forbade the women to do their washing near the spring. He marked out a special place for doing laundry, he outlined where to wash dishes, and he'd sit whole days on the steps of the locked bathhouse near the mosque making sure the women didn't break the rules.

It was quiet in the village, very quiet. Only the water bursting from the pipe into the reservoir—very much like its counterpart, the letters Yakub sent one after another from prison—reminded everyone of how things had been before. "First things first: I send greetings, Honored Mama. Second, of course, I want to know what's happening with you. Don't be too upset about me, and don't worry that I'm enduring the torments of martyrdom here. Everyone should be lucky enough to live the way I do: I eat hot food three times a day. I've even put on some weight, may my enemies choke on it! I'm satisfied with my situation. God willing, I'll return soon. Honored Mama, if possible, have Hasan circumcised. He's a big boy already, it's embarrassing... Husein will wait, we'll celebrate his circumcision when I get back. Keep a closer eye on Rakhib, don't let him be lazy; times are such now that we can't do without learning. God alone can help the ignorant!"

And once again Aunt Nabat tramped around the fields with a bag from morning until night collecting dropped sheaves of wheat, seeking out potatoes left behind in the ground, picking up spilled peas. But in the evening she tied on a new, sateen chador, donned new slippers, picked up her gleaming, red tea kettle, and headed to the spring for water. Aunt Nabat stopped in front of every house, shoved yet another letter from Yakub in front of everyone she met, and announced loudly, so that all her mortal enemies could hear, that her son was just about to return. Going a bit over the top sometimes, Aunt Nabat would suddenly start carrying on about something ridiculous. "I have mutton simmering at home," she'd throw out offhandedly. "I ordered my daughter-in-law to put on the samovar and decided to come to the spring myself—we wanted some fresh water." And it was done so convincingly—the air even started to smell of mutton cooking, just like before the war! And you even started to believe that they had a samovar and that Sadaf was adding coal to it right now, although everyone knew that the house had been completely cleared out when Yakub was arrested; they managed to conceal the tea kettle somehow.

It took Aunt Nabat a long time to reach the spring with her kettle. She kept talking about her son, and although her voice had already long grown hoarse from tiredness, she tried to speak as loudly as possible. "I'll wear myself to the bone and raise Yakub's sons—they won't be hungry or cold!" she repeated over and over.

The "mortal enemies" for whose ears these words were intended were, for the most part, old women like her who also wore the chador and slippers. The only difference was that roses grew in pots on their iwans, and real samovars smoked in their homes. Catching sight of a person with whom it wasn't necessary to stretch the truth, Aunt Nabat immediately dropped the pretense, her voice growing quiet, her movements weak—the old woman's strength deserted her. Forgetting about mortal enemies and about the tea kettle, Aunt Nabat leaned back against the wall or sank onto a stone in exhaustion. "I suffered through the soldiering, but prison—I can't take any more!" Aunt Nabat only said that to those whom she considered friends.

And the tempting smell of lamb immediately melted away, and the samovar disappeared, together with the kindling with which Sadaf had lit it. I'd see Yakub's empty yard; Sadaf's sunken eyes; Hasan, whom his father hadn't managed to have circumcised; little Husein, Aunt Nabat's favorite; and Rakhib, who was settled somewhere in a corner with a schoolbook, choosing the more difficult problems. Today's Rakhib was absolutely not who he'd been a year ago—when his father egged him on, he could have laid anyone flat on his back. He'd turned into a lamb, not a guy. It hadn't been necessary to say a thing about his studies; it probably hadn't even entered Yakub's head that his Rakhib—a D student, quarrelsome, the terror of the whole school—now solved problems in a way that simply amazed the teachers.

If even Yakub understood in prison that "you can't do without learning," it meant times truly had changed. It was all they talked about in the village: "Study, children! Learning will bring you bread. God alone can help the ignorant!" Maybe Rakhib took to his books because he believed those words and because nowadays he wouldn't be able to grab hold of any of the goodies of life without an education. Many reckoned this way, but it seems to me that the reason for Rakhib's new-found interest in his books lay elsewhere. His mother, Sadaf, had recently started coming to the school as a cleaning lady. And when she swept the yard, washed the toilet, or carried wood from the shed and lit the fires in the classrooms, I noticed that Rakhib hung his head each time she bent down, reddening in shame—threadbare, dark-blue pantaloons with large, gray patches peeked out from under her skirt. Other people probably had patches, too, but no one saw those.

We studied. And not only because "learning brings bread" or "God alone helps the ignorant." It's possible that Salatyn, who lived over the river at the other end of the village, had never even heard those words, and all the same, she didn't miss a single lesson; even in a hard frost, she ran barefoot to school. We teased her, but not because she ran barefoot in the snow. It was just because her name immediately reminded us of the words to the song:

Salatyn is coming, a white swan swimming...

I don't know which Salatyn those words were meant for; perhaps that Salatyn really was a swan, but when I hear that old folk song, I don't ever imagine a proud, solemn beauty, but our barefoot Salatyn, chilled to the bone, and no matter how merry the song, it doesn't give me pleasure. Even now, looking at flocks of elegant, satisfied girls coming out of school or the institute, I sometimes hum this song under my breath. Each time the stove appears before me. I even hear how the firewood sputters in it because while Salatyn warmed herself, no one dared say a word. The bell had rung long ago, but the lesson still hadn't begun, and you could hear how Salatyn's teeth chattered and how the firewood crackled in the stove. It sometimes happened that Salatyn's feet wouldn't warm up; her blue toes didn't want to turn pink, and then the girl would start to cry, unable to hold back. There were so many tears that it seemed something had frozen in Salatyn's head, something that was now thawing in bright drops that coursed down her cheeks. From her face, it didn't look like she was crying: it seemed that the most ordinary water was flowing from her eyes. While the little girl warmed her feet, Teacher Leyla, who'd just graduated from the Baku Pedagogical Institute, paced quietly behind the blackboard; clicking her bright, elegant shoes, she listened to the crackle of the firewood. Then she stepped out from behind the blackboard and started the lesson, as if nothing had happened. Leyla spoke more than once of some shoes she had lying around at home, unused—she very much wanted to give them to Salatyn. But as soon as the shoes were mentioned, the little girl immediately started to cry, and those tears no longer looked like thawing ice: those tears were completely real.

It was quiet in the village, very quiet. And in this quiet Aunt Nabat stole in the morning to the cemetery where the orchards began, a small bag in her hand; she returned at dusk, hiding behind the walnut trees that grew thickly on the slope. And a little later she'd bustle around the quiet village streets, red tea kettle jingling, and the latest letter from Yakub rustling. Then she'd go home and smudge the letter with herbs for protection from the evil eye.

In the evening the shrill voice of Ebish could be heard from beneath the dense thicket of almonds in Aunt Sadat's yard. Aunt Sadat's son was hard of hearing, and therefore he tried to sing as loudly as possible:

> No one to shine my samovar,
> No one to tell about my sorrow...

It was just a song, but it was impossible to listen to it with indifference; everyone knew about Ebish's troubles. It even seemed to me that Ebish was intentionally lying about the samovar: they didn't have a samovar, and you couldn't get married without one. For years they'd been talking about when to buy one, but it didn't depend on Ebish or his mother. The problem was the almonds. They had plenty of almond trees—the whole yard was full of them—but the almonds had to ripen. Then they'd earn enough money for tea and sugar and a samovar. But for five springs in a row, frost had killed the flowers, and Aunt Sadat couldn't buy a samovar and marry off her son. The trees were right in front of me, just over our fence, and I knew for a fact that Ebish didn't possess a samovar.

Across the street, just opposite the thicket of almonds, was the yard of Teacher Leyla, and during the quiet evening hours her wicket gate stood wide open. Each evening at exactly the same time, Leyla diligently swept the yard, watered it from the doorway to the iwan, even watered the street in front of the house. Then she covered the table with a snow-white cloth, put out choice, washed pears and apples on a plate, washed her hands, combed her hair, and sat down at the table. During those hours Leyla usually corrected our workbooks or read. She left the door open so that Beanpole Husein, walking nearby, could see her—each evening he showed up on our street. Leyla didn't talk to Husein; they didn't even say hello to one another. When he approached, Leyla lifted her head and smiled—that's it. I never heard Leyla sing, but each time I passed by her home, for some reason I recalled the same song:

> I pour water on the street
> So there's no dust on my love's feet...

It was quiet in the village, very quiet. Returning from the fields in the evening, Aunt Medina would stand for a long time by the wall dividing our yard from Ebish's, thinking and thinking. When I banged the door latch on returning from the street, my aunt shuddered, straightened up, put on a carefree face, and began picking pebbles off the wall, chucking them at the birds that were making themselves at home in the trees. That curious woman—as if I didn't know what she'd been thinking about! As if I understood less well than she did that this fall, again, the collective farm wouldn't pay anything for days worked. That if winter didn't surprise us today, then it would tomorrow...

Many people thought that I should go to the collective farm, at least in the mornings before school, to rake hay or turn on the water. I was still a boy, and a boy could shove stolen apricots into his shirt or collect firewood—a child couldn't be held accountable for that. Then things would have been much easier for us. It didn't occur to anyone that Aunt Medina would never permit me to steal. And everyone looked in bewilderment at the empty bucket she carried out of the orchard, as empty as it had been when she carried it in.

Quiet reigned, complete quiet. And we three—Azer, Rakhib, and I—spent the most wonderful hours of that quiet on the mountain behind the village; we lay there, looked at the village, daydreamed. The quiet gave birth to daydreams about a road that was smooth, straight, and clean. Someday a road like that would run through our village, and our girls, just like the girls we saw in the movies, would walk with us through the village along that straight, smooth road. They'd tear down the mosque near the spring and build a giant Palace of Culture in its place. There would be a park in front of it. We'd seen that park in the movies. We also dreamed of the reservoir described by Azer's father in the papers he left along with the poems and plays he'd written. A place had been marked to show where the reservoir should be built. And a sketch was even attached. Uncle Hasan had written about which orchards could be irrigated with water from the reservoir and which fields could be made fertile again. We just added the park, and we planned to water the road because without that, there was no point in either the sketch or the reservoir for us.

The note attached to the sketch didn't say anything about a park. However, the poems left by Uncle Hasan were full of parks and palaces, and there boys and girls passed hand-in-hand along smooth, clean roads. Sometimes Azer and I sat on the slope until late at night reveling in these verses, even learning them by heart. Rakhib wasn't interested in poetry; he was completely absorbed in the sketch. He even tracked down the place where Uncle Hasan had planned to build the reservoir—he tramped about fifteen kilometers along the riverbank. When we returned to the village after studying at the institute, we'd undoubtedly build that reservoir: that was a given. And although we hadn't agreed on the division of responsibilities, none of us doubted that the engineer of our building project could only be Rakhib.

We were in the seventh or eighth grade then. There wasn't much time left before we'd go off to the institute. We knew geography, and we knew that Baku was located over the mountains to the northeast of us. But in the evenings when we lay on the slope of the mountain behind the village, geography would vanish from our heads. There, where the sun went down behind the furthest peak, there was so much light in the evening that it was as if not one but a thousand suns were gathered, pouring across the peak to light up the mountains. Baku—our Baku, with which we connected our brightest hopes and dreams in these quiet hours—could only be there, in that ocean of sunlight.

Sometimes we'd sit out on the mountain until dark, until the women, finishing up with dinner, went out onto the street and arranged themselves in a cozy group near Aunt Sadat's house. The girls from our street also gathered there, and we, remaining at some distance, instantly started discussing them. Not all of them, naturally, we were mostly interested in girls our age, those who studied in our class or the one above ours. Our main subject of consideration was their breasts, of course. We couldn't think of anything more pleasant or exciting— after all, we were thirteen or fourteen. I'd never have started talking about Aunt Shakhrabanu's illness, but she herself harped on it all the time. Every night the discussion in front of Aunt Sadat's house was about hemorrhoids. Some healer had advised Aunt Shakhrabanu to treat herself with hedgehog fat, and the poor woman pestered us with tearful requests to catch a hedgehog; she even lay in wait for us at school. But in the evening she didn't dare approach us—the kids met her with deafening laughter.

It was quiet, very quiet. The women sat on one side of the street; we teenagers crowded the other. We talked about Dinara more than the other girls: she had the biggest breasts. Aunt Susen's son, Khashim, knew this better than anyone. One evening he went with Dinara to the mill to turn off the water and, placing the lamp on the ground, took her in his arms. Dinara was a beautiful—a very beautiful—girl, but none of us fell in love with her, and of course, we didn't dream of marrying her. And generally speaking, although each and every one of us necessarily had a beloved—either real or imagined—we were all in love with just one girl: Teacher Leyla. It was impossible not to love her—she had very beautiful dresses. And in the deathly quiet of those evenings, there was nothing more wonderful than her little window hung with a white curtain. Leyla corrected workbooks or read, and it seemed to us that her window was lit up far, far away in another world, where there weren't any of our streets, our conversations, or any of us either.

* * *

The women sat in front of Aunt Sadat's house until midnight because there was no one to yell at them, no one waiting for them at home. Only Aunt Jamila, Leyla's mother, kept track of the time; at exactly the same time each night, she put out her daughter's light. Aunt Jamila left, the light went out in the far-off, little, white window, and our street seemed even emptier, even sadder.

2

On one of those quiet nights in the village, Uncle Elmurad—Aunt Susen's husband and Khashim's father—returned. His appearance was strange. First of all, the war had been over for three years already, and people had long ago stopped waiting for those who hadn't returned. Second, a message had arrived saying that Uncle Elmurad had been killed in battle, and no further information had come.

And third, he appeared suddenly, when it was nearly dark; had he appeared a half-hour later, there wouldn't have been a soul on the street.

We were so engrossed in chattering about girls that we didn't pay any attention to the heavy, soldier-like steps. But then we noticed— the women suddenly jumped up one after another, pressing themselves against the wall—that a grown man was walking along the street toward us with a large suitcase on his shoulders. The women watched him walk past in silence. And only as the man was passing them did Aunt Sadat suddenly scream in a strange, shrill voice like Ebish's:

"Good gracious me, it's Elmurad! Susen! Elmurad's come!"

Uncle Elmurad stopped. He steadied the heavy suitcase on his shoulder and turned to the women, seeking his wife among them. Aunt Susen pressed herself against the wall, and it seemed that she'd stopped breathing.

"Oh, are you here?" asked Uncle Elmurad. "You've been hanging around here all this time?"

"All this time" meant "since before the war," that is, seven years already, and when Uncle Elmurad said it that way, everyone immediately felt easier. Aunt Sadat exclaimed in her own voice, not Ebish's:

"Still cracking jokes, Elmurad! Always a joker, still the same!"

The women started talking with great animation, but Uncle Elmurad kept walking. Aunt Susen hurried after her husband, got ahead of him, and ran toward the house. The door opened with a bang. A fire was lit on the iwan. But Khashim remained standing still; something seemed to have come over him. Uncle Elmurad walked up to us. He stopped, but he didn't put down his suitcase. He was probably looking for Khashim but was unable to recognize him—he looked at all of us the same way.

"Well done, indeed; you watch over our women. That's the right thing to do. Keep your eyes peeled, or just you wait, they'll steal your mothers right out from under you!"

Only when Uncle Elmurad turned and walked on did Khashim shoot ahead of his father and rush headlong toward the house. Soon after, we all headed there. Khashim came out to meet us, not quite himself. He blocked the path and said that his father was tired, he was sleeping. In other words: "Go back where you came from!" We turned around, but then Aunt Susen came out and hung the lamp by the door. That could only mean one thing: "To hell with that numbskull Khashim, who doesn't know how things should be done! Customs are customs; if someone wants to come in, come on in!" Leaving the door open, Aunt Susen walked further up the street. She wasn't looking like herself either. Her face was completely white, and she was shaking all over. Muttering something under her breath, Aunt Susen walked past the women, all of them still clustered in front of Sadat's house, and knocked at Teacher Leyla's door. They opened the door, and for a long time Aunt Susen's trembling whisper could be heard through the doorway—she was crying. When she came out with some lepyoshka in her hands, the women still clustered in the street suddenly began bustling around, buzzing like an agitated beehive, and with one accord started to congratulate her. But it was as if Aunt Susen didn't hear a thing. She just muttered something, shaking all over, and every vein in her face pulsed.

"Did you see? He came back! Could death really take someone like that? Allah himself wouldn't fool with him, with that dog, to hell with that Allah! You saw him: sticking out his pot belly, shoulders like a bull's! Did anyone come back from the army with that kind of fat face? Looks like he found himself a whore there, too, wherever he's been lounging around until now! Three years since the war was over— and here he is now! Welcome him! Ooh, the damned bastard! He won't just get under my skin now, the wicked man, he'll flay it off my back! He should've perished, disappeared in a foreign land. But no, he's arrived home! His whore pined for him! Well? What are you gawking at me for? Go see her—it's a holiday for her! Let her get dressed up to greet her special guest! Let her smear henna all over herself!"

"All over herself!" Aunt Susen shrieked, walking past us. If we hadn't still been little ones, she would have said something else— "Let her smear herself *there*!"—but we understood everything all the same. She went into her house; the women started chewing over the situation. Some were convinced that Susen was now out of luck: once again heads would be slapped, ears boxed. Others said that didn't have to happen. One had to think that Elmurad had sown his wild oats, gotten wiser: would he really start visiting Gyulshen again?

I don't know who thought about what, who dreamed what dreams that hot summer night lying in the yard or on the iwan: I just know that I lay down to sleep on the roof. And that as soon as I lay down, the moon immediately set. And I also know that when I lay down on the roof and the moon went down behind the mountains, I no longer wanted to be a doctor or an engineer—or anything I'd dreamed of becoming before. I wanted to be Uncle Elmurad—that big, that powerful. And that night I became Uncle Elmurad. No, no, I didn't sleep—I looked at the stars. And no matter how sorry I felt for Aunt Susen, when I became Uncle Elmurad, I immediately found myself at Gyulshen's house: I have no idea how. The moon hadn't yet touched the walls, the door was in shadow. Gently, unhurriedly, I knocked at that dark door. Somewhere a dog started to bark. And I began to feel that I couldn't wait any longer. Not one second longer. But no one asked, "Who's there?" and no one fumbled with the latch. The door opened instantly, and Gyulshen stepped forward to meet me. She was wearing just her shift, a white shift for sleeping; her breast was exposed, her hair loose about her shoulders. I embraced her, pressed her head to my chest, clasped her in my big, strong arms. "I came back for your sake, Gyulshen, only for you!" Gyulshen didn't say anything; she smiled. I said, "I love you, Gyulshen." She started to cry, and I pressed her head even harder to my chest so that the tears moistening my shirt pierced my chest, my heart. Then I began kissing Gyulshen: first I kissed her hair, then her eyes, then her lips, her breast... Then I heard Aunt Susen's voice: "Let her smear henna all over herself! Let her smear henna! Smear henna! Henna! Henna! Henna!"

At noon the next day I caught sight of Gyulshen near our house. She was walking along the empty street, head hung low. At Aunt Sadat's house she looked cautiously around—besides me, there was no one else near—gave the low-slung door a push, and was then hidden behind the almond trees.

I don't know how I'd found myself at Gyulshen's house the previous evening when the moon set and I turned into Uncle Elmurad. I don't know how long I was there, and I don't know how long I hung around by the crack in the wall separating our yard from Aunt Sadat's yard either. First Aunt Sadat and her guest stood by the window and whispered about something secretly and mysteriously, the way only women can whisper. Then Aunt Sadat went into the house and dragged out her enormous mattress. Dear Lord, it had been a long time since she'd brought that out! And to think that Aunt Sadat had solemnly dragged that splendid, enormous mattress out of her house several times a day before the war! One of the women who visited Aunt Sadat every day would stretch out blissfully on the mattress, and the hostess, giggling and whispering something in her ear, would set about plucking her eyebrows. She'd always been able to pluck eyebrows; it was practically a profession for her, but for some reason I'd completely forgotten about both Aunt Sadat's skill and her enormous mattress.

And now she pulled out the mattress and spread it on the grass in the very same spot where she'd always spread it before. Gyulshen yawned, stretched out, stuck out her large, round breasts, and then she smiled that special, curious smile that I always noticed on women as they lay down on Aunt Sadat's mattress. She pulled the gauze scarf from her head and, throwing it over the branch of an almond tree, spread herself out luxuriantly on the mattress. I couldn't exactly say when she was more beautiful—lying now on the mattress beneath the almond tree, or lit up by the moon at night (something I'd had to imagine because the real moon had set)—I simply don't know. But I do know for a fact that the grass around the mattress on which Gyulshen lay was uncommonly fine. And the almond tree on whose branch her headscarf hung white was astonishingly beautiful. And even the wart on Aunt Sadat's nose was attractive then... Many years have passed since that time. The grass on which the mattress lay is probably not the same grass. But the almond tree stands as it stood then, and the buds still pop out in the spring, and its flowers bloom, and each time I look at that almond tree, I remember how beautiful it was: that tree was incredibly, unbelievably beautiful then.

3

Where we live, no one says simply "a tree." We can't imagine such a thing. In every garden, in every yard there are trees by the dozen, and each one has its own name; some even have nicknames. And every small child will tell you who in the village has the sweetest cherry plums, whose apricots ripen first, whose walnuts have the thinnest shells. For us, a tree is a living creature. There are favorite trees that are like actual children to the people who look after them, and those caregivers can receive the kind of bounty from certain trees that you won't see from any son. It's not for nothing that we have the saying "Better a tree that bears fruit than a son who bears none."

But this certainly doesn't mean that trees in our region are valued only for their fruit. It may be that the tree produces no fruit at all but is cherished: one fine day you suddenly find out that you first saw the light of day "under that apple tree, my son." And that your mother's contractions began "under that cherry-plum over there." Or it turns out that "your cradle hung from that walnut tree over there." There are trees that perished long ago from old age but to this day live in people's memories. Many a time my grandmother, laying down her troubles and sorrows, would suddenly start talking about some out-of-this-world pear trees that apparently once grew on our land back before it was taken by the collective farm. And what grapes there were, each one as big as a cow's teat! But the main thing was the mulberries. As soon as my grandmother started talking about mulberry trees, she couldn't stop: I don't think any other person on earth could talk about mulberry trees the way she did. When my grandmother started talking about mulberries, her face was transformed, lit up. And the silky, young grass was already turning green around the mulberry trees, strewn with light-filled, ripe berries, like amber. Young girls appeared in the green meadow, not today's drab women—lazy, heavy-footed—but the way they were before: agile, nimble-fingered. With songs and rhymes, they picked every last berry over the course of an hour. And the next morning the glade would again grow yellow with ripe mulberries—large, juicy, transparent, like amber.

Why did my grandmother talk so passionately about mulberries in particular? Could her firstborn son perhaps have come into the world under one of those trees? I don't know. But I do know that in spring, when the silkworm breeders went into the collective farm orchard with billhooks in their hands to chop off the mulberry branches, my grandmother would be overcome with distress. Sometimes it seemed to me that the complete rejection of and even enmity that my grandmother felt toward the collective farm sprang from this annual hacking of the mulberry trees. My grandmother never set foot in the collective farm orchard—she couldn't bear to see the mutilated, abused trees. My grandmother often said that they just needed to plant more saplings for the silkworms; that's what people had always done in the past. And to raise one's hand to an old tree, hack at it with a billhook—my grandmother thought that was shameful. She was quite elderly, and it was probably difficult for her to witness such disrespect for age.

We also had mulberries in our yard, and pears, and every other kind of tree. And all of these trees belonged to me, although that doesn't mean, of course, that they were all equal in my eyes: I knew their shortcomings too well. The "idlers" stood out for their capricious ways:

while the fruits were green, just look, the branches broke, and when the time came for them to ripen, the tree would suddenly up and drop half of its fruit. I particularly remember one apricot tree: in spring it was completely covered in flowers, but you wouldn't get any fruit from it, the miser. Oh, how those idlers angered me! I cursed them roundly and sometimes even hit them with stones. And yet I bawled all day when they sawed down the pear tree near the cowshed—and what a hateful tree it was, you wouldn't find a stingier one in the whole village. I bawled, but my father chuckled; that time, for some reason, he was pleased that I was crying.

I divided the trees into male and female. The black cherries and plums were of the female sex, of course, and the apples and pears were male. Where this division came from, I don't know. In any case, it didn't depend on height, nor on girth. Otherwise, the enormous plane trees wouldn't be young girls, and the short, sprawling hazelnuts wouldn't represent young men for me to this very day. This division had been worked out in my head immediately and for all time. Only the quince gave me pause. This is how it happened: one spring morning the quince flowered, and on that same spring morning Teacher Leyla came to school in a blindingly white scarf. When I glanced at the quince spilling its dazzling, white branches over the wall on my way home from school, I immediately understood that it was a girl, and I wondered why I hadn't understood that before!

4

In the fall of that same year, Uncle Elmurad planted four mulberry seedlings in the street in front of his house. There wasn't really anything special about that; anyone might have thought to plant trees. But we never planted mulberries, not because we were lazy but because we didn't want our work to go to waste—we knew that when summer came, once again there wouldn't be enough food for the silkworms, and even if you screamed or howled like a wolf, they'd hack off your mulberry trees, leaving only the trunks. And who needs trunks? So people didn't plant mulberries, although what's better than a mulberry tree in front of your house? But Uncle Elmurad planted them. He said they could hack off the branches, if necessary; the silkworms would die without food. He also insisted that if everyone planted young mulberries in pairs in front of their houses, then the "repersentative" with shoulder marks wouldn't prowl around the yards but be satisfied with what was on the street. He said this with good reason because every spring at the end of May, when there was nothing left to feed the silkworms, something unimaginable happened in the village. A few women fell on their knees in front of the representative, crying and pleading. There was always some woman who embraced a tree, shielding it with her body: "Go ahead," she'd say, clutching it so tightly that you couldn't tear her away, "hack off my head, but don't touch this tree!" In short, other than Uncle Elmurad, only Aunt Nabat resolved to plant a mulberry tree in front of her house. I watched as she dug a large hole, panting heavily. Then she dragged a crooked, humpbacked sapling from somewhere and planted it in that hole. No one else in our village wanted to plant trees in the street.

If Uncle Elmurad had set about the business more firmly, if he'd explained, if he'd made his case, then perhaps he'd have convinced our fellow villagers to plant mulberries. But Uncle Elmurad didn't like making long explanations. On the whole, he was a bit different. Although it had been many months since he returned to the village, I never once saw him sitting in front of the mosque. Uncle Elmurad had no patience for idlers, couldn't bear smokers. The second he appeared on the street we immediately hid our cigarettes, although there was never an instance of Uncle Elmurad scolding or expressing disapproval of anyone as he passed by. Now Khashim hid his smoking from his father and took pains to sneak away when he went out into the street. Uncle Elmurad himself worked tirelessly; in the morning he went out to the fields with his shovel on his shoulder, and in the evening he puttered around his garden until dark. Not only did he transplant dozens of young trees to his own yard, he stuck poles between his and the neighboring fence and draped grapevines over his fence, attaching them to the poles with thin twigs of quince. Uncle Elmurad transplanted trees to his yard, reinforced the walls with wood chips, coated the roof; Khashim maintained that his father was also getting ready to build a bath.

Uncle Elmurad was always so busy, so engrossed in his own affairs, that it seemed nothing else mattered to him, that he didn't have any idea how people lived in our village.

But it turned out that he did have an idea. When the accounting and re-election meeting was convened that winter, it became clear that Uncle Elmurad knew quite well how the village lived, what was happening in the streets, and even the fact that a few girls went to school barefoot. Indeed, he began his remarks with those barefoot girls. He looked at the people sitting in the hall and said very angrily that real men wouldn't let girls in our village go to school barefoot. And to make things clearer, he began talking about some place called Europe as an example, saying that the girls there were painfully clean, so clean that after seeing them, one wouldn't even want to look at our grubby girls. We could keep our own children just as clean and comfortable, but we were exceedingly lazy, we didn't like to work—we just looked for something to steal. We sat with our mouths wide open and waited until the Soviet authorities put bread in those mouths.

Uncle Elmurad talked most of all about theft. Where there's theft, he said, there's no point in waiting for the harvest, for prosperity. And he spoke again about life in Germany: there, even if owners leave their shops open, no one takes anything. And he said that there was even the kind of country where housewives leave a container and money for milk on the porch at night; the milkman comes in the morning and pours out the right amount of milk, takes the money, and goes on his way— those are the kinds of miracles that exist in the world. Uncle Elmurad said that we should introduce this state of affairs in our village. In fact, Uncle Elmurad spoke longer than anyone else at that meeting, and at the end he looked at the district committee official sitting behind the red table in a well-pressed black suit and suddenly changed the subject. He spoke exactly like the drummer, Imamali, had once spoken; he talked about the Communist Party and the government and said that for us, the collective farm workers, all the appropriate arrangements had been put in place.

Everyone really liked Uncle Elmurad's remarks. The district committee official was the first to clap his hands, and he hadn't clapped for any previous speaker. Then he got up and said that as the district committee of the Communist Party had authorized him to hold this accounting and re-election meeting, he proposed that Comrade Elmurad be elected as the chairman of the collective farm, seeing as how the aforementioned comrade clearly understood the tasks set before us at present by the Party and the government. And he proposed that everyone in favor raise their hand. Everyone immediately raised their hand, and Uncle Elmurad was chosen as the chairman of the collective farm.

5

To everyone's surprise, that winter Uncle Elmurad did indeed build a bath in his yard. But he didn't forget about the public bathhouse. It was refurbished inside over the winter; when things warmed up in the spring, the outside was plastered. Then donkeys and mules spent a long time carting in firewood (enormous tree stumps), and just before Nowruz-Bayram, having heated the bath to the proper, scalding temperature, they re-opened the bathhouse.

And once again boys swarmed the square outside the bathhouse. Languid, clean, rosy-cheeked women again came out of the bath in the evenings. And although Uncle Elmurad didn't allow anyone to linger idly about, the square in front of the mosque was no longer silent.

Dawn had barely broken when crew leaders went around the houses rousing people for work. Immediately after the milking, Uncle Nazar, who'd been appointed chair of the inspection committee at the same meeting as Uncle Elmurad, appeared in the cowshed with a notebook in his hand: everyone who went to the field could receive a liter of milk. Uncle Elmurad divided the grain—what little remained from last year—among the collective farm workers. They gave a cash advance to those most in need. In short, the collective farm began to resemble a collective farm.

All the same, that spring Aunt Medina wasn't terribly eager to head to the fields. She kept trying to find work somewhere where there was a salary: in the library, as a caregiver in the kindergarten, or in the worst case as a cleaning woman at the first-aid station. Each day she went to the village council, but she never received anything definite from the chairman. Each day he put off his answer until tomorrow, and each day when she came home from the village council my aunt stood for a long time, leaning against the wall that separated our yard from Aunt Sadat's yard. My aunt was either silent, or else she cursed the new "executive committee" with all her might: a blockhead, a stump of wood, a dolt. Abutalib had been an able "executive committee," but this new chairman was the "executive committee" in name only. Apparently, there truly were no capable people left in the village.

That spring, as always, the trees flowered. The almond trees in Aunt Sadat's garden flowered so gloriously that it now became possible to hope: Aunt Sadat would finally buy a samovar and marry off Ebish. In the middle of April, as always, the silkworms were distributed among the houses, and in the middle of April the buds unfurled on the humpbacked sapling that Aunt Nabat had planted. And although at the end of May, as always, there wasn't enough food for the silkworms, the "repersentative" didn't come to the village, and those who were responsible for feeding the silkworms didn't walk around the yards with billhooks—Uncle Elmurad had procured several loads of mulberry leaves somewhere in a neighboring village. At the same time, people brought seedlings and planted a new mulberry grove.

That spring, as always, we celebrated both May Day and Victory Day. But that year we didn't stop by the collective farm orchard on the morning of the holiday and didn't haul armfuls of jasmine and roses to school—Uncle Elmurad had categorically forbidden people who didn't work there from entering the collective farm orchards. And the roses that had been planted from time immemorial just for their beauty and that ordinarily faded away without anyone noticing—and if they lived, it wasn't because of anyone's care—now became "collective farm property." Their petals were plucked and taken by the bucket to the receiving point at the canning factory.

One May morning Gyulshen suddenly appeared in our yard, although she hadn't visited my aunt regularly before that. She drank tea, took one of the three eggs that had just been boiled in the samovar, salted it heavily, and ate it. Then she collected my aunt, and they left together to gather rose petals. With those rose petals, my aunt's work at the collective farm began anew.

It was an unforgettable summer. Uncle Elmurad ordered us, the students in the upper grades, to go out into the fields. When the crew leaders came by in the cool mornings to rouse us for work, we were the first to leap up, and there was a special kind of pleasure in that early rising. How marvelous it was to eat a quick bite on the orchard grass or right at the edge of the field! We even brought the tea kettle with us and boiled tea on a fire. Right up until midday we mowed, collected fruit, harvested crops. And when the midday heat set in and the water was diverted to the orchard's reservoir ponds, we splashed in the cool water for hours. Uncle Elmurad forbade people to wander idly around the orchards; he posted guards with guns. I don't know how it was for the adults, but it gave us boys great pleasure to walk past the guard vigilantly protecting our collective farm goods.

During the daytime, we worked together: Azer, Rakhib, and I. Rakhib also worked in the evening, when everyone else had already departed for their homes. Well, he wasn't exactly working—he was walking around the mountain in that same place where we usually lay around reading poems or puzzling over Uncle Hasan's drawing. The chairman appointed Rakhib to guard the water, the same water that, bursting free of the mountain, rushed under the collective farm storehouse and fell into the reservoir with a roar that reminded me of Yakub's voice; in the evening they released that water over the collective farm fields. But even if Rakhib hadn't been on the mountain, no one would have dared take the water: you couldn't steal from Uncle Elmurad! For his duty at the reservoir, Rakhib was credited with fifteen workdays each month. Uncle Elmurad didn't discuss it openly, of course, but he said more than once that it was necessary to help Yakub's family because if there were five worthwhile men in the village, Yakub was one of them. I don't know why, but when Uncle Elmurad talked that way, I always remembered that Yakub beat his wife. Having thought it over, I even came to the conclusion that there was something secret, transcendent, some kind of special wisdom accessible only to real men in the act of giving a beating—after all, Uncle Elmurad himself often thrashed his wife soundly; it was precisely for that reason, of course, that he had such a high opinion of Yakub.

Rakhib walked around the slope by himself until it was quite dark. Azer and I rarely climbed up there now because the square in front of the mosque had again become noisy and interesting. Now the men gathered here in the evenings, sitting up late on a wooden platform set near the fence. Even Uncle Elmurad frequently put in an appearance here. However, he never sat down; he remained at a slight distance, standing there with his hands in his pockets, his legs in their heavy soldier's boots planted wide apart.

Most often the talk would be about the diverse countries many had chanced to visit during the war or about the harvest—they were figuring out how much they'd earn per workday this year. Uncle Khilal usually said that the Soviet authorities, okay, that was one thing, but these days there were way too many officials of all kinds. Uncle Isfendiyar considered the Soviet authorities to be a great power: if they wanted to, they could conquer the world in five years. From that, he somehow came to the conclusion that it was absolutely necessary to open the border with Iran. Talking about the border, Uncle Isfendiyar would worry a great deal; he'd start to curse and for good measure beat himself on the chest with his fist so hard that the dust flew from his jacket.

Uncle Murid always began with the same thing: "I'll tell you straight out: I'm not afraid of anyone!" After that, he'd generally say what he'd wanted to say. And no matter what anyone else was saying, Uncle Nazar stuck his own silly maxim into the conversation: "To each his own spoon, to each his own food."

Uncle Elmurad didn't get involved in these conversations; he mostly just joked from time to time. And everyone liked that except Uncle Isfendiyar, who couldn't bear his jokes—he immediately began thumping himself on the chest. He was angry because Uncle Elmurad told people not to listen to him. According to Uncle Elmurad, Uncle

179

Isfendiyar had his own interests in Iran: his father had left seven carpets in Tabriz during the time of Tsar Nicholas, and Isfendiyar was impatient to receive his inheritance—if they opened the border, he'd take off after his carpets.

Uncle Elmurad could joke for hours on end on any theme but one: he always spoke about women seriously, from the heart. A man should have the kind of wife, he'd say, that when he comes home from work, he sits near her until morning, until he goes back to the fields—as if he doesn't have the strength to tear himself away. The kind of wife, he'd say, that when you sit in a meeting of the Party district committee and they ream you out—you might be shaking in your britches, say—you suddenly remember that your wife is waiting at home, and consequently your soul grows so light that you forget the plan, and the report, and that they're preparing to slap you with a reprimand: you'd drop everything and fly to her as if you had wings. "A wife," he'd say, "isn't just a woman, she's the spring flowering of the soul." Every time Uncle Elmurad said "flowering of the soul" he nodded at the tree growing near the spring or pointed at the orchards beyond the river; I immediately recalled how they looked in flower, and for some reason I imagined a quince tree weighed down with white blossoms. Uncle Elmurad said all of this in complete seriousness, but the others chuckled: stop beating around the bush, Elmurad, they'd say, we know what kind of "flowering" you mean. Several of them probably thought that the chairman was starting such a conversation on purpose: he wanted to flaunt what a fine woman he had. Maybe that was the case, but for some reason it seemed to me that if even the slightest chance had arisen, Uncle Elmurad would have taken Gyulshen into his home and stopped all those conversations. The reason he kept having the conversations was that he couldn't take Gyulshen into his home.

Uncle Elmurad always turned out to be the center of attention, but this certainly didn't mean that Uncle Nazar, the chairman of the inspection committee, remained in the background or that no one paid attention to him. By no means. How could anyone miss him? Every evening he put on his beautiful black suit! Uncle Nazar took great pains to preserve his precious suit, but he didn't want to show it, so he sat together with everyone else on the wooden platform. But he didn't fool anyone: the suit gave him no peace, and everyone saw that the poor man was in agony. Another concern also plagued him—he kept jumping up, kept looking at the spring; if some hussy was heading for the water with her cooking pots, Uncle Nazar would immediately scold her, as was right and proper. I think he came up with his saying about the spoon, which he stuck into the conversation time and time again, while keeping an eye on the women with their spoons and pots here by the spring.

* * *

When it got dark, people gradually dispersed, and Rakhib came down from the mountain and went home. In the evenings, as usual, Ebish's song could be heard from Aunt Sadat's yard, and people thought with relief that this year, at last, Aunt Sadat was certain to buy a samovar and marry off her son. Teacher Leyla watered the street in front of her house and placed pears and apples on the table, as usual; and when Beanpole Husein passed by her yard, she smiled at him quietly and tenderly. But now things weren't limited just to smiles; they'd stand on the riverbank under the large, spreading walnut tree until dawn.

We worked at the collective farm until the last day of vacation. Azer and I were credited with forty-seven workdays. Rakhib was credited with sixty-five. That summer, without telling us, he finally caught the hedgehog that Aunt Shakhrabanu had tearfully begged for. I don't know if the hedgehog fat helped or not, but the woman lavished all kinds of praise on Rakhib and prayed to God that his father would be released from prison as soon as possible.

I don't remember whether anyone walked barefoot to school that winter. However, it's burned into my memory that a new director appeared that fall—a woman by the name of Ziyanet Shekerek-kyzy—and it immediately became known that there was a "mass of serious shortcomings" in the workings of the school. The most important shortcomings were detected among us, the students in the upper grades. To name just one, not a single member of the Komsomol— the Young Communist League—wore the Komsomol badge. Teacher Leyla, our homeroom teacher, found out about this before everyone else. She immediately traveled to the district center, bought badges with her own money, and pinned a badge on each of us at the very first lesson.

Then a campaign began against our fabric bookbags. All of our bookbags were, in fact, torn because our mothers had sewn them for most of us before the war. A few people immediately bought satin and sewed new bookbags; the rest began wrapping books in newspaper.

On the whole, many things in our school changed with the appearance of the new director. Tardiness, for example. That was the very first item. The bookbags, Komsomol badges, and all the rest of it— those came later. Ziyanet Shekerek-kyzy announced that we students in the upper grades must set an example for the younger students, and therefore the instant one of us arrived late, running up a minute after the bell, Ziyanet Shekerek-kyzy led the guilty party from classroom to classroom and the little ones chorused, "Shame! Shame! Shame!" so joyfully, so sincerely that it absolutely touched the heart.

Then our headmistress got her hands on a large church bell from somewhere and hung it from a beam above the school iwan, and it was decreed that Sadaf had to appear at school an hour before the beginning of classes to ring the bell. During the hour remaining at our disposal, it was expected that we would "rouse ourselves from sleep," "run through some calisthenics," "complete our morning toilets," and "break our fast." The only one of these that I fulfilled faithfully was washing my hands and face. The question of calisthenics only bothered me for a couple of days; I was afraid that Ziyanet Shekerek-kyzy had placed spies somewhere. Then I satisfied myself that there was no one behind the wall, no one peeking through a crack, and I calmed down. There was still the question of breakfast, but this was out of my hands: if my aunt was not too tired from the day before, she got up early and put on the samovar. Then we'd drink tea. If there was no tea, I grabbed a piece of bread and ate it on the road to school. In general, I could get by—it was enough to wash in the morning! However, someone managed to violate even that rule every day. Ziyanet Shekerek-kyzy regularly led those students around the classrooms, subjecting them to general opprobrium. Sometimes all the violators were immediately lined up on the athletic field; the director selected the cleanest and tidiest first graders, led them to the field, and they loudly shouted, "Shame! Shame! Shame!"

Of the three of us, none had been caught yet; none had been late even once. Each morning Sadaf began to ring her bell at the crack of dawn. To tell the truth, I immediately went back to sleep as soon as she stopped, but all the same I got up on time because I just knew when to get up—I'd had my own signal since the first grade, a signal that hadn't once let me down. Depending on which rock face of the mountain the sun had climbed, I knew exactly how much time remained until class began and could unerringly determine whether I'd be able to run to the spring or would have to "complete my morning toilet" at home, whether I should walk to school or run. I even knew how to drink my tea, whether I should pour it into the saucer to cool or had time to drink it out of the glass.

Each morning, having barely opened my eyes, I'd see the mountain lit up by the sun. I didn't just tell time by its light. For many years I immediately remembered whether or not we had bread as soon as I opened my eyes and looked at the mountain.

That fall everyone had bread; by the end of the summer, the grain had already been divided. Then they gave out walnuts in payment for days worked, and when they brought in the harvest from the melon fields, it turned into a real holiday. We kids raced to the melon fields three times to get the muskmelons and watermelons we'd honestly earned; then my aunt brought two more sackfuls of them on the mule.

At the end of autumn, money was distributed for days worked. Our tiny shop was cleaned out in a single day. And at the accounting and re-election meeting that winter, Uncle Elmurad said that next year there would even be butter in payment for days worked—not a lot, to be honest, around ten or fifteen grams—and sheep's cheese and, God willing, they'd manage to find honey.

In the fall Leyla got married. But Aunt Sadat again postponed Ebish's wedding for a year. She decided not to buy the samovar: "A samovar, so what? His bride can bring it in her dowry." Aunt Sadat had grand ideas of buying a carpet; she started up a conversation about the carpet with anyone planning to go to Baku or Yerevan.

That fall Aunt Nabat bought a samovar, although she had no intention of giving up her red tea kettle yet. She arranged Hasan's circumcision. She might have arranged circumcision for the youngest boy, too, but she couldn't make up her mind; she very much wanted Yakub to do everything himself when he returned.

We had a great many boys who ran around in girls' skirts after circumcision that fall; they ran around the streets in droves or romped on the square in front of the mosque. When the kids launched into games in front of the school gates, Aunt Shakhrabanu, who lived across from the school, shouted at the girls; for some reason they liked to tease the fellows in skirts, and for some reason Aunt Shakhrabanu didn't like that at all.

6

Uncle Elmurad had a leather field bag that he carried across his shoulder and a red fountain pen—he tucked the pen into the breast pocket of his soldier's shirt. And although I never once saw him open the leather bag or write with the red fountain pen, it never even occurred to me that Uncle Elmurad was illiterate. I found that out in the spring when there was a rumor about a merger of collective farms. It turned out that Uncle Elmurad was against the merger because he was illiterate; in a large, consolidated collective farm, they'd never let him remain chairman. Uncle Isfendiyar made that point on the square in front of the mosque: Elmurad, he said, was unlettered, he couldn't possibly manage two collective farms. The majority of those sitting nearby didn't agree with Uncle Isfendiyar; they even laughed at him, and he grew incensed and started to beat himself on the chest again. He shouted that there was nothing funny here and that even Murid's blind dog could see that Elmurad was beside himself when talk turned to the merger.

Uncle Murid, who had been dozing off to the side near the bathhouse, immediately jumped up, as if he'd just been waiting for Uncle Isfendiyar to say something about his blind dog. He started to shout about Isfendiyar, that Isfendiyar was a thousand times nastier than any dog because envy had rotted his guts: worms were swarming in his stomach. Why did Elmurad always stand in his way? Because that man spared no effort, he'd planted a new garden and put together a new bath and draped his vines on poles: whenever Isfendiyar looked at his trees, the worms raised a ruckus! He'd die of his worms! He'd die and lie around without burial—no one would want to dirty their hands! And the blind dog, God willing, would raise his leg over Isfendiyar's gravestone! In a word, Uncle Murid shamed him as well as he could and then, sitting down in his former corner, calmly added that Uncle Elmurad could easily manage not two, but ten collective farms.

Three days or so after that conversation, a meeting was convened in the club on the question of merging the collective farms. Incidentally, it didn't in the slightest seem to me that Uncle Elmurad was beside himself. On the contrary, his mood was excellent. He gave the first word to Uncle Nazar. Nazar picked up two thin pieces of printed paper about the merger, began reading, and read the papers to the end. The chairman didn't call on Teacher Misir for help, and while Uncle Nazar was reading, the teacher fidgeted uneasily in his chair.

Then Uncle Elmurad himself started speaking. He generally couldn't speak without joking, but he led the discussion about those two thin papers sent us from the district committee in all seriousness. He said that the Communist Party never took unnecessary decisions, that everything written on the sheets was correct and timely, and that we, the collective farmers, were in no way against it. We just thought that what was written on those papers didn't pertain to us. Large collective farms, those were different matters—they had thousands of hectares of land, and their fields were flat, no mountains or ravines there. But what about us? Where could tractors drive here? Orchards, melon fields... Well, if there were fruit growing or sericulture on that collective farm, then of course. We could join them with great pleasure. But their land was flat: wheat, beans, onions. And you can't put apricots and onions in the same storehouse. It's the same with cucumbers and tomatoes: they don't "share a bed" very well. With that, Uncle Elmurad indicated that serious conversation was finished and that we could now joke. Everyone started to laugh, and a few women covered their faces with their hands in embarrassment. Even the furrowed brow of Uncle Nazar, who'd been sitting tensely and gloomily as he read the papers, not knowing what to say, smoothed out after Elmurad's joke. And the stupid saying he'd thought up while watching the dishes being washed suddenly fell into place. Nazar loudly announced:

"To each his own spoon, to each his own food."

Then Aunt Zokhra was given a word because she worked in the mountains at the summer pastures, and if she'd climbed down to the village and come to the meeting, it meant that she had something to say. Aunt Zokhra got up and, placing her red, weatherbeaten hand on the secretary's shoulder, said the following:

"Write this down! The collective farm was dead, completely dead. Now it's come back to life. He brought it back to life—write that, write it!—he, this very Elmurad! He revitalized it! Did you write that? Good. Now write that I'm against the merger! Write it, write it! And write my whole name and the name of my father! I, Zokhra Khanoglan-kyzy, a collective farmer since 1933, a member of the Communist Party since 1934, do not agree to the merger! Write it down, don't be afraid! You understand, sometimes a husband and wife can't get along; how can we suddenly force two different villages to live in a single household?!"

Everyone liked the joke about the husband and wife as much as the recent one about the cucumbers and tomatoes because it hit Elmurad right between the eyes. Well, he was never at a loss for words, and he blurted out such a thing that the women started to squeal. On the whole, the meeting was remarkably cheerful, and a resolution was approved to write to Baku from our village. The resolution was adopted unanimously. We boys standing in the back by the wall also raised our hands so that our apricot collective farm wouldn't be merged with an onion farm.

Part Two

1

But either the quiet in our village doesn't depend all that much on what's taking place on the square in front of the mosque, or else I'm giving the word "quiet" some special meaning. When they called a second meeting a few days after that happy, noisy meeting, there couldn't possibly have been quiet on the square. That day the club was stuffed to bursting. There were more kids in front of it than had ever gathered before. They watered the street from the tearoom to the little square where cars parked in front of the administration building because on that day the director of the Zemotdel—the agricultural department—was supposed to come to the village.

What kind of quiet could there be when even performers from the House of Culture arrived? Two women—powdered, made up, their hair gleaming—walked along the club iwan; the male performers sat in the tearoom. Onstage, the tar and pipe could be heard behind the curtain; backstage, in the "Red Corner" room where adults usually read books and studied Party propaganda, Ziyanet Shekerek-kyzy tyrannized over the little kids. Today the collective farms were being merged, and an amateur concert was being given in honor of the event.

Maybe the people who'd been sitting in the overcrowded club since lunchtime awaiting "the Zemotdel" were sitting quietly. Or maybe the quiet was a function of the table that had occupied its appointed place since morning, and not even of the table itself but of the roses and the carafe of water that stood on it—the table covered in red satin, the bouquet of roses, the carafe of water. The director of the club had picked the roses somewhere, and the water was ordinary water from the spring, clean and clear. Maybe I wouldn't have remembered that water and wouldn't have been so frightened for the roses if the person whom the village called the Zemotdel hadn't walked into the club with such a threatening air; if at this meeting, as was usual, the chairman and secretary had been chosen; and if that person we called the Zemotdel hadn't towered over the table decorated with roses in such menacing solitude.

The director of the Zemotdel towered menacingly over the table decorated with roses and the carafe of water, but in the Red Corner, the first graders howled as before.

Uncle Elmurad was sitting on a stool off to the side. It was as if he'd deliberately positioned himself farther away, somewhat as if he'd sidelined himself. On the other side of the table, but much closer to it, sat Uncle Nazar and Aunt Zokhra. Those two certainly didn't look like people who were sidelining themselves from anything; on the contrary, both were waiting with great hope for the Zemotdel to propose that they take places behind the table covered with red satin. But the Zemotdel didn't call anyone to join him. Sitting at the table, he pulled out a cigarette, smoked, and was silent for a while, looking angrily around at the crowd. Then he suddenly turned to Uncle Elmurad:

"Stand up, crook!"

When the director of the Zemotdel shouted these words, fear fell upon the meeting, and it became so quiet that it was as if the people sitting in the club had disappeared, dissolved in the silence; the red table remained, the carafe of water remained, and the director of the Zemotdel remained. The roses also remained, but when the director started shouting at Uncle Elmurad, the roses trembled; I saw with my own eyes how they trembled, I swear—I swear by everything holy I've got left in the world.

Uncle Elmurad did not stand up. In the first place, why should he stand up? He surely wasn't a schoolboy. In the second place, he couldn't stand up because Gyulshen was in the hall. When the Zemotdel started shouting at Uncle Elmurad and the people sitting in the club disappeared for a moment, I instantly saw—besides the table, the carafe of water, and the roses—Gyulshen. Without looking at her, I distinctly saw her light-blue jacket, the white scarf on her head, even the watch on her wrist—the same gold watch that people said Elmurad had brought her from Berlin.

"Just you look at him! Look at this disrupter! A crook who goes against the Party!"

This time the Zemotdel said "crook" much more quietly. It would have been possible not to say it at all because the hall was still completely empty: there weren't any people. There was only the table, the carafe of water, and the bouquet of roses. And there was Gyulshen, but maybe no one besides me noticed her presence.

It was quiet. Completely quiet. Except that from time to time, the sound of children's voices reached us from the Red Corner. Then the voice of Aunt Zokhra rang out.

"Fine, Comrade Representative," she said. "We see that you can threaten us, but when are you going to get to the point?"

And here even Uncle Nazar plucked up his courage.

"We misjudged, Comrade 'Presentative," he said. "Forgive our mistake."

People began whispering in the hall. The fear eased a little. But the representative evidently needed that fear. And he again started shouting at Uncle Elmurad:

"Well, out with it, how many beehives do you have?"

Uncle Elmurad really did have a great many hives. He was known as an expert on beekeeping, not just on our street but throughout the whole village, because he spent entire evenings near the hives. If anything went wrong with bees, you went to Elmurad. As soon as the warm weather arrived and the hives were opened, the bees were everywhere, all around; they flew into the gardens, buzzed about the flowers, hummed in the branches of the almond tree bending over the spring.

I had no doubt that as we were now talking about bees, Uncle Elmurad would certainly say something. But once again he didn't answer. Then the representative shouted even louder. Uncle Elmurad got up unhurriedly, and it was the right thing to do—otherwise, I wouldn't have seen how much taller and heavier he was than the director of the Zemotdel. Uncle Elmurad smiled, by God, he smiled; I wouldn't have believed it if I hadn't seen that smile with my own eyes. And he said this:

"Comrade Zemotdel, you'd better conserve your cigarettes, because it seems that this conversation is going to be a long one. You might not have enough cigarettes, and we'll be embarrassed before you: we don't sell that kind in our little stall. And the second thing is, this performance is of no use to either of us because the real performers have arrived—they're going to give us a concert. And the kids are worn out—rehearsal after rehearsal. So leave my hives out of it! Don't even think of laying a finger on them—I won't let you! After this kind of meeting, you have to eat honey for ten years so that your guts don't burn out!"

"Your guts have already burned out! The venom of ownership has poisoned you! And yet you carry a Communist Party membership card in your pocket!"

"Excuse me, Comrade Director of the Zemotdel, but I have to tell you: I don't carry my Party card in my pocket. It's at home, locked in the trunk. It lies deep in that trunk, under the seventeen orders and medals I brought home from the war. It's a bit difficult to get it out of there—you have to lift the medals. And they're heavy, Comrade Zemotdel! So heavy that not everyone has the strength to lift them: you could strain yourself!"

The Zemotdel was instantly transformed. It's hard for me to explain exactly what happened to him, but looking at his face, it was possible to say without a shadow of a doubt: he hadn't earned any orders for distinguished military service. In fact, it seemed to me that even if the director of the Zemotdel had earned such an order, he wouldn't have said the word "crook" again. Because when he'd repeated it before, no one had been frightened; no one had disappeared from the hall. On the contrary, the crowd had grown bigger; a few people even started laughing. And a curious thing happened. The third time he said "crook," the director of the Zemotdel suddenly began to look remarkably like one of those fellows who loves to cheat at a game. It's impossible to express how much he looked like that. I saw many of those cheaters in my boyhood, and I remember them all as if it were today; one bit me on the hand when I knocked him flat on his back. Another, having lost at alchiki, attacked me with a stone in his hand. Once I won several raw eggs from a fellow on Nowruz-Bayram: the lowlife threw the last one right in my face. And they tore my shirt and cut my head with stones, and yet I remember nothing so well as the cow manure with which one scoundrel plastered me. When the representative shouted "crook" at Uncle Elmurad for the third time at the meeting that day, I immediately recalled that fellow and the meaty slap of manure.

So they tore my shirt and drew blood from my head; that happens sometimes even now, and each time I force myself to smile. But when matters get to the point of manure, I can't smile. I immediately remember how desperately I howled on the square then, smeared from head to toe with manure, and it's all I can do not to burst into tears. He laid me out flat many times, and I didn't respond—I just lay there. I went to great lengths to avoid getting hit in the face with manure again. But my God, you can't always lose, can't always give in!

When the director of the Zemotdel shouted "crook" for the third time and began to look remarkably like that scoundrel with the manure, it was clear that he was uncomfortable—he kept fidgeting in his chair. People in the hall were whispering, laughing softly. The Zemotdel left Uncle Elmurad in peace and turned to the meeting.

"Well, everyone who's against the merger, raise your hands!" he said, and his face again started to resemble the face of someone who's playing dirty.

Among those sitting in the front, only Aunt Zokhra raised her hand. In the back rows, Azer was the first. Then other kids raised their hands. I raised my hand last, but not because I was the most cowardly: this all smelled very much of manure, and I knew better than all the other kids what that was.

They quickly booted us kids out of the hall—small fry who didn't even belong to the collective farm had no business hanging around meetings. I don't know how things went after that, but I've remembered the Zemotdel's face my whole life. And the table covered in red satin, and the carafe of water, and the roses trembling in fear—I could swear, even now, that they were afraid, swear by everything holy I've got left in the world.

We kids hung around the gray Willys jeep in front of the administration building until the end of the meeting. The meeting concluded, the director of the Zemotdel left, and probably because the merger took place anyway and Uncle Elmurad was replaced, the gray jeep twisting along the mountain slope hummed loudly and cheerfully, like a boy who's won a game and scampered away without allowing his opponent any chance to recoup his losses. Then came the concert. First our kids sang in chorus. Then the performers gave a show. And immediately after the concert it became known that Uncle Elmurad would be put in prison. It turned out that he'd plundered Berlin and that ten kilograms of gold lay in the suitcase he'd carried on his shoulder at that time. I don't know who launched the rumor about gold, but Aunt Susen immediately confirmed it all. That evening she circled around the spring until dark—first with her bucket, then her pitcher, then her tea kettle. And with every step she stopped to whisper to someone.

Aunt Susen reckoned that if they didn't put him in prison now, it meant that the Soviet authorities had absolutely no brains. She kept harping on the gold watch that that "whore" wore on her wrist and about the ten kilograms of gold brought in the suitcase from Berlin; by nightfall, ten kilograms had grown into a pood. On top of that, Aunt Susen reported that besides gold, there was also a pistol in that suitcase—he'd brought it to kill her one night, and the next morning he'd lead the whore home.

Aunt Susen's holiday ended with nightfall. As soon as it got dark, I heard her usual wailing in the yard, and I couldn't believe my ears: for some reason I'd been certain that Uncle Elmurad would spend that night with Gyulshen. That was most likely the case, and it probably wasn't Aunt Susen's husband but her son Khashim who'd decided to school her.

At the end of first period the next day, Ziyanet Shekerek-kyzy sent for us. Azer, Rakhib, and I were expected to appear on the iwan— we'd been caught after all. As soon as the bell finished ringing, Azer dashed home for his Komsomol badge, and Rakhib and I stood on the iwan and couldn't figure out what was happening—if this was about badges, we both had ours. A few more students from the upper grades appeared, and they were made to stand next to us. Then Ziyanet Shekerek-kyzy arrived and explained that yesterday, in voting against the merger of the collective farms, we'd shamed our local school. This could only mean one thing—now the first graders would be led in, and affairs would take their regular course: "Shame! Shame! Shame!" But no chorus was convened that day. On the contrary, the little ones running up from all sides to shame us were chased from the iwan, and Ziyanet Shekerek-kyzy said she had something serious to say to us. I don't remember whether our headmistress spoke for very long, but I remember extremely well that in talking about the masks and disguises that people such as Uncle Elmurad put on, Ziyanet Shekerek-kyzy cited examples from two plays, *Almas* and *Khayat*. Without those two examples, I'd never in my life have believed that our former chairman had been wearing a mask. But when I saw Uncle Elmurad returning from the fields at sunset with his shovel on his shoulder, I no longer had any doubt that he had been disguising his true face.

Lying on the slope of the mountain that evening, we worked out a plan for a single, grand operation. Thoroughly wracking our brains, we thought up a wonderful name for our plan: "Operation Lightning." The name wasn't an accident—in the coming night when everyone went to bed, we'd redirect the river water in the irrigation canal and turn it on

Uncle Elmurad's garden; with lightning speed, the water would level his garden to the ground. And that night we did it: we redirected a large portion of the river water in the irrigation canal and released it into Uncle Elmurad's garden. But it turned out the next morning that the water hadn't washed out the garden at all, but streamed, gurgling, along the street. It had undermined Aunt Sadat's wall, and she, up to her knees in water, dammed the flow with stones, cursing the wretches whose idea it had been to release the stream into the village... That was the end of "Operation Lightning." For a long time we couldn't figure out who might have diverted the flood from the garden. Only much later did we find out that Rakhib had done it; after leaving us, he'd gone back to the irrigation canal and redirected the flow of water, but as he had been too lazy to go all the way to the stream, he released the flow directly into the street.

2

That spring we celebrated May Day and Victory Day just as before. They hung banners on the tearoom and the collective farm administration building and portraits over the doors of the club. Now we ran freely around the collective farm orchard; we carried armfuls of jasmine to school for May Day, and after Victory Day the square and the schoolyard and all the streets were strewn with rose petals.

At the beginning of May, as always, the mulberries unfurled their leaves, and at the end of May, as always, their leaves were insufficient to feed the silkworms. Silkworm breeders with billhooks in their hands and ropes at their belts walked around the village, spreading horror and confusion everywhere. They hacked off the top of Aunt Nabat's crooked, hump-backed sapling and stripped bare the thin branches of Uncle Elmurad's seedlings. The silkworm breeders hacked down one of them, and he hacked down the others himself. He chopped and grumbled: "And what are you doing, you scoundrels? Mutilated the whole tree! If you mangle them this badly, there won't be anything left to hack next year!"

But the next year they also chopped, only this time they chopped even more of the trees in the yards. The shouting began at dawn near Aunt Sadat's house and gradually shifted around the village, reaching Aunt Nabat's house around lunchtime. We heard it in school right before lunch, and soon after lunch Aunt Nabat's famous "sugary" mulberries stood without a single twig; toward evening Sadaf ran around the streets shouting that her mother-in-law was dying. A crowd of women flocked to say goodbye to Aunt Nabat. There was no goodbye, however. Running into their yard, I discovered the old woman walking around; Aunt Nabat was wearing a white shirt that looked very much like a shroud, but in her hand was a long pole. With the pole, Aunt Nabat chased the women from the yard. Huddled in a knot, frightened, they ran to the gate, and Aunt Nabat shrieked after them in a raspy voice:

"Get out while you can! Dead! How can I die, if my son hasn't come home from prison? Yakub hasn't come home from prison, and they're saying I died! I won't give you the satisfaction of dying! Get out of here, godless heathens!"

Aunt Nabat drove the women through the gate and even chased them a little way down the street. The women ran away from her in a crowd. I also ran, and Aunt Medina too. But we had to turn around midway because Aunt Nabat suddenly shouted loudly:

"Medina, where in the world are you going?!" And running out of breath, she said, barely audible: "Oy, sweetie, I'm dying!"

We turned around and followed Aunt Nabat into the house. She lay down on the bed and, paying no attention to me and Rakhib, showed Aunt Medina how swollen her legs were. Then she talked for a long time, and what she said very much resembled a farewell. Aunt Nabat ordered Rakhib and me to always live in friendship and agreement: we were men, the clan depended on us, and our clan had always had plenty of enemies.

Aunt Nabat talked about Yakub—the pride of our clan—for a long time, then about Yakub's father and my grandfather. She even commanded that when she died, she should be laid to rest between Yakub's father and my grandfather. But Aunt Nabat didn't die then.

* * *

After a couple of days, she rose from her bed. After a week, the swelling went down. That spring Aunt Nabat bought a pregnant goat from Gyulshen's father, but before the goat gave birth, Sadaf died. One night she suddenly started bleeding from her throat; the next day they washed her in the yard near the irrigation canal, and toward evening we lowered Sadaf into her grave. Then the three of us—Azer, Rakhib, and I—walked a long way off and climbed the mountain behind the cemetery. We sat down there, not looking at our village; then Azer proposed that we swear our brotherhood. For that, it was necessary to prick our fingers with a thorn. We pricked our fingers with the thorn, each sucked a little blood from the others, and we became brothers. Rakhib had lost his mother, but now he had us. Azer had had a good idea.

3

It grew quiet again in the village. Perhaps we'd never experienced such quiet. The bathhouse had been closed a week after Uncle Elmurad was driven from the chairmanship. The door stayed locked for a long time. And then one night some son of a bitch—who, as Uncle Nazar said, could have cut off his mother's breast without a second thought—made off with the door. From time to time Uncle Nazar attempted to protect the bathhouse, to save it from desecration. But mischief-makers did their business, and now it was impossible to walk near the bathhouse because of the stench. The walls were covered with indecent drawings, and although naked women had been drawn by various people, the caption beneath all the drawings was one and the same: "Gyulshen."

But Gyulshen didn't know anything about the drawings. She didn't go to work; she never appeared near the bathhouse. That summer her father promised her in marriage to one of his friends in a neighboring village, and she was supposed to leave soon for her husband's house. Gyulshen didn't talk to anyone about that and didn't consult with anyone about anything. More and more, she busied herself with grapes. My aunt said that Gyulshen hadn't left a single bunch of grapes in her own yard intact. She also visited us, as if her only purpose was to spoil the grapes. She wandered silently under the vines, thought, then became attracted to some bunch, took it in her hand, and started picking the grapes. She'd pick out one or two grapes and throw them away. It was as if she wanted to spoil the entire bunch, to not leave a single one whole once she left the village.

Gyulshen and Aunt Medina spoke very little; my aunt said nothing about the bunches of grapes, of course. Gyulshen walked around the yard picking grapes off the bunches, and my aunt sat in front of the window and patched up old clothes. Let's say that there was something they couldn't talk about because of my presence. But I noticed that even when I wasn't there, they were silent. Several times I came into the yard and found the following scene: Gyulshen wandering among the trees and Aunt Medina standing a little way off, leaning against the wall and silently thinking. That summer the wall dividing our yard from Aunt Sadat's yard again became my aunt's preferred place because everything was going badly at the collective farm, and there was absolutely no hope of receiving anything in payment for days worked. Once again everyone pilfered what they could, but as before, Aunt Medina couldn't bring herself to steal. The orchards gradually fell into neglect, and there was no point in even talking about the melon fields.

That summer, contemplating things by the wall at length, my aunt thought mostly about me. In the fall I was supposed to go to Baku. I'd already sent my documents to the university and received notification that I'd been accepted. They accepted me without any exams—I finished school with the gold medal—but I had nothing to wear, I didn't have a suitcase, and we'd saved up only the hundred rubles I earned at the receiving office for fruit.

That summer I thought about my aunt no less than she thought about me. I went to the collective farm only because of her; from morning to night I stood on the threshing board, and in the evening I tended the oxen that had dragged that board during the day. All for the sake of an armful of firewood that I hauled home every evening; I was stocking up firewood for my aunt for the whole winter, dry walnut wood. And then a remarkable thing happened. One morning when I brought the oxen in from the pasture—the threshers hadn't arrived yet—Uncle Murad, who was assigned to guard the threshing floor, gave me a strange order. Without pausing his morning prayers, he ordered me to pour some grain into my sack and take it home right away. I was taken aback—that wasn't something you decided to do on a whim. Uncle Murad even seemed a bit scared himself. But he immediately got angry and started shouting at me:

"Get a move on! Why are you standing there like a lump? I'm looking the other way—do you hear?!"

He certainly should have been looking the other way because Uncle Murad observed the fast and completed his prayers, and a person who completes his prayers and observes the fast shouldn't see such things. Especially as this wasn't just theft, but theft on the threshing floor, and Uncle Murad had told me more than once: "A place where they steal grain from the threshing floor won't have a harvest for a thousand years!"

One evening when I came home, my aunt, beaming with happiness, showed me a smart, dark-blue suit; a small, blue suitcase; and a whole stack of ten-ruble notes—these had been brought to me by Gyulshen.

Walking once along the street near some women, I overheard that the gold watch Uncle Elmurad brought Gyulshen from Berlin had been seen on the wrist of Misir's wife: Gyulshen had sold it to Misir.

Returning home one night, I found out that Gyulshen had gotten married. She'd left forever. My aunt pointed at the setting sun—the village where Gyulshen's husband lived lay in that direction. Then my aunt glanced at the bunches of grapes plucked by Gyulshen. I also glanced at them: how pitiful they were, unneeded by anyone.

One night in August I transferred the oxen to the drover and said a final goodbye to Uncle Murid. The next morning, dressed up in the blue suit Gyulshen had given me, I traveled to the bathhouse in the district center, and there, sitting in the barber's chair, I suddenly saw Yakub in the mirror. The barber had just started cutting my hair, Yakub's face was covered in soapy lather, but on seeing me, he jumped out of his chair, put his arms around both me and the chair, and began to kiss me. Yakub and I couldn't stop looking at one another in the mirror. Then we drank tea in the tearoom at the bazaar. After that, I visited the bathhouse, and returning home in the evening, I saw Yakub in our yard at home. He was sitting on the palas carpet and drinking tea. My aunt was walking under the grapevines in the same place where Gyulshen had recently loved to walk. The only difference was that my aunt wasn't plucking grapes from the bunches and that, in contrast to Gyulshen, my aunt was crying; on seeing me, she began quickly wiping away her tears.

I sat next to Yakub. My aunt poured tea for me. I saw how difficult it was for her to ask even the simplest questions: how was my bath? How did I get home, in an open car or one with a roof? My aunt would get angry when I returned home after the bath in an open car. That day I'd actually gotten a ride in a traveling movie van. Hearing this, my aunt immediately started talking about the movies.

"What movie is it?" she asked.

Aunt Medina divided all films into three types: funny ones, sad ones, and those with songs. She liked the ones with songs best of all because in those films there had to be orchards, sunrises, and sunsets; in those films young men and women strolled around under flowering trees and sang, in chorus or alone. I don't remember which film they'd brought that evening. But I remember very well that while asking me about the film, my aunt didn't stop walking around. And that the film didn't interest her at all, that she was asking me questions simply to drive away the quiet, and that driving away that quiet was very difficult.

The quiet continued, such quiet. In the distance beyond the trees, the sun was already settling into a grayish haze. But it was still hot, all the same; in the thicket of almonds in the neighbor's yard, the cicadas moaned from the sweltering heat, and it seemed that the heat itself was moaning.

Yakub sat by the wall, leaning his shoulder against it. He kept trying to straighten up, to sit the way you're supposed to, but he was very tired; it was clear from his face that he was falling asleep, that he didn't have the strength to say a word. He just lifted his head and smiled from time to time.

The quiet continued, the quiet. Except that my aunt walked under the grapevines, and the bees buzzed tirelessly. They circled around the spoiled clusters of grapes, attached themselves to our glasses, crawled into the sugar bowl. Yakub glanced at the bees, then at me—he wasn't even able to wave a hand. It was necessary to drive away the bees, but I didn't want to: the sun would sink behind the mountain, and the bees would fly away by themselves.

For some reason I very much wanted them to fly away on their own that day. And for the cicadas in the thicket of almonds to stop chirring on their own. Soon they'd stop. And hauling water from the spring, Dinara would water the street in front of Aunt Sadat's house and sweep the spot extra clean where the women gathered to gossip in the evening. Dinara was now Ebish's wife, a young housewife, and a young housewife must haul water and water the street in front of her house so that everyone can see that she isn't lazy.

The bees would soon fly away, crawl into the hives, and Uncle Elmurad, returning home, would close them up to rest until morning. I very much wanted Yakub to go away and lie down to rest until morning. But he sat there, leaning his shoulder against the wall, and was silent. Only my aunt kept talking and talking, walking ceaselessly around under the grapevines. She was talking so that it didn't get quiet. And so that Yakub wouldn't fall asleep. Finally she came up to me and stopped.

"And our Sadyk is leaving for Baku," she said. Smiled. Fell silent. "What places he'll see! What beautiful suits he'll buy... He'll never want for anything!" She was saying this like a poem, like a story: "And I'll start working at the collective farm. And Yakub. We'll send Sadyk money..."

She'd had to walk a long time under the grapevines until she found the strength to say those words. Words that meant just one thing: "I've agreed to marry Yakub." It was a good thing that she finally said them. She said them and grew calm; she sat down near me and looked at Yakub. Yakub brightened up, smiled sleepily, but didn't have the strength to say a single word.

We sat there a long time afterwards in the quiet, but it was now a completely different quiet. The cicadas in the thicket of almonds still moaned from the sweltering heat, and the heat moaned from their moans. The sun had already touched the mountains and was just about to disappear behind the heights. It was a strange sun: tired, in some kind of sleepy haze. As if it weren't to blame for this terrible heat, as if it weren't its fault that the cicadas were moaning from the heat. As if it weren't the sun, but one of us: maybe Gyulshen, whom they'd forcibly sent there, beyond the mountain; maybe Aunt Medina, who'd said what she had to say and been drained of all her energy except for the light in her eyes, light that was veiled now by the haze; maybe Yakub, who'd arrived dead tired from prison and wanted only to sleep, sleep, sleep...

First the bees flew away, then the cicadas quieted down. When the sun set, Yakub finally stood up. I went out into the street with him in my new, blue suit. And everything all around was dark blue like my new, blue suit. It was noisy, full of people. Up on his roof, Uncle Elmurad was busily stamping the earth, securing the gutters—after such sweltering heat, it was bound to rain.

I don't know if it rained then or not. I remember only that the street that night was vivid, dark blue like my new, blue suit—and I ran away from that overpowering blueness, scrambled up the mountain to where the three of us always sat together, and sat there a long time alone. And while I sat there, Uncle Elmurad still busied himself on his roof, and along the mountaintop behind which the sun was sinking, a thick, black cloud slowly climbed. It grew completely dark, and the only thing visible in the twilight was a clean area the size of the threshing floor—the area Dinara was watering.

In the morning I'll leave, but Dinara will water the street for a long time to come, demonstrating that she isn't lazy. And those who lounge around the village or hang out on the square in front of the mosque these days will probably never convince Uncle Elmurad that they aren't idlers. And he'll never again tell these people about the various faraway countries, about the gardeners and beekeepers of those places. In the morning when everyone else is still just waking up, he'll be silently setting about his affairs, having risen before dawn. And he'll return home just as silently in the evening with his shovel on his shoulder.

In the morning I'm leaving. But each year the grapevines will stretch overhead along the poles that Uncle Elmurad set in the street, and each year in the springtime Uncle Elmurad will open his hives, and the gardens and yards and the crown of the almond tree bending over the spring will be filled with the buzzing of bees.

I'll leave, but Aunt Susen will catch hell, as always, and as always, Khashim will hide his cigarette in the hole in the wall. They'll gather the grapes, the grapes will grow again, the hives will be sealed up and then opened again, and together with all of this, in the suitcase—under seventeen orders and medals—will lie a thing that no one on earth has the power to take from there: the Party card of Uncle Elmurad.

The Tale of the Silver Tweezers

instead of an epilogue

My father sold muskmelons from the collective farm in the district center, and we saw him only in the evenings. There was just our house then, there was the yard of shady trees, there were the mountains and the sun; there was me, and there was my grandmother. We also had a cow who, like my father, went out in the morning and came back only in the evening.

Everything else was out there, beyond our fence. There were different houses on the other side of the fence, different trees, different people. There were big kids there: they hit the little ones. There were scary dogs there: they bit the little ones. There beyond the fence, weddings took place: people rejoiced. There were also funerals, funeral feasts: people cried.

There was me, and there was my grandmother, and in the evenings my father and the cow came back home to us. There was also another place, the "other world," and on Thursday nights when we lay down to sleep, my grandfather would come from that other world to visit us. On Thursdays my grandmother soaped and scrubbed the whole house. She shook out my grandfather's black khurdzhin bag and hung it on a nail in the room. She turned down the wick of the lamp and placed it to burn in the hallway, trying to keep it secret from my father. My father grumbled when he saw it because kerosene was expensive and heavy to carry from the district center, and then, you all know, my father didn't believe in any kind of other world or any kind of God.

My father slept alone in the small room. My grandmother and I slept here in the big room, and on Thursday nights the lamp burned nervously in the hallway next to our room, trying to stay hidden from my father. I was also nervous on those nights. I was very afraid of my grandfather, although my grandmother insisted that he wasn't frightening at all. He'd never in his life scared anyone, never said, "Boo!" to a goose—that's the kind of man he was. And he didn't walk among us to scare us—he was checking on us, seeing how we were doing, whether we had kerosene, whether we had enough bread. And he was also finding out whether we'd strayed from the path of the righteous. And because my father had strayed from the path of the righteous, my grandmother turned her face to the heavens each time she completed her prayers, urging God at length to forgive my father for his sins. My grandmother even taught me the prayer. I also began to beseech God. "Lord," I'd say, repeating my grandmother's words, "you are merciful and just: forgive my father! You see yourself that they've worn the man down, always on the run, everyone treats him badly: forgive him his sins, show your mercy!" My grandmother said that my prayer would reach the Almighty quicker because I was an innocent child and because the angels that sit on everyone's shoulders hadn't yet inscribed a single sin on my forehead—and that God had to forgive my father because my father didn't eat stolen food; he earned his bread by the sweat of his brow. There were certain people whom God would never forgive: thieves, haters, blasphemers, those who wrote words on the mosque and washed dirty things in the spring. But at that time those people were a long way away from me, a very long way—on the other side of the fence.

There was yet another kind of place on the other side of the fence— school, where the bell rang over and over. There was a shop on the other side of the fence near which people always shouted, quarreling over kerosene. There were all kinds of things on the other side of the fence, but all of them were a long way away, a very long way.

There was me, and I had a grandmother, and the two of us understood one another very well. When the sparrows twittered in the crowns of trees or the magpies screeched, we were certain that they were talking among themselves: I was certain, and my grandmother was certain too. In the evenings when the sun sank behind the mountain, neither of us doubted that the sun was going to sleep. We both knew every single one of the magpie chicks that nested in the old pear tree, my grandmother and I. Catching sight of a bat, we'd both freeze in fear, my grandmother and I... And it was only on the other side of the fence that my grandmother became different: she knew everyone there, I didn't know anyone; she wasn't afraid of anyone, I was afraid of everyone.

There was me, and there was my grandmother, and in the evenings my father returned home, and the cow returned home. The sparrows and magpies talked among themselves in their own language. And the sun went off to sleep behind the mountain. And somewhere far, far away on the other side of the fence, strange people lived, scary dogs barked. Somewhere a bell rang. People quarreled over kerosene near the shop. We had kerosene and we had bread; my grandfather came from the other world on Thursday nights to make sure of that. On Thursday nights the lamp in the hallway burned nervously until dawn; my grandfather's black khurdzhin bag grew even blacker, turned even more terribly black on its nail. There were also my grandfather's black prayer beads. And my grandmother's silver tweezers. In those days there was also a young woman, Sadaf: she came twice a week and used the silver tweezers to pluck out some kind of coarse hair from my grandmother's eyelids. Those hairs really bothered my grandmother when she threaded a needle, and because of them my grandmother's white hairs often ended up in the pan; I got terribly scared when they fell onto my father's plate.

One day my grandmother's tweezers disappeared: they fell into the grass under the apple tree and were lost. I looked for them and looked for them but didn't find them. Then Sadaf came; she also looked for them and didn't find them. Our neighbor Aunt Shaiste ran her fingers through every blade of grass under the apple tree and didn't find the tweezers. My grandmother pestered me to death with her needles and thread, and nearly every evening my father found white hairs on his plate. Then my grandmother died. They carried her away and buried her in a grave. They told me that my grandmother had gone away forever and would never come back again. My grandmother went away forever, but my grandfather came as he had before. Now my Aunt Medina came to visit quite often. On Thursdays she washed the floor, shook out the khurdzhin bag, and put the lamp in the hallway. And the sparrows and magpies talked in their own language, as before, and the sun went off to sleep behind the mountain. And then Aunt Shaiste came, and it turned out that my grandmother hadn't gone away forever after all.

Aunt Shaiste was standing in the yard, leaning back against the duval. Aunt Medina was baking lepyoshki. And under the apple tree, in the spot where my grandmother had lost her tweezers, a large, dark-blue butterfly was flying. I wanted to catch it, but Aunt Shaiste suddenly shouted extremely loudly:

"Lookee there, Medina: under the apple tree! Look under the apple tree! It's really Esmet, bless my soul, Esmet! Don't touch it! Don't touch it, son! Let it fly! It's your grandmother, come to look for the tweezers!"

I froze, paralyzed with fear. First I grew heavy like a stone, and then light like a feather. Then I lifted my head, looked around; everything around me was different, not at all like it had been. And my aunt wasn't the way she had been, and the yard wasn't the way it had been. The sun went off to sleep behind the mountain—I'd never in my life seen such a sun. Never again did I see a world of such color, or such mountains, or grass, or trees!

My grandmother had become a butterfly and was fluttering around the yard above the grass. When she flew far away from the apple tree, I wanted to call her back to show her, maybe she'd forgotten, where the tweezers had been lost. Sometimes my grandmother didn't fly alone: sometimes she flew with friends, but I didn't touch them either. I helped them look for the tweezers.

Once upon a time there lived talking magpies, and there were talking stars. And on the other side of the fence, scary dogs barked. Near the shop, people cursed over kerosene. But we had kerosene, and there was bread, and to make sure of that, my grandfather visited us as before.

One night my grandfather came again. This was during the war, and I no longer had a father, nor was there kerosene, nor bread. And when my grandfather came, for the first time I wasn't frightened: I even rejoiced. "Grandfather," I said, "we haven't got any bread, did you bring some?!" My grandfather thrust his hand into his khurdzhin— it was that same black bag that hung on a nail in the room—he felt around in one pocket, no bread, felt around in the other pocket, no bread there either. My grandfather picked up the khurdzhin, shook it, and my grandmother's tweezers clinked on the floor... I immediately found the tweezers—they really did turn up there in the khurdzhin. I took the tweezers, hung them on the apple tree, and my grandmother, appearing in the garden, flew around and around the apple tree. But for some reason my grandfather didn't come back after that. Sometimes I dreamed of a bat instead of my grandfather—gigantic, black, like my grandfather's khurdzhin, and each wing was a half-khurdzhin.

One fine day I unfastened the wicket gate and went out for the first time without my grandmother into that secret, somewhat terrifying world on the other side of the fence. I wasn't brave enough to go far; I ran back. Coming back, I walked up and down for a long time in our yard under our trees, and I pictured to myself the people and trees I'd seen today for the first time in my life without my grandmother; I wanted, very much wanted for those trees to be exactly like our trees, but those trees for some reason didn't want that.

Eventually, those strange trees did come to be just like our trees. I grew braver and made it all the way to the spring. I looked at the people crowding the square in front of the mosque: they were strangers, but not nearly as frightening as before. If Blind Islam hadn't been among them, I might have plucked up my courage and made it all the way to the mosque. But Blind Islam was there. Blind Islam was always there; he sat on a stone and leaned against the wall of the mosque.

The kids crowded around Blind Islam. They always asked: "Uncle Islam, who am I?" and held out their hands to the blind man. Uncle Islam recognized everyone by their hands; first he said the name of the boy, then the name of the boy's father.

And then one day I also went up to Uncle Islam.

"Uncle Islam, who am I?"

Uncle Islam was surprised, even a little taken aback. He took my hand, stroked it. He ran his fingers over my fingers, felt my wrist. Then he turned his head and fixed his coal-black eyes on the spring, looking at something only he could see. He was surprised anew and grew a bit thoughtful because there, where he was looking—the place only a blind man could see—he didn't see my name: I wasn't anywhere there.

I said to Uncle Islam:

"I'm Sadyk, son of Nadzhaf."

And there on the square in front of the mosque, among many other names, my name also began to be mentioned: Sadyk, son of Nadzhaf.

Then it started to be heard more often than the other names:

"Sadyk's a terrific boy!"

"That's my boy, Sadyk!"

But that came later, in a completely different time, when I was finally able to go to the shop for tea and to the spring for water. I'd buy Uncle Islam tea and haul water for him, and for that reason he shouted my name louder and more cordially than the names of the other boys.

An enormous, spreading walnut tree grew in Uncle Islam's yard. Its mighty branches hung over the lane that led to the spring. This was still the time when people were strangers, and the older strangers, the aksakaly, spoke mysterious words under Uncle Islam's walnut tree. Coming back from the spring, old women put down their pitchers and buckets under the walnut tree and whispered, lifting their faces to the heavens: "Glory to you, All Merciful, for your great benevolence!"

"You don't abandon your mercy for this poor man!" "O Almighty, don't abandon me, your poor slave, either! Show your generosity and benevolence to my unfortunate orphans too!"

They said these things under Uncle Islam's walnut tree because the tree was completely covered in walnuts; the branches were literally breaking from the weight. There were also years when there wasn't a single nut on the walnut tree, and then the women went to the tree and said: "It seems, Almighty, that you've closed your eyes to our sorrows! And you're no kinder than others, may you be overthrown! You're destroying wretched orphans!"

The conversations with God under Uncle Islam's walnut tree would start in the spring and end only in the fall when it came time to shake the tree. All this happened in those years when folk came from all over the village to shake the nuts from Islam's tree. "Beanpole" Kamal, who was the best at shaking down walnuts and the best at dancing at weddings, would climb to the very top of the tree, whistling merrily. There he shouted, whistled, and danced up and down as if he were at a wedding, and a hailstorm of walnuts pelted the ground under his heavy stick.

The women and girls collected them right up until sunset. In the yard, on the street: they picked them out of the thick grass, fished them out of the irrigation canal. The women were in a hurry because they had so much work to do at home: fetch water, cook dinner, feed the children. The sun set, and the women went home to boil water for tea, make dinner, feed the children. And this was precisely the time that we badgered Uncle Islam until dark:

"Uncle Islam, who am I?"

"Uncle Islam, who am I?"

* * *

Then I became a first grader. But the sparrows and magpies still chattered away in their own language. And the sun still went off to sleep behind the mountain, and there were still strangers in the world, and there were secret, incomprehensible words...

Then for some reason Uncle Islam also stopped hearing, but he could still recognize our hands, regardless. I'd hold out my hand to

Uncle Islam. He'd stroke it, run his fingers over my fingers, feel my wrist, and always know exactly who I was:

"Sadyk, son of Nadjaf!"

"Sadyk, my fine fellow!"

"That's my boy, Sadyk!"

Then the women whispering those stern words under Islam's walnut tree also came to know my name well: Sadyk, son of Nadjaf.

"Nadjaf's Sadyk gets straight As!"

"Sadyk's a sensible fellow, God bless him."

"I'll marry my daughter to Nadjaf's Sadyk—he's growing up so smart!"

"Hey, Sadyk, son of Nadjaf, where are you going at this early hour?"

"Hey, Sadyk, was it you who hurt our dog's leg?!"

And the time arrived when they called me and four other kids out of class one day and led us to the school iwan—we had to go to the district center and join the Young Communist League, the Komsomol. Azer, Rakhib, Salatyn, and a girl by the name of Menzer were sent to join the Komsomol along with me.

They lined us up on the iwan to see how we looked. Menzer was more fashionable than the rest of us, her father was the chairman, but the rest of us also looked presentable because we'd cut our nails, washed behind our ears—after all, they'd told us the night before—and everyone wore shoes that fit. Only Salatyn didn't have properly fitting shoes; she was wearing big galoshes, old and full of holes. She'd washed them well, but all the same, the galoshes were really ghastly.

Of course, they noticed the galoshes. Salatyn was so frightened and distraught that even our headmistress, Ziyanet Shekerek-kyzy, felt sorry for her. We walked to the district center on foot. It was a chilly, damp spring day. And although the day was chilly and damp, the girl called Menzer somehow grew warm; she took off her jacket, and for some reason I threw that jacket over my shoulders. As soon as the jacket touched my shoulders, everything immediately became different—as had happened once before. The damp chill disappeared, and the cold cliffs immediately warmed up; they thawed out and turned not yellow, but reddish. And they became incredibly lightweight. I don't know why this happened. Perhaps I'd been chilled to the bone. Or maybe it had happened because the jacket's lining was silky, soft, and never before had I felt such softness and silkiness.

And then and there it began to seem to me that Menzer was exactly like that: soft and silky, and her hands were silky, and her legs, and her breasts. And that invisible, girlish softness and silkiness trickled into my soul to remain there forever.

One night, waiting for the crowd to disperse after a movie, I climbed onto Rakhib's shoulders and wrote two names on the enormous, old plane tree that grew right next to the tearoom: mine and Menzer's. There were already a great many names there.

And Menzer's father noticed that writing on the plane tree. Right there next to the tearoom, he gave me a hearty box on the ear. Then he took me by the ear, dragged me to the tree, and forced me to scrape off what I'd written.

Then Rakhib and I once again stayed around after a movie. I clambered up to the very top, to the very highest, thinnest branch. It was a moonlit night. It was spring, and the crow chicks in the nest rocking on my branch were, had to be, still without feathers. The mother crow flew out of the nest. She cawed, circled around me, and beat me in the face with her wings, but I didn't give up, I held on and wrote these two words on the branch: "Sadyk + Menzer."

This time what I'd written remained hidden under the leaves all the way until autumn. But the leaves fell, the writing became visible, and being afraid of the chairman, I didn't go anywhere near the tearoom. Then one day Menzer's father caught me in the collective farm orchard and yanked me out of a walnut tree by my foot. He dragged me to the square under the plane tree, chewed me out in front of everyone, dragged me to the administration building, and only then did I understand that it was all because of what I'd written on the tree.

At the administration building, Menzer's father didn't beat me—he just picked up the telephone receiver and threatened to call a policeman. But he didn't call the police. He sat me on the sofa, sat down next to me, and started talking with me softly and gently. "Aren't there any other girls whose names you could write?" asked the chairman. "The school director has a beauty, you don't write her name!

The tearoom manager, Kurban, has a daughter who's a real bitch, who doesn't she run around with—why don't you write her name? Write the doctor's daughter's name! Misir's daughter is much more beautiful than mine—write her name! Then I'll say, 'Well done,' then I'll say, 'You're a real man!' After you write that, come into the orchard and take whatever your heart desires. But what good does this do? Have you decided to disgrace your chairman? You're making a fool of me in front of my enemies! After all, I was friends with your father. And you and I will be friends!"

No, Chairman, you're lying: Misir's daughter is absolutely not as beautiful! And there are silky cliffs in this world, there are lightweight mountains, light as down.... In the office I was able to hold back my tears, but coming out of the administration building, I began to sob uncontrollably. The doctor, the school director, the tearoom manager, and Teacher Misir were all still standing under the plane tree. They were standing there and looking at the administration building. "Loudmouth" Asad was also looking at the administration building and shouting, waving his arms. Farther off, Grandfather Aslan stopped, and boring a hole in the ground with his stick, he shook his head discontentedly from time to time. But Loudmouth Asad was literally yelling at the top of his lungs.

"Here's justice for you!" he shouted. "Feast your eyes, people! Feast your eyes on how soldiers' orphans are mistreated in state institutions! They're torturing an innocent child! A sinless baby is being tormented for a handful of walnuts!"

Loudmouth Asad shouted for a long time about orphans and state institutions that torture the children of dead soldiers. That's the sort of man he was; it didn't matter to him that the chairman hadn't laid a finger on me, who cared, he wouldn't be quiet until he'd shouted to his heart's content.

That same night I decided to scrape my words off the plane tree. And I climbed almost to the top, but suddenly got frightened: the branch was much too thin. In fact, just the summer and fall had passed, but my weight wasn't what it had been, and neither was my courage.

And then the branch disappeared along with what I'd written on it, and the crow's nest disappeared, too, for "interfering with the power line."

At the spring the women whispered:

"You know, Nadzhaf's Sadyk is in love with the chairman's daughter..."

But later:

"Nadzhaf's Sadyk is moving to Baku!"

"It's Sadyk! He's come back from Baku!"

"Good heavens, is that you, Sadyk? Have you come home for good, son?!"

Islam has a strange memory: his hands remember everything. Or perhaps he's made some kind of special note of my hands; no matter when I arrive, he immediately recognizes me. Uncle Islam takes my hand and won't let it go for a long time; it's as if we're conversing with our hands. And each time my hands answer Islam's main question: "No, I haven't come home for good."

Each time I arrive, I tell him the exact same thing, and each time he repeats his question anew. For some reason Uncle Islam is convinced that a person who grew up here, by this spring, can't possibly go away forever: sometime he has to return.

At the spring everything is the same as it was before.

"You know, someone saw Mukhtar's Kamal in Moscow. They say he's rolling in cash. A whole packet of twenty-five-ruble notes in his pocket! And that's just the start of it, they say, there's more where that came from!"

"And they wrote about Yakub's Rakhib in an American newspaper: he wrote some book about the atom..."

"And Kazym's Gafar was sent packing. He took bribes from students. He shamed the village, may someone wring his neck!"

"Did you hear how clever Khasandzhan's Salman has become? He grew into a man himself and dragged his brothers along with him. Now they're living off the fat of the land in Sumgait!"

And the spring babbles along.

Uncle Islam sits, as always, leaning against the wall of the mosque, sits and stares at the water, looking at something that only he can see.

Maybe he really can see? Maybe there, where he looks so fixedly, the sparrows and magpies chatter among themselves, and the sun is going to sleep behind the mountain? Maybe it's daytime there now, the heat has already passed, and a butterfly flutters over the grass, looking for silver tweezers. Or maybe it's night there, and a lamp blinks timidly in a hallway, watching for someone from the other world.

Or maybe there's no one in that place he's gazing at, just the blackest darkness.

And some little boy, frightened of Blind Islam, not daring to go out into the street. And a boy who earns nothing but straight As: maybe his name is Sadyk, or maybe Ali, or Akhmed...

"Ali's Akhmed gets straight As!"

"Akhmed's a gentle fellow, God bless him!"

"I'll marry my daughter to Ali's Akhmed—he's growing up so smart!"

"Hey, Akhmed, was it you who hurt our dog's leg?!"

1966-1968

About The Author

Akram Aylisli (b. 1937) is an Azerbaijani novelist, playwright, and editor. His works have been translated into more than twenty languages. Publications in English include *Farewell, Aylis*, a trilogy of novellas that includes the controversial *Stone Dreams*. *Stone Dreams* explores themes of understanding and mutual accountability among Azerbaijanis and Armenians; its publication in 2012 led to public burnings of Aylisli's books and an ongoing harassment campaign against the author by the Azerbaijani government. In 2014, Aylisli was nominated by an international group of supporters for the Nobel Peace Prize. Since 2016, he has been the target of a politically motivated criminal investigation by the Azerbaijani government that has imposed significant restrictions on all his activities. Aylisli lives in Baku, Azerbaijan.

About the Translator

Katherine E. Young is the author of the poetry collections *Woman Drinking Absinthe* and *Day of the Border Guards* (2014 Miller Williams Arkansas Poetry Prize finalist) and the editor of *Written in Arlington*. She has translated work by Anna Starobinets (memoir), Akram Aylisli (fiction), and numerous Russian-language poets from Kazakhstan, Russia, and Ukraine. Awards include the Granum Foundation Translation Prize, the Pushkin House Translation Residency, an Arlington County (Virginia) Individual Artist Grant, a National Endowment for the Arts translation fellowship, and a Hawthornden fellowship (Scotland). From 2016-2018, she served as the inaugural Poet Laureate for Arlington, Virginia.